TOPE OMOTOSHO

Dance with Me

LEVERAGE
PUBLISHING

First published by Leverage 2020

Copyright © 2020 by Tope Omotosho

This novel is entirely a work of fiction. The names, characters and incidents portrayed in it are the work of the author's imagination. Any resemblance to actual persons, living or dead, events or localities is entirely coincidental.

Designations used by companies to distinguish their products are often claimed as trademarks. All brand names and product names used in this book and on its cover are trade names, service marks, trademarks and registered trademarks of their respective owners. The publishers and the book are not associated with any product or vendor mentioned in this book. None of the companies referenced within the book have endorsed the book.

First edition

Advisor: Dapo Omotosho

This book was professionally typeset on Reedsy.
Find out more at reedsy.com

To the Lover of my soul, my First Love,
Thank You for giving me yet another message to write.

Tope Omotosho returns with another great book showcasing God's love. A good example of what Christian Romance should be - godly romantic relationships and a romantic relationship with God. Dance with Me is an enjoyable read.

Acknowledgement

To my Sweet Caramel, Dapo. I love you.

Thank you Mayowa for making me smile. *kisses* Thank you Morayo for bringing joy into our lives.

My financial partners and helpers too numerous to mention that said yes to God, may yourdance with God be never ending.

Editing by Niki Igbaroola

Cover Design by Leverage Press

Author Photograph by Ajibola Animashaun Photography

www.lifegodandlove.com

Dancing requires trust.

p.s This is not your typical love story.

Chapter One

March 2019, present day

He walked into the bathroom, the familiar smell of mint and honey filling his senses - resistant to fade even years later, bringing forth ever present bittersweet memories. Her toothbrush and favoured toothpaste, sitting in their pink cup holder caught his eyes as it did every morning. As was now a familiar routine, his eyes followed on from the toothbrush to the face cream next to it, the dent of her finger as it absentmindedly reached for the cream ever visible. A glance at the clock she'd put over the bathroom sink, one she claimed helped keep her on time in the mornings, pushed him to the sink where he brushed his teeth around the wistful smile he couldn't seem to erase.

His mind wandered to yesterday's events and he knew he needed to share them with Kiki. Knew he had to because of how happy it would make her.

Flicking off the light switch, his smile turned to a chuckle as he walked out of the bathroom, thinking about Kiki's reaction to his news. That he knew her so well was a testament to their bond. A bond that he would forever be thankful for. He buttoned his shirt and pulled on his trousers. He slid his wedding ring down his finger; the glint of silver from the band catching his eye, sending a sharp tug to his heart. He didn't mind if people thought him silly for still wearing it even when it was Kiki shooting him disapproving looks.

Ambling down the stairs, he found her seated beside the couch flicking through a magazine. The smile she threw his way caused him to lightly stumble, still not used to the brilliance of her smile and the way it always could shift his world.

In a few strides, he was at her side, falling gracefully into the couch with a perfect view of both her face and the picture she'd taken years ago to mark her birthday. Her mouth opened as though about to say something but he interrupted her, eager to share his news.

Micah took a deep breath. "So it finally happened. What we prayed about." He pinched the bridge of his nose before continuing, "Well, at least God answered this one." He knew she would object to that: his current distrust in God and unbelief in His will for their lives. He could also predict her response, hear her voice say that no matter what, God was involved in their lives and He was sovereign.

Her voice always came to him at different moments of his day respective of where he was - giggling, chastising and intimating him of her opinion from time to time.

God is faithful, Micah. He always is, she said to him then.

He wanted to argue. Wanted to say that God had failed, but instead said, "I've heard. Well, I just wanted to let you know before I head out that I love you, always." He pressed his lips to his fingers and placed them on her lips.

Then he left the house.

* * *

"I think it's time you consider meeting someone new. It's been three years already."

Micah covered his eyes and groaned, "Big sis, please don't start." He had endured a long day of meetings at the church, meetings that revolved around issues he knew could have been resolved easily but

2

CHAPTER ONE

instead had become endless cases of back and forth.

"Don't say that. I'm worried about you." She clasped her hands in front of her. "We are all worried about you. I know you miss her. I miss her too. She was like a sister to me with that her strong British accent and terrible *pidgin English*."

Micah smiled a little.

"Life is full of ups and downs. I understand how you feel bu-"

"You don't understand what I'm going through!" He countered.

She jolted and only then did he realize he might have raised his voice a little too loudly. Her brown stained lips parted in shock, her bulky frame motionless for a few seconds. He hated himself for having come to this.

He took a deep breath and tried to speak calmly. "Yo-", he paused. "You don't know, Belinda." He buried his face in his hands briefly before raising his head once more, "You don't know what it's like waking up to an empty bed; stretching your hand to the other side and realizing each day that she's not there. After seven years of every day together. After months of watching that person die slowly. Sis, don't tell me you understand."

Her eyes pooled with tears, mirroring his. Her voice heavy with grief as she said, "You're right. I don't. But I know that the Bible says we shouldn't mourn like unbelievers do because we would see those dead in the faith rise again. I believe it. Don't you?"

"*Oh, please,*" Micah thought. He couldn't count how many times he had heard those words or how many mouths had uttered them since Kiki's passing but hearing them from his sister was the last straw.

"Are you mocking me?" Micah asked, unable to contain his anger at her statement.

"*Haba!*" she cried in agony; the veins on her neck in clear view. "I'm not! This is a difficult thing you have gone through. But you have to allow yourself heal, Micah. You have to."

God, you knew all those years back that this was going to happen. Why didn't you tell me? Why didn't you warn me? He uttered in his heart, the same question he'd been asking for months now.

However, Micah knew he wouldn't trade those few years of bliss for anything in the world. He welcomed thoughts of his past. Thoughts of Kiki. Thoughts of what had once brought him so much joy. . . thoughts that were all he had to live on.

Chapter Two

Zainab shivered and drew her kimono tighter across her body. The silk material felt extremely light against her skin. It was special to her, a gift from her best friend last year on her thirty-third birthday; a gift her friend had hoped wouldn't be for her pleasure alone.

Take it as something to enhance your femininity, Adesewa had said.

Too bad, Zainab thought. For the last two years she had stopped bothering herself about the ticking of her biological clock or any other drivel people had said about the fact that she was in her thirties and had amassed a small fortune of her own. Whether or not it scared off men no longer bothered her.

She heard a shout, looked towards the window and noticed a troop of people going into the next compound, talking and laughing too loudly about something. The clouds were dark with the residue of rain lingering in the air. She yearned for a hot cup of green tea and so put on the kettle. The warmth from the cup seeping into her palms, abating the chill that had come with the rains.

There was loud music coming from the house next door. She settled down on a sofa, her feet tucked underneath her bum and took a sip. The taste of the slightly bitter tea invigorating her.

The bass from the music next door caused the centre tables to shake, making it impossible for Zainab to put her mug down. She couldn't believe that her father;s neighbours had a party raging this loud and long on a Tuesday evening, especially given how heavy the rain had been all day. She was just about to call out to her father to complain, when he walked out of his study to join her.

"Why did your former neighbours move out again?" Zainab asked, placing a palm on her forehead and squinting.

"Because they found a better place in Lagos." He coughed into his handkerchief before settling down on a couch opposite her.

She snorted. She had never been a fan of Lagos but was living there based on God's instructions. The two reasons she came to Ibadan were to see her dad and enjoy some peace and quiet as she waited on God. Her business line was switched off to avoid distractions.

She had been up all night, preparing for an upcoming conference up north. A revival program. It didn't matter that her eyes were burning and her limbs felt sore. Her tummy felt knotted, partially from nervousness and excitement for all the things she was sure God was set to do for all that would be in attendance at the programme. Public speaking wasn't her forte especially when it involved sharing parts of her personal life. The parts of her she'd rather keep buried.

But God had shown her that her life wasn't hers any more and she knew that to hold back was to resist that knowledge.

"I guess we share similar distaste for the city life," her father said. "Back in the day, though, Lagos was my city " her father continued, becoming animated before succumbing to a coughing spasm that had become a regular occurrence.

She watched her father for the next few seconds as he battled with the spasms until they subsided. - his eyes teary and his breathing slow.

"Are you sure that cough is going? What did your doctor say?"

"I just happened to miss my appointment."

She narrowed her eyes. "Or you just so happened to deliberately forget it."

He smiled. "How did you get to know me so well?" He cleared his

6

throat. "I'm very much okay. Stop pestering me with your incessant worries."

He winked at her.

Zainab knew her father appreciated her concern. Who would have known their relationship would be so free and easy considering the circumstances of their first meeting.

Zainab's mother, Samira, despite being the daughter of a religious extremist, had fallen in love with a young Christian man who had been everything her father hated. According to Zainab's mother, her father would have killed her if she remained in the relationship - a fear that caused a great deal of friction between them. When the time came for Zainab's father to leave Jos at the end of his NYSC year, leaving wasn't the hardship he imagined. The lack of a possible future with Samira sealed their fate. So he boarded the bus, leaving behind the possible love of his life but also a child he wouldn't come to know until much later.

For much of her life, Zainab was under the impression that her biological father was no longer alive - something her mother had led her to believe. Finding out that he was alive had made her so angry. To young Zainab, she had been abandoned to a life with a step-father who had punished her for the sins of her mother. A step-father who had always let her know she wasn't a part of his family, just someone he had to take on to secure the woman he had desired for years. The woman he had still married, despite her status as 'damaged goods'.

To grow up in that house was for Zainab to never feel fully loved or wanted, feelings that made her spiral into many of the bad decisions that had shaped much of her late adolescence and twenties.

Finding out that her father was alive had left her feeling a deep hatred for him, convinced he had abandoned her. At this point, her mother had passed away so it was easy for her to feel abandoned and create an image of her father as this monster, avoiding, for a long time, all his attempts to meet her.

But now things were different.

Zainab stared at the man seated in front of her. The grey hair on his head slowly overshadowing the black. His tired eyes and frail hands. She was worried about him. His health. Praying desperately that God would give him more years so she could enjoy his presence in her life. She was also glad for the half-sister her relationship with her father had given her. A sibling who had no prejudices against her.

"You're making it difficult for me to not care by skipping your doctor's appointments . You're going to leave me no choice but to let Efe know how stubborn you are."

"You and your sister shouldn't be policing me. I'm the parent. Besides, I'm an old man. My body can't work as well as yours."

Zainab scoffed. "You're just fifty-eight."

He widened his eyes comically. "Just?"

"Dad, please stop with the theatrics."

He looked at her then, the smile faltering from his lips and replaced with a solemn look. "I will fix another appointment and I promise to go."

She smiled. "Thank you." The music suddenly came to a stop and while welcome for a moment, the silence was deafening.

"It's good to see you smile. So, any man yet?"

"You've been asking that question for the last two years and the answer is still no."

Her phone beeped then and she grabbed her phone from the stool beside her. Leke, a photographer colleague she worked with from time to time, was saying hi. He was asking when she would return to Lagos.

"And why is that?" her father asked as she typed a reply, "I hate to break it to you, my dear, but you're not getting any younger."

She took her eyes off the messages and smiled at him. "I know."

He narrowed his eyes at her. "Tell me the truth, Zainab. What's going on? Are you afraid?"

She laughed. "Why would I be afraid?"

He lifted his slim shoulders in a non-committal way. "You tell me. You're a young, beautiful, successful, Christian woman. Any man in his right faculties would be blind not to notice you."

"I'm fine being single. Besides, the work of my Father consumes me."

"Zainab, talk to me," he pleaded, concern causing worry lines to form across his forehead.

She looked at him, and for a brief moment considered dropping her guard and sharing her fears with him. Opening up about the incidents in her past that still haunt her today. How much she had hurt at being abandoned close to the altar because of her sins. How she felt she wouldn't be good enough for a man because of her past. How a tiny part of her still believed IK's words that she was sick in the head. But as always, she shrugged it off, smiled and said, "I'm satisfied with what I do and who I am. Marriage does not define me or make me a person of worth or value. Jesus does and I'm satisfied with Him."

Her father looked at her intently. "I guess I have no reason to question or doubt you . . ."

He didn't say the word, but Zainab sensed a 'yet' resting at the tip of his tongue; waiting to be voiced.

She changed the topic.

"This may sound stupid, but do you ever think of what life would have been if you two stayed together?"

"Your mother and I?"

She nodded. This was a thought she'd entertained during her childhood when she believed he was dead. Laying in bed at night, she'd imagine a world that included her, her mother and biological father living together.

He gave a broad smile, one triggered by a pleasant memory. He had shared some with Zainab - retelling funny tales and adventures he had with her mother. Times he taught Zainab's mother how to make chocolate coated pancakes; a meal that had unwittingly been one of the highlights of her childhood.

"Yes, I have thought about it. Maybe we would have been over thirty years married or we would have gotten sick of each other and parted ways. I loved your mother. Her poetic nature and stubbornness. Something you seem to have inherited from her." Zainab withheld a smile. "But one thing I do know is I'm in God's will right now and I believe that's what matters."

Zainab bit her lip and nodded. Her father always seemed to have the right things to say. She also knew she couldn't predict the future and God's ways were the best.

"How's your step-dad?" he asked.

"He's fine."

"And your siblings?"

"They are good. Attending Arabic school and following their father's orders like their life depends on it." She used the tip of her thumbnail to pick at a stub of dirt underneath her forefinger. "The man is set in his ways. He always wants to be present whenever I go visiting. Apparently, I'm a bad influence."

"Little does he know how much you've changed and for the better."

She lifted the black mug to her lips and took a sip of her green tea which was now lukewarm. If she had been told five years ago that she would be drinking tea she would have laughed and said over her dead body. But here she was, drinking green tea as a way to trump the urge to get a wrap of weed or smoke a cigarette. God had totally lifted her from a deep abyss to His light.

Thinking back now, she was disgusted at the way she had lived.

"You know, there was a time I was so high I couldn't get up from my bed for hours. I would just stare at the ceiling." She looked down at her tea. "IK always knew where to get the best weed from." For much of their relationship, the two would sit on her bedroom floor smoking seemingly endless joints, talking and exploring one another's bodies. She wondered if IK did similar things with his wife.

"You know the past is the past. We all make mistakes. I, for one, have surely made plenty in my many years on earth. Mistakes make us human but learning and leaning on Christ to make us better – that's the journey to perfection. Because then, we become more like Him."

"True," she responded, taking comfort in her father's wisdom.

"Was IK – was he the one who introduced you to marijuana?"

"No. It started way back in uni. Like I said, he just managed to always have the best weed."

"Well, those days are behind us."

Zainab silently agreed with her dad. She had come a long way.

* * *

She threw her head back, her laughter carrying a tune he knew too well. Then she said it again, her eyes teasing and pleading at the same time, as though she held on to a secret, *"Dance with me, Micah."*

Micah forced his eyes open and released a sigh. She'd come to visit for the umpteenth time that week. Walking through the house with authority, singing along to the radio and dancing around him as he made dinner - her ever present smile an invitation to him to reach out and touch her, hold her, initiate any physical contact.

He let out another sigh. March was always a tough time for him. A time when he had to remember. A time he had to let go of her physically. But after all these years, he was yet to let go in his heart.

And he was used to her frequent visits.

He groaned softly, threw his bed-cover to the side and dropped his feet on the floor. He hunched forward, his head in his hands.

"God, when would it stop? When would the torture come to an end?"

11

he questioned.

It was painful enough that he couldn't hold her. Painful she would forever be out of his reach in this part of the world, a very lonely one without her. He couldn't tell anyone her voice kept him company most of the time.

Willingly invading his thoughts.

"I miss you, Kiki," he whispered to the empty room, even though there was no one else in his three bedroom apartment. "More than you know."

Awww . . . I miss you too. You know you ought to stop thinking about me so often and talking to yourself. People might start to think you're a complete nutter if you keep this up, especially in public.

Micah sighed. "I know, I know. I can't help it."

You can help it. You just don't want to. Don't do this to yourself, love. We'll still see again.

Micah shook his head. He wasn't ready to let go. Not yet. He didn't think he ever could. His heart couldn't take it. His eyes shifted to her wardrobe. A few of her clothes were still in them, the rest, stored away, carefully preserved so they didn't lose her unique scent. He didn't have the strength to give them away. Belinda and him had engaged in an argument when he came home an evening after service to find out she had taken a great deal of Kiki's clothes and given them out.

Things were still shaky between them.

You know you would heal faster if you did give them away, right? Kiki's voice filled his thoughts.

"I know," he whispered to himself.

He stood and made his way to the window, pulling the grey and blue curtains aside to gaze at nothing in particular. The security guard was sitting on a wooden bench, a pair of black boots at his feet as he took a rag and began wiping them clean one after the other. His mouth shaped in a tiny circle as he whistled; the wind carrying the tunes all the way to him.

It sounded like Prince Nico Mbarga's 'Sweet Mother'.

Micah scanned the street. A couple of kids were riding their bicycles with parents behind them, dressed in matching black joggers, walking leisurely, chatting animatedly while keeping an eye on their children.

He stepped back and headed to the kitchen.

There were a lot of memories in their kitchen. He often came back to one - Kiki sitting on the black granite counter-top while eating his famous concoction rice out of a pot.

"Honey, this is so good! I really can't imagine my life without this." She *chucked a spoonful into her mouth and chewed silently. How she managed the latter, he didn't know.*

"I'm glad you like my cooking," he said, amused.

"I-love-your-cooking." She pointed a spoon at him. "You should seriously consider opening a local restaurant or something."

Micah chuckled. "Not my thing."

Her eyes popped like something dawned on her. "Then let me open the restaurant, manage it and you'll be the cook."

"I don't think so."

"I can seriously do this." She went on like she hadn't heard a word he said. "Let's put my MBA to work."

He ran a sponge over a pot. "I know. It still doesn't mean I should go into the food business. There are a lot of things that have to be put into consideration aside from the end product of a delicious meal. Besides, what time would I have to do all that cooking as a pastor?"

Her face fell. "Right."

Frowning, she dug her spoon back into the pot and raised it back to her mouth. Her gaze thoughtful.

He smiled to himself. He knew she was thinking up possible ways it could work, and that was one of the many reasons he was in love with her. Her optimism in difficult situations.

"What if we get someone you could trust and you pour all your knowledge into the person? That could work, right?"

"Maybe. But the truth is I'm not really keen on the restaurant deal." He dropped a clean spoon in the plate rack and dried his hands on a napkin.

She rolled her eyes. *"You're so boring! Micah, we should do exciting things. Explore a little in life and try something new. I assure you that this restaurant business would kick off."*

"I'm not saying it won't be a success."

"Then what are you trying to say?" she asked dryly.

"That this isn't what I'm called to do, sweetheart."

"Mmm-hmn, I hear you."

Micah chuckled. *She sounded cute and funny whenever she was trying to imitate local Nigerian dialect.*

"But you want to know something?" he asked, closing in on her and taking the now cold pot off her hands.

"What?" she whispered. Her lips tilted to the corner.

"I get to be your personal chef all the days of your life."

Her lips spread to a full blown smile as she leaned close to him. Her breath carrying the smell of the dry fish in his signature concoction rice. "I think I like the sound of that, Mr. Oramah."

He wrapped his arms around her waist and pressed his lips against hers.

Micah discarded the memory. A wave of sadness tugging on his heart. He pulled open the fridge and fished out something he could eat quickly. There was a wedding at church - fellow workers were getting married. The groom had requested his presence and Micah had promised to be there. Now he wished he could go back on his word.

Kiki loved weddings. The decorations, wedding dress and the couple dancing into the reception.

"Nigerian weddings are the best! Nothing like a good intro dance into the rest of their lives."

14

He tossed his half-eaten sandwich on the plate and glanced at the wall-clock.

Nine-thirty.

He might as well start getting ready.

* * *

11 Years earlier (2008)

She was there again.

They were at a church in Manchester. She was seated at the front, dressed in white and looking almost angelic in a blindingly white dress. A peacock-looking hat perched on the side of her head, her eyes fixated on the pastor, her pen furiously scribbling in her notepad as she followed every word he uttered.

Micah couldn't stop staring at her. And it wasn't just because of her flawless mocha skin and incredible body. There was a grace to the way she moved, like she was fully comfortable in her body.

"Sorry, is that seat taken?" A blonde lady asked him, cutting off his thoughts and forcing him to focus on something other than the stranger who he couldn't keep his eyes off. Her grey eyes both questioning and hopeful.

He shook his head and stood up to allow her to move into the empty seat. She offered him a smile of thanks and focused on the pastor whose salt and pepper hair, despite being well groomed, failed to hide the excess thinning that comes with old age.

Micah sat down and tried to do the same but it wasn't long before his eyes strayed back to the lady in white.

He had been watching her for the past month and a half, coming to every service in the hopes of catching sight of her.

She smiled all the time and was courteous to everyone. She was in the choir and a great dancer, moving her small frame in tune with the beats from the drummer.

Micah shifted his eyes back to the pastor. He was determined to at least catch a couple of words of what he was saying. He was talking about God's perfect timing in everything. That God had His calendar for things to happen in their lives and nothing was coincidental as the world liked to think.

Micah wondered if this was perhaps God's timing for him. His cousin, Demi, had forced him to take a train ride from London to Manchester over a month ago for the duration of his brief vacation from his Master's program. And then Demi had invited him to church and since he saw her, she was all he could think about. Finding himself hopping on a train any weekend he could, taking the three hour journey to see her, fantasising about what talking to her would feel like.

For the past few weeks, he'd told himself that each Sunday would be the day he walked up to her, introduced himself and finally asked her out to lunch and each Sunday, he chickened out, too shy to make the move.

"Oh for goodness sake, would you give it a rest and just *talk* to her, Micah," his cousin furiously whispered, jolting Micah from his obsessive staring.

"I'm not so sure," he replied over the sound of his racing heart. The truth was he was also scared of what being in a relationship again would look like after the mess his last one had deteriorated into. And moreover, he wasn't even sure if a relationship with her could work.

He shook his head. "How would this relationship work *sef*? I overheard her talking the other day. She has a British accent. Would she now up and leave her life here? *Abi*, I will move over to the UK to live here?" Voicing it aloud iterated how silly considering a relationship with her was.

It could never work.

"You never know," Demi maintained. "She might be the one. And if

16

you guys marry, you just might really become a Britico," she continued, winking at him.

He looked at her, slightly irritated. "That's not what I'm looking for."

"I know, silly. I'm just pulling your legs. No need to get annoyed."

When Micah finally did ask her out a week later, she smiled shyly at him and agreed to go to lunch with him after service.

That day was one of the best of his life. They had lunch at 19 Café Bar and headed off to Piccadilly Gardens - strolling around the park and taking in the historical buildings but mostly talking with an ease that elated him.

Her voice, contradictingly soft and raspy despite the strong Mancunian lilt, enraptured him.

"So, how long have you lived here?" he asked as they strolled despite the chill in the air.

"All my life," she countered. "My parents moved here a long time ago. I was born here."

"Do you ever think of going to Nigeria?"

She exhaled a foggy breath and he caught a whiff of the minty gum she chewed. "I don't know, actually, I have thought about it but not seriously. I mean, my mum and dad don't go often so I never really considered it. My life is here, unless God says otherwise."

Kiki looked at him and smiled.

He smiled back.

"Tell me more about you, though. Do you have any siblings?" she asked, hopping over one of the many puddles that the endless rain created around the city.

He gave a slight laugh as his elder sister's face flashed across his mind. Their last conversation was about him finding a nice girl over here. "Yes. Belinda."

"Just the one?"

"Yes."

"Younger or older?"

"Older. And you?"

"Let's see. There's Solomon, Felix, Cassandra, Elijah and me.'"

Micah blinked. "You have four older siblings?" Micah knew his mother had stopped at two because she couldn't stand the thought of going through another six hours of labour.

She laughed. "Fortunately or unfortunately. I can't seem to decide which of the two."

"Wow." He watched as a man walked by with his white-haired dog on a leash while talking on the phone. "My father agreed to have just two children, but I guess his words didn't match his desires. He ended up with two more outside his marital home. My mother never forgave him."

"Really!" she exclaimed blinking twice. "That must have been hard for your mum."

"It was. She tries to act tough and strong, but deep down I know she still misses him."

He still recalled times his mother would set the table and cook extra food just in case his father showed up hungry or because the other woman was mistreating him.

"Apparently, my parents like a big family. They also thought it best to give me an African name as a first name to make up for their sins of abandoning their Igbo heritage with the first four." She turned her gaze to him. "So my grandmother said." She looked back at the tall hotel and shop buildings that stood afar. "I'm not bothered by it though. I like to believe I'm the unique one."

"So, no English name?" His teeth chattered. His hands balled into a fist in his leather jacket.

"I have one. Rayna," she said, her long coat, trimmed with fur across the collar and sleeves inducing slight envy in him.

"Nkiruka Rayna Nnadi. You have a beautiful name."

She smiled. "I think so too. Tell me more about yourself. What university do you go to and what course do you study?"

Inwardly, he was doing somersaults that she was interested in learning more about him. Pleased when she had noticed the small scar on his forehead; a trophy from younger years of playing football.

"London Met. Public health."

"So, you're a science geek?"

He chuckled. "I guess you could say that. But I sense God calling me to a different direction."

She arched a brow. "Really? Like what?"

"Probably to become a pastor."

"Interesting," she said, the expression on her face unreadable so he decided to switch the direction of the conversation.

"I couldn't help but notice your dance moves in church."

There was a gleam in her eyes. "I love to dance. I took ballet classes in school, but didn't go far with it. Something about standing on your toes and trying to find balance *unbalanced* me."

They spoke, laughed and got to know each other better as the hours hurried by. Daylight fast running out and the temperature dropped even further. Micah noted two important things as he headed back to London later that evening - he wanted to see her again and he was going to take her dancing no matter how silly it made him look. All he wanted was to see her smile and make her happy.

Two months and seven dates later, Micah officially asked her to be his girlfriend.

Chapter Three

Guilt and a tinge of betrayal set in on her. Her thumb deliberated on tapping her name amidst the other names her Instagram search offered. Betrayed by a twitch of her forefinger, Tobi's phone came to life with enough photos for her to feed her eyes on. Photos she now considered as the only way of being intimately close to her.

Tobi swallowed hard as she scrolled through picture after picture, unable to peel her eyes away from them until she tapped on a particular option. She brightened her phone screen, the illumination helped sharpen how beautiful the lady was in her dress which perfectly highlighted her figure. The curves on her body carefully sculpted. Her teeth evenly perfect.

Maureen's smile did all sorts to her.

Maybe that was why she spent over thirty minutes of her daily self-allotted time stalking her crush on every social media platform. Tobi had discovered that she spent more time on Instagram. Putting up pictures of herself with friends or taking selfies of her latest outfit or hairstyle. Pouting seductively, laughing or pulling a funny face.

The sound of a door opening and closing alerted Tobi that Detan was most likely doing his toilet routines at 3 a.m., a strange habit and routine developed over the years.

Tobi thought about Maureen's hair and realized she liked it more in a long, brown weave with side-swept bangs that covered a part of her face - her current look.

She turned her phone face down on the bed and rested her head on the pillow. It's cool, fluffiness against her head relaxing and comforting.

Maureen was nothing like Tobi and probably would never be.

* * *

"I haven't slept as good as this in the last one month." Detan said, massaging the back of his neck with one hand while the other reached out to his steaming cup.

Tobi grimaced; the strong aroma of coffee granules churning her stomach. Even more the sound of him slurping on his cup.

"Good for you."

"What about you? How was your night?"

"My night was fine." She shrugged. "Spent most of it trying to sort something at work." She pulled open the fridge door and peered in. Half a loaf of stale bread, margarine, four eggs, bananas that were half-rotten and two bottles of wine were its only contents. She slammed the fridge shut; the sound of bottles jiggling against each other reaching her ears as though in protest.

Detan threw a quizzical look her way. "I thought you were supposed to be on leave?"

"I thought so too." She jerked a thumb at the fridge. "How come you didn't load up the fridge? I told you I was coming over *nau*."

He slurped his coffee again. "You said over the weekend. Not Friday close to midnight."

What's the difference? "I decided to come a few hours earlier. Is that a problem?"

"No *o*! I wonder why your husband would let you drive all the way here at such a time. Anyways, it only means you have to shop yourself.

21

I have to go to work." He downed the rest of his coffee and burped a little.

She grimaced. "*Urrgh!* You're such a pig, Detan."

"*Na you sabi.*"

She scratched her scalp and could literally feel her nail dig out a part of her dry skin. She was sure there would be proof of that under her nails. "Is there anywhere I can get plantain?"

"Yeah, the woman down the street sells. Buy a lot 'cause I intend on eating some when I return."

Tobi snorted. "I didn't come here to be your personal cook.'"

He came to stand next to her, hanging his arm around her bare shoulders, all six foot frame of him. A great feat considering he was the only one in the family with such poise. Their father still said he wasn't his son. No one could decipher if it was a joke anymore.

"But you're my baby sis. You need to help me." He winked and added his cup to the pile of dirty dishes. Surely he didn't expect her to take care of his mess. "Besides, my babe isn't here."

Tobi's stomach growled. She wrapped an arm around her tummy and leaned against the fridge. "How's she by the way? Mummy was asking about her the other day. Said it's been a while since she last saw her."

"Don't mind her. She's pushing for us to get married and wants to find more ways to cajole her into pressuring me. Can you imagine?"

"I can." She tilted her head. "What exactly is she suggesting?"

"She wants her to get pregnant."

Tobi's lips parted slightly. "So?"

"Maureen would never do that. She's one of those good girls. Bringing a child out of wedlock would destroy her."

"Good for her."

Detan shook his head. "But you know Mummy. She would not let down. I've told her I will propose when I'm ready. *Abeg*, nobody

22

should stress my life." He picked his phone off the table and headed out the kitchen. "See ya."

"Later." Tobi murmured.

Her eyes scanned the room wearily. Eyeing the kitchen sink which was filled with dishes, pots and all sorts. She wasn't in the mood to sort out the pile. She wondered how any woman could deal with her brother and his disgusting habits.

"Well, I didn't jump from frying pan to fire," she mumbled, deciding to leave the pile alone; ignoring her long developed instinct to set everything right.

The woman selling plantain was yet to arrive and Tobi didn't think she could wait. There had been an argument with Shola last night before finding her way to her brother's house, and she hadn't thought about dishing herself the fluffy *amala* with *ewedu* soup she had spent time cooking.

The smell of roasted yam wafted to her then and Tobi searched the street for where it was coming from. Making her way to the old woman who stood by the charcoal-lit fire; turning hot pieces of yam with her bare hand. Sweat beads trickling down her neck to her chest despite the cool of the morning.

Tobi purchased what she needed. As soon as she got back she went to her room and lay tummy down on the bed.

She fished out her phone underneath her pillow.

Four missed calls from Shola. Tobi ignored them. Instagram notified her that there was a new post from her crush. Tobi tapped it and a picture of Maureen showed up on her screen. She was dressed corporately in a grey pant-suit and white collared shirt. Her weave packed up in a bun. Her lips painted in a shade of fuchsia. Her smile alluring.

Tobi blew softly on the yam and bit into it.

* * *

Shola had called five times that evening and still, Tobi wasn't ready to talk to him. It was only a matter of time before he came looking for her.

Tobi popped some pop-corn into her mouth, a novel in another hand.

"Your ringtone is beginning to irritate me. It's either you turn the phone off or put it on silent." Detan complained, his eyes refocusing on the basketball game.

"Sorry," she muttered.

"Who's calling you *sef*?"

"Shola."

He looked at her again. Eyes narrowed. Disbelief on his face. "Pick his call *nau*. *Abi wetin happen*? You guys are fighting again?"

"Somehow."

Detan muted the game and faced her. "What happened?"

"It's not that serious for you to mute your game." She picked her phone and decided to send her husband a text. "We will be fine."

"Talk *jere*."

"I'm serious. Married couples have misunderstandings all the time." Detan raised his hairy brows. "Okay." He turned and resumed watching the game. The sounds of the commentators filling the room once more.

"Did you tell him you are here?"

"Yes." A lie. She told her husband she was going to a work-related conference and not that she was on leave.

Me:

Please, stop calling me. I'm fine. I just need to cool off. Can't you at least understand that? I will call you later.

She tossed the phone aside and tried to focus on her novel but that wasn't working. She stared at the black-lettered fonts on the cream pages but her mind was elsewhere.

She realized she liked girls as a student of an all girls secondary school. She remembered seeing Victoria, her best-friend back then, undress in front of her when she had stained her uniform. Tobi couldn't explain the different emotions running through her at seeing the faded pink underwear on her friend's privates. The pull to run her hands over her young, smooth body had been alarmingly strong.

At first, Tobi thought something was wrong with her. That the devil was on to her and maybe the fall on her head her mother had always said happened when she was just three years old had somehow reset her brain. But holding hands with Victoria felt too good to be a side effect of brain damage and despite it costing her a best friend, the electricity that had raced through her body when she dared brush her lips against Victoria's was a memory she still cherished.

Tobi didn't tell anyone about her thoughts or emotions. More out of fear than anything else. Telling herself her emotions were out of the ordinary. Absurd . . . and so she kept it under. Twelve years later was when it dawned on Tobi of how much she was living in denial. She had already married Shola in an attempt to hide her secret.

Shola was a good guy. He didn't deserve how she treated him.

Her phone beeped. She had a text message.

Shola:

Tobi, this can't keep on. Every time I talk to you about God and bring up church, we have an argument. You can't keep running.

I can't keep tolerating this.

Tobi didn't reply. There was nothing to say. Every time she stood before Shola, she felt dirty. Like he knew her darkest secrets and would use it against her. Like she would never be good enough for heaven as he liked to preach.

Nowadays, Tobi didn't know what was right.

And little by little, she was starting to believe she would never be good for heaven.

Chapter Four

"Seyi, remove that key from your mouth! Now!"

Zainab stifled a yawn with a tired hand and smiled as her best-friend tried to manoeuvre the car key from her son's hands. Her victory brought eminent tears from his face that rolled down his chubby cheeks within seconds. It brought memories of Zainab's nephew who was around the same age.

"See, you have made him cry," Adesewa accused.

Zainab slapped a palm against her chest. Still trying to shake the sleep from her eyes. "Me? How? It's you that took the key from him," she half-heartedly countered.

"I told you not to give it to him. I told you he has started putting things in his mouth. Just admit you dozed off while I said that." Adesewa tossed the key to Zainab with one hand and produced a set of toy keys with a range of colours in her other.

Seyi kept quiet instantly. A smile filling his face. Zainab looked at Adesewa who was smiling triumphantly.

"Problem solved," Zainab said.

"No thanks to you," Adesewa said while carrying her son to the play pen at a corner of the lounge. Coming back into the kitchen area, she walked to the fridge and brought out two cans of Coke from the fridge before coming to sit next to Zainab at the breakfast bar. "So, how was your trip?" she asked, opening her can and taking a sip. "How is your dad and how did the conference go?" She managed to continue between sips, leaving little time for Zainab to respond to one question before throwing out another.

"Oh my days. The conference was amazing, Ade. Souls won for Christ. Deliverance from oppression. It was beautiful. Yeah, there were a few obstacles but God sorted those out. I was half-expecting to go there and talk to only a few people – twenty max. But a lot of people showed up. There was even a Christian couple who walked up to me, saying the message was what they needed at that point in time 'cause they were so discouraged." Zainab gushed, quickly invigorated by the memory of her time at the conference .

"Awww, why the discouragement?" Adesewa asked, concern causing her forehead to lightly wrinkle. This was part of the reason Zainab loved Ade, her ability to empathise with others at a moment's notice.

"Why live in the heart of trouble when you can be far from it like other Christians and enjoy your walk with God without fear of being killed the next day," was Zainab's response.

"Hmm, I totally get. Korede and I were still discussing it yesterday. Beating ourselves up at how infrequently we are in praying for Christians facing persecution."

Zainab thought of the young girl she met who wanted to give her life to Christ but was afraid of what her family would say. It made Zainab think of her mother and the battle she had to face for loving her father. "We should also pray for those who want to be Christians but are afraid of the repercussions."

Adesewa nodded. "Most definitely. I will add it to my list of prayers on my prayer wall."

"What's that?"

"Prayer wall, *nau*. Remember the movie *War Room*? Writing prayers on a paper and sticking it on the wall."

"Oh, yeah. I remember."

Adesewa took a long sip of her drink. "What about your dad?" She dropped the can and stood up.

"My father is stubborn. Refuses to see a doctor for his cough. I'm worried about him."

Her best friend returned minutes later with three small bags of plantain-chips and chin-chin. She'd barely tossed a bag of chin-chin at Zainab before tearing into her own.

"Is it that serious?"

"He complained of chest pain as well. So yeah, I guess it is. But I made him see a doctor before I left. We're waiting for the results."

Seyi shrilled and they both looked in his direction. The keys were a distance from him so Zainab went to pick it up for him. His toothy smile of appreciation gripped her heart.

"He'll be fine. Don't worry too much."

When Zainab returned, Ade was more than halfway through a second bag of chin-chin.

"Babes, if I didn't know better I would say you are pregnant."

Adesewa's eyes widened. "No. Pregnant *ke*? I'm breast-feeding *nau*. I would eat a lot."

"Aren't you supposed to be eating healthy stuff like *pap* or fruits?"

"I'm tired of it. Seyi is eight months old. He can take pap as well."

"Okay."

Zainab checked through her phone. A few WhatsApp messages from a couple of unknown folks and acquaintances asking for her availability to do their makeup.

"Is it only your dad's issue that's bothering you?"

"I'm fine."

"Liar. You have always been secretive Zainab. Spill it."

"Did you put *jazz* in your mouth?"

Adesewa pressed her lips together. "I saw a picture of IK and his wife."

Zainab didn't look up from her phone. "So?"

"Why didn't you tell me?"

"There's nothing to talk about. Nothing to say. My ex got married. That's not something worth discussing."

"For real?"

Zainab raised her head and looked at her friend, touched by the concern. "For real."

"You aren't saying anything because it hurts. Over six years of friendship, Zee, and I believe I should know you a little."

"Whatever."

"If you want to talk about it . . . I'm here."

"Thanks, but there shouldn't be a need."

"I miss Audrey. If she was here, she would have bugged you."

Audrey was the third lady in their girl-squad. She'd travelled abroad to pursue her dream of being in the movie industry, she was currently taking courses towards getting a degree in a bid to become the next Kemi Adetiba.

Zainab shook her head. "I would have ignored her. But Audrey decided to relocate to the U.S so you two can Skype, she can call me herself and I can ignore her."

Adesewa's mouth opened like she wanted to say more. But she stood, her petite frame crossing over to the pantry. "You know what? I'm going to make you my designer cupcake coated with chocolate and whipped cream."

"Is it for me or you?" Zainab joked, liking the idea of a thousand calories to lift her spirits.

Adesewa wrung her hands and bit her lip. "Actually, it's for both of us . . . because I also think I'm pregnant."

Zainab raised a brow, careful not to let the "I knew it" at the tip of her tongue fall out, instead she asked. "Does Korede know?"

"I haven't told him yet." She folded her arms and looked up at the wooden beams, biting her lip. Then she covered her face with the sleeves of her denim blouse. "It's so embarrassing."

"Means your husband can't seem to get enough of you." Zainab winked in an attempt to comfort her distressed friend.

Adesewa's eyebrows came together as her forehead formed tiny lines.

"Please, make the cake *jor* and be happy you're pregnant. Or do you want to have an abortion?"

She bit her lip and turned her eyes to where Seyi sat.

"Ade?"

"I don't know. I haven't healed fully from the surgery and now I'm pregnant?" She shifted her eyes back to Zainab no longer hiding her tears behind her clothing, "I don't know. I know it's wrong for me to have these thoughts. I know I should be happy I'm pregnant." She placed her palms flat on the kitchen counter. "But the truth is, I'm not ready for another baby. I'm still getting used to having a son. Gosh, you saw how crazy I got after Seyi. Recovering from all those nights I had to get up to feed him and cuddle him back to sleep. The way he kept eating and I felt like he was going to suck the blood out of me. I'm still trying to enjoy being a mother and now I get pregnant again?" Adesewa rubbed her forehead. "This can't be happening to me. I'm just very stupid to have gotten pregnant."

"Hey," Zainab said tenderly, "Don't be too hard on yourself. It's not like you planned it."

Adesewa dropped her hands, a frown on her face. "But I wasn't wise enough to consider protection or family planning."

"Can we agree that maybe this is what God wants for you? Also, breastfeeding is supposed to act as a contraceptive. It just didn't work for you."

Adesewa covered her mouth with a hand right after a sob escaped her lips and she closed her eyes. "Gosh, I'm so silly. There are a lot of people out there desperate to be called parents and here I am, blessed with another and considering a termination. I'm a bad mother."

Zainab winced at how cruel her friend was being to herself, unable to relate but feeling desperately empathetic. She stood and walked over to Adesewa, rubbing her back gently. "Don't say that. You're a great mum. You haven't made a final decision. Talk to Korede and you guys would surely know what to do. God provided this baby, so He would also give resources to take care of him or her."

Adesewa wiped the tears from her eyes with a fist. She sniffed. "Yeah, thanks." She forced a smile. "I'm definitely pregnant. See how I just had a mini meltdown. Let me make the cupcakes. Please, could you help rock Seyi? He needs to take a nap."

Zainab walked over to Seyi and picked him up. His baby soft skin and the smell of the cocoa-butter vaseline Adesewa used on him drifted to her. His small body resting against her chest. Sometimes she wondered if she could be a good mother. If she would ever *be* a mother. She thought of a lullaby her mother often sang to her while she was little and she crooned the same to Seyi. Forcing thoughts of ever having a child far from her mind, Zainab settled to be the best god-mother to her god-son and the best aunty to her niece and nephew.

* * *

Maureen finally made an appearance on Wednesday after work. Her chic look was a print wrap dress and strappy sandals. Her hair cascaded down her shoulders and her make-up as fresh as morning. Her perfume filtered the air.

"Hi." She pressed her lips against Detan's cheeks and waved cheerily at Tobi. Tobi waved back, the familiar flutter in her tummy returned. "How are you enjoying your leave?" Maureen asked, dropping her bag carefully on a red love-seat and taking off her shoes. Her toenails painted baby blue.

"I don't know if I should still call it a leave. The office keeps calling me."

"Her phone is a hotline," Detan chipped in.

"It means you're valuable to them."

Tobi shrugged. "Maybe."

"How was work?" Detan asked, pulling his girlfriend to himself and shifting her hair aside.

"Fine." Maureen grinned. "I only stopped by to greet you guys. I'm on my way to church for Bible Study. The youth pastor is teaching this great topic on social acceptance and homosexuality."

Tobi's drink went down the wrong way and resulted in a coughing spree.

"I would have liked to follow you, babes, but I have work related stuff to do."

Tobi snorted at the lie. Her brother only had a load of laundry and a basketball game with his street friends. Maureen might have guessed as much because of the quelling look she threw his way.

Smart girl.

"I will come another time," Detan said.

"Oluwadetan, why are you always giving me excuses when it comes to church?"

Tobi almost rolled her eyes at the mention of church again. *Must you follow me everywhere I go? Can't I be left alone?*

My love for you is a strong fire that cannot be quenched, Tobi.

"Did you guys hear that?" she asked the couple.

Maureen shook her head, looking clueless. "Hear what?"

"Never mind. I'm going to my room."

Maureen looked at her wristwatch. "I have to go. I don't want to be late." Detan started saying something but Tobi was already half-way to her room. She sprawled on her bed and plugged her ears. She closed her eyes. Bobbing her head to the tunes of 'One Dance' by Drake and singing along. She thought of how it would be like to live her life as she wanted.

No restraints. No condemnation. Just freedom.

She felt cold hands on her thigh and screamed. Her eyes snapping open.

"What are you doing here?" she squealed.

Shola raised his hands. His look apologetic. "I'm sorry. I didn't mean to scare you."

She yanked the ear-buds off her ears and got up. "You also aren't supposed to be here. How did you -"

"Know you lied to me about the conference and ran to your brother's house? Your brother gave me a call."

Tobi tossed the ear-phones on the bed and it landed at the far end of the bed. She should have known something would give. "I told you I needed some time."

He reached out to hold her hand but she stepped back from him. He sighed. "Sweetheart, you know you can't keep running from our marriage every time you get upset."

"Please, stop with all that running away nonsense. If I was running, I would have left you a long time ago." She ran her fingers over her uneven, black hair with gold highlights. A reminder that she needed to visit a salon to get it trimmed, to also touch up her nails and paint them black or something bold. "You shouldn't have come. You also shouldn't have called my mother."

He sat on the bed, the bed creaking with his weight. "I didn't have a choice. Tobi, talk to me! What's the matter? What have I done wrong this time?"

"Does it always have to be about you?"

"You are my wife," he said quietly. "We are one. You are me."

Tobi let out an expletive. "Please, spare me the Romeo and Juliet recitation. I'm tired of your holier than thou attitude! Tired of hearing you make out God as someone waiting to rain brimstones on me." She ambled over to the wardrobe and murmured, "I'm tired of this marriage."

"You would only be tired if you're guilty of something. Are you?" She laughed. "Stop trying to go all psychologist on me. I'm not one of your patients." She turned. "I haven't done anything wrong. All I ask is that you respect my opinions and ideals. You are a Christian and serving God. That's fine. But don't try to convert me. That's all I ask."

He let out a sigh and hung his head. "Okay. I've heard. It doesn't mean I won't be praying for you. So, can we go home now?"

"No." She turned her back on him. There was nothing keeping her from going home with him, but she wasn't ready. He needed to know she couldn't be bullied into doing what he wanted and if he tried to, there would be repercussions from his actions. "I will be back home by the end of the week."

"Okay." She heard the bed creak as he got up. Heard his footsteps as he walked up to her. "I love you, Tobi." He placed his hands on her shoulders. "See you at home."

The door closed behind him as he left. Tobi heard some voices before all was quiet again. She sat on the bed. Shola was a good guy. They met at a club six years ago and dated barely a year before she decided to accept his proposal of marriage. He loved her wild side. Said she complemented him. Then, he became a hard core Christian and everything changed.

He changed.

Tobi slowly reclined on the bed, knowing in her heart, she could never change.

* * *

"Pastor Micah! How are you, sir?" a young lady asked. Micah recognized her as one of those who recently joined the Wednesday Bible study meeting in church.

"I'm great, and you?" He couldn't remember her name. He asked.

"Maureen. Maureen Daniel. The message was really good, sir. I learnt a lot." She said, walking alongside him towards the lead pastor's office. The man had requested to see him after the service.

"Thank God for that."

"Sir, I've been meaning to discuss something with you. It's kind of personal."

He stopped and turned to face her. "Is it urgent? I have a meeting with Pastor Wilson and I don't know how long it's going to take."

She hugged her Bible to her chest. "Oh. I can wait."

It was past eight and he didn't think it would be right to have her wait for him when almost everyone in the church was gone. "I don't think that would be good. Give me your number and I can give you a call later tomorrow so we can talk. Is that fine?"

"Yes, sir."

They exchanged numbers and Micah made his way to the office. The familiar potpourri air-freshener greeted him. Pastor Wilson's bulky frame was seated behind a mahogany desk with a pile of files on them.

His large bible, opened directly in front of him.

"Micah, how are you? I was beginning to think you forgot our meeting."

"No, sir. I had to see to some things and cut short a counselling session."

Pastor Wilson nodded. "Have a seat."

Micah sunk his weight into the soft cushions. "Shepherding God's people is not an easy task. It must be done with grace and prayer." Reclining his back on his chair, he clasped his fingers and placed them on his extended waistline. "The youths like you a lot. I've seen a lot of improvements from them and the testimonies received are impressive."

"I can't imagine doing any of this without God's help," Micah responded.

"Yes, yes. God is an important factor in church growth."

Factor? Micah tried to relax his features, hoping not to betray his disdain at what Pastor Wilson had said.

"Micah, we are thinking of you heading the church permanently. It was a trial before. We wanted to see if there was any potential for the youths gathering in a separate section of the church. But with the increase in numbers and the financial reports; I can gladly say it's a good decision. Do you accept to pastor the church fully?"

He was short for words then finally managed, "Can I have time to pray about it?"

"Of course, but know the position is already yours."

"Thank you, sir."

Pastor Wilson glanced at his watch. "I have to leave. *Madam* doesn't like me staying out too late. Too much fear and superstitions going around these days." He rose to his feet and Micah followed suit.

"My regards to her, sir."

"She will hear."

Micah drove home, mulling the idea of being fully responsible for over a hundred souls. Was he ready for it? Could he handle it?

You can, Micah. If God is with you, you can.

He wasn't sure.

* * *

The soft bristles moved front and back on her nose, eyes and forehead. Her eyebrows were filled and priming had been done. Zainab looked up at the time. She dipped the tip of the brush lightly on the foundation at the back of her hand and applied. She had to move fast so there weren't any delays.

Her two assistants were working on the last two girls of the nine bridal squad. The photographers were standing at a corner of the room, waiting to take a photo of the finished work. Zainab shifted her eyes to gaze at Leke. He was looking down at his camera, probably looking through shots he had taken.

Zainab went for a nude-matte lipstick to complement the bride's gold blouse above the traditional George wrapper.

"All done," Zainab announced.

Leke was by her side in an instant.

Zainab watched him work as he gave directions to the bride on her posture and asked her to show how happy she was about her traditional wedding. The bride in turn gave a slight smile that teetered on the edge of anxiety, shyness and love. Her eyes, brimming over with joy and excitement. Zainab didn't doubt her love was true and pure; definitely the real deal.

"That's it," Leke said as he took shots, moving his muscular frame back and forth as though building rhythm to a dance in his head. "Okay, show me dance moves. Show us how you're going to dance towards your husband."

The bride began to move left and right, the smile fixed on her face. She even bent low slowly and rose back up. Her friends cheered her on as she danced. One of them actually got her phone out and played a song Zainab didn't know but noted had a catchy beat. Soon, the atmosphere was high on laughter and joy. Another photographer who accompanied Leke started taking pictures of the bridal party in their coral attire as they hooted and cheered.

The mother of the bride burst into the room.

"*Ehn-ehn*! You people are having fun without me. Me too I want to dance *o*." The woman started dancing. Her hips swaying in steady motions, her hands balled in fists. The sides of her lips spread apart and her shoulders bouncing. The cheers and hoots went to her. The bride throwing her hands in the air as well. Her long, coral beads jiggling against her chest.

Zainab found it all amusing. The joy, laughter . . . it was always the highlight of her day after hours of back-bending work, inhaling a mix of mint, coffee or bad breath while covering up pores with thick layers of makeup. Some layers were heavier than others, with more blemishes to conceal.

The dance ended with the bride and her mother embracing.

"She better not cry after spending two hours on that."

"It's tears of joy, Zee. Let her shed them even if it's just the period of the weddings."

"Ouch. You are so cynical."

"Nope. I'm a realist. I love weddings but I've seen too many to not know mishaps happen."

"What do you mean?" She took out a bottle of water from her backpack and gestured at her team to take a break. They would still be available for any touch-up. Part of the agreement with the bride was to stay the duration of the Edo-Igbo wedding because there would be a change in attire.

"You spend a lot of money on an engagement and at the end of the day, the couple never make it down the aisle. I believe in marriage, but I think too many people rush into it without proper thought and consideration to the fact that marriage takes hard work."

"True. I've made up some brides that looked like they were being forced to get married. The sadness in their eyes almost made me encourage them to put their foot down to whatever threats or self-sacrifice they have sold themselves to."

"Did you?"

She folded her arms across her chest. "I did one time." She felt his gaze on her.

"For real? What happened?"

"I was slapped hard on the face and asked to leave." This was followed by the obscenities the mother of the bride rained on her in heavy Yoruba dialect.

Leke looked at her. "Ouch."

"I guess there are some battles best fought on your knees."

"There are also some you can't fight because their minds are set on it." His jaw tightened as he said the words. "I have seen a lot in these weddings. I see all and know all there is to know."

She raised a brow at how cocky he sounded.

"I'm like Hawk Eye in Marvel. I see everything." He raised his camera.

"I see," she said dryly.

"Nope. You don't," he teased before walking away to take a couple more shots of the bride and excusing himself to the venue of the occasion.

Zainab shook her head as he left.

The two had crossed paths at a pre-wedding photo shoot a year ago. Leke had been impressed at how adept she was with time and makeup, and collected her contact. He called a month later to inform her he had a job for her. Hence, their work together on a few occasions in the last few years.

She checked her makeup in a compact mirror and decided to leave on her *ankara* gown and not change to anything over the top. She hated the scratchy material of the lace she brought with her for the event.

A lot of money had obviously been spent from the looks of the tasteful ornaments. A crew of camera men stood on a corner of the room, gisting among themselves while waiting for the wedding to begin. There was a time when all this was set up for her, but she had never known, and probably would never know, the extent of it. Never experience the joy of a man waiting for her.

Never say never.

She felt a nudge on her arm before she could capitalize on the words whispered across her heart, igniting a spark of hope within.

"Nice kicks by the way," Leke said.

Zainab looked down at her black lace-up sneakers and back at him. "Thanks."

The traditional wedding lasted well over three hours and Zainab was relieved to take off her shoes and soak in a Vanilla scented bath to relax. Her back ached badly and her body screamed for a massage. She went through her phone - discovering a long list of unread messages and missed calls. A text from Leke read:

Hey. Thought to send this to you. You looked intense. Have a good night's rest.

Zainab scrolled down and downloaded the image. It was a black and white photo of her. The background was blurred but there was an intensity in her eyes. She knew what she was looking at. The couple's dance, love evident.

The tears came heavily and she succumbed briefly to the shroud of loneliness enveloping her.

Chapter Five

Five years earlier (2014)

"I can't believe you came!" She wrapped her legs around his waist as she jumped on him, throwing her hands around his neck and hugging him tightly; her head pressing hard against his windpipe as he struggled to take in the cold air. His arms went around her waist, taking in small whiffs of the flowery scent of her perfume.

Kiki planted little kisses on his neck and dropped to her feet, pulling back to look in his eyes. Her piercing brown eyes gazed up at him with amazement and love, making his months of planning worth it.

"Happy birthday, sweetheart," he said, the sacrifices he had made and how he counted the days and set aside the money just to be here with her at this moment.

She smiled. "Thank you."

He pulled her close again. His fingers massaging the back of her scalp. Her hair feather-like on his fingertips. His forehead pressed gently against hers.

"God, I've missed you Kiki. You don't know how much," he declared, breathing in her intoxicating scent.

He felt her grin against his chest. Her fingers playing with the buttons on his grey coat. It was early March and the weather, brutally windy, had a biting chill that despite his thick coat, he couldn't help but feel.

"I've missed you too. My sister came up with a ton of scenarios on how I should react if you did indeed surprise me. I thought she was being super silly because all that I expected was a video call but she told me to pray hard and now here you are!" She stepped back again and raised a brow, "was she in on this?"

Kiki's elder sister stood in the background, holding bags of groceries from Sainsbury's. She gave a brief nod at him, grinning from ear to ear at having helped pull off the surprise before heading into the apartment to give them a few more minutes of privacy.

"I might have had some help. But did you?"

"Did I what?"

"Pray hard."

Kiki pursed her lips, her expression surrendering to guilt. "Not really. I didn't for one second think you'd be able to be here at all. You're here and that's all that matters." She brushed off invisible specks of dust from his coat while answering in a bid to avoid meeting his eyes.

"Now you can take me for that lovely dinner you were chatting about."

"Don't you have plans with your family?"

She lifted her shoulders. "Yeah, the usual birthday family tradition. But I don't think they would mind if I broke the tradition just this once."

"I think we should just have dinner with your family tonight and tomorrow we can have the whole day to ourselves after church."

"You really have thought this through," she gushed looking him in the eyes with all the love she had for him.

He winked at her.

The warmth in the apartment was a much welcome relief from the cold outside. Kiki peeled off her nude coloured coat to reveal a black off-shoulder dress that stopped just at her knee. The heart shaped pendant he gifted her when he left the UK a year ago, rested on chest. He felt his heart constrict against his chest. His mouth went dry all of a sudden at how beautiful she looked. Her permed hair resting on her

43

shoulders.

He could still remember their first kiss. He'd come up to Manchester early on a Friday so he could catch her as she came out of class. The smile on her face when she saw him waiting, with two Styrofoam cups of hot chocolate outside the building, had validated his desire to see her that day. They'd grabbed a quick dinner at a local restaurant before going to watch a movie, sharing a big tub of sweet and salt popcorn while Kiki slurped a huge Tango Ice Blast. Walking her home had been nerve-racking, his palms sweaty as he tried to muster up the courage to finally go in for that kiss he had dreamt about since setting eyes on her.

The knowledge that all he had that night was Demi's lonely couch before a long journey back to London. That's what pushed him to finally lean in for that kiss when they arrived at Kiki's. His heart rate sped even further as she leaned in also, their lips touching, lightly at first but slowly intensifying as he brought his arms around her waist and she his. He tasted the artificial sweetness of her ice blast and thought he'd never tasted anything more intoxicating.

It had taken a lot for him to pull back from her that night. To keep his desires a bay.

Letting go of the memory, Micah reached into his pocket and held the small box nestled there briefly before releasing and joining her family.

"I remember when Kiki was little and she would run to get her shoes when we were going out. She wanted to go everywhere I went," Solomon said. "I will never forget the day I had to bribe her with two quid just so she wouldn't tell our mum and dad about me sneaking out of the house at 1 in the morning."

"Two quid?" Elijah asked. "She asked me for five!"

"Weren't you going to see your girlfriend? What was her name again – Ngozi Amaka?" Felix chipped in.

"And she was totally gutted when I couldn't take her with me to London for the Hillsong Christmas concert," Solomon said, ignoring Felix's taunts.

Kiki wagged a finger at Solomon. "You still owe me."

"I know." His eyes shifted to Micah for a moment then back at his sister. "I promise to make it up to you?"

Kiki's eyes narrowed, "You promise?"

"Cross my heart and hope to die," he responded with a mock solemnity that had the whole table laughing. It was a throwback to their childhood.

Joining in the faux seriousness Solomon had adopted, Kiki got up from the table pinky finger raised, walked over to Solomon and made him cross fingers and salute; their special promise agreement.

Unable to keep the serious looks for long, they both started giggling, egged on by the sniggers coming from the rest of the table and Kiki quickly hugged her brother and planted a kiss on his cheek to show that all was forgiven.

"Love you too, baby sis," Solomon responded, laughter still spilling over his lips as Kiki made her way back to her seat.

Micah looked at Kiki's parents who were seated, enjoying the meal and their children's banter. Kiki's father nodded, an affirmation of his blessings on what Micah had in mind.

"Kiki . . ." he started once she sat back down. He went down on one knee in the presence of the people she loved most in the world. People she may have to leave behind to begin a new journey with him in a new place.

"Kiki, I love you like I have never loved any other woman in my life." She pressed her hands together against her lips as tears pooled her eyes. "Words fail to express how much I love you. But every day, I thank God for bringing you into my life." He brought out the black velvet box that held the ring he had purchased in London. "Kiki, will you do me the honour of being my wife?"

Micah heard someone sniff behind him, but his focus was on the woman alone - the woman whose teary eyes were staring back at him, not fully readable.

"Kiki?"

"I- I." She was at a loss for words, possibly for the first time ever. She looked into the eyes of the man she loved so dearly, looked around to see her family waiting with bated breath, noticed the tears shining in all of their eyes before turning back to Micah.

"Kiki?" he prodded, nervousness causing a fine sheen of sweat to coat his upper lip.

"I-yes," she whispered, too overcome with emotion to speak any louder.

"Yes?" he asked, hopefulness making his eyes appear to shine brightly.

"Yes!" she said even more loudly, handing over her left hand so that he could slip the beautiful ring on her finger.

Micah quickly got up and pulled his new fiancée into a kiss, one that quickly turned urgent and much more steamy than present company needed to see.

"We are still here," Kiki's father announced and the rest of the family laughed.

"Welcome to the family." Solomon embraced Micah, patting his back emphatically, while trying to mask the tears, clear as day, in his eyes.

"Thanks." Micah said not at all bothering to stop the tear that escaped his brimming eyes.

* * *

Micah dialled Maureen's number and waited till she answered on the third ring.

46

"Good afternoon, Pastor Micah."

He shielded his eyes from the sun and glanced at his phone briefly before returning it to his ear. "Maureen?"

"Yes sir."

"How did you know it was me?"

"Truecaller."

He nodded. "Right. How are you?"

"I'm fine. And you?"

"I'm better than good." He went back into the house and leaned against his dining table, shifting his note

book and Bible aside. He was preparing his study notes against a Wednesday sermon alongside praying about Pastor Wilson's offer.

"That's good to know. Thank you for calling as promised."

"You're welcome. What's up?"

She breathed heavily and he felt her hesitate. "It's about my relationship. I'm in a relationship with a guy like that and, he claims he's from a Christian home and also claims to be a Christian but I'm seriously in doubt."

Micah sighed inwardly. He should have guessed it would be another relationship issue. He was getting a lot of those these days. Why was it so hard for people to make a choice when it came to a marriage partner? He had thanked God everyday when he and Kiki were an item. Grateful to God for bringing her into his life. Grateful for her love.

"What makes you doubt him?" His eyes found a silver-framed photograph of Kiki and him at Demi's wedding four years ago.

"He brings up various excuses as to why he can't come to church with me. Pastor Micah, I like him a lot but I'm not sure. Even his mother has funny ethics."

"What sort of ethics?"

"She's insisting myself and Detan, that's his name, should try to have a baby. That way I can get her son to commit to me quickly. Frankly, I'm not in a hurry to get married. My parents aren't pressuring me."

"Then why are you still with him? Have you prayed about it?"

"Yes, sir."

"So?"

"I'm unsure. I know the right thing to do would be to leave him. But, I really like him."

"I understand how you feel. But regardless, you have to do what is right. God knows what's best for you. If this guy gets away, it doesn't mean the world is over. There are more. There are others out there you can be with. Do you understand?"

"I understand. Thank you, sir. But to be honest, getting a partner this day and age is really proving difficult. There are a lot of things I would want in a man, but because of my beliefs, it seems I would have more things to look out for than the average woman who isn't a Christian."

Micah sat. "Explain more."

"What I'm trying to say is, there are Christian guys out there who view settling down with a woman is the norm. Like it's no big deal to sleep with a girl you're going to end up marrying. Like sex is not a major issue."

"Have you and Detan had-"

"No!" He could hear the disdain in her voice at his prompt assumption.

"I'm sorry. Please, go on."

Micah heard a woman's voice in the background and Maureen responded by telling the person she was fine.

"Are there still Christian guys who are willing to wait it out to the wedding or is there really no hope?"

Micah remembered the scripture that talked about the very elect falling. "There's hope, Maureen. Concerning this guy, if he doesn't share your values . . . you already know what to do. Do what you have to."

The call ended shortly after that.

Micah hoped he hadn't been too harsh with her. He rubbed his eyes with his thumb and forefinger. There were times the idea of standing in front of a group of youths, who looked up to him, frightened him. There were days he had picked up a pen and written a letter to Pastor Wilson, stating that he didn't want to go on being a pastor.Minutes later, he would yank out the letter from the envelope and tear it into pieces.

He pulled his Bible closer to him; the pages worn from use. There was a time when the words in it meant everything to him and he couldn't go a day without taking it in like a fish needs water for survival. Now, all he did was live off crumbs of yesterday.

God, where are you?

I'm right where you left Me, son.

The reassurance was calming but brought back memories. *Where were You when Kiki needed You? Where were you when she was crying out in pain? Where were You when she was dying?!*

I was there, as I am here for you.

Micah shut his eyes, as the jaws of pain seized his heart. He had begged God. He had fasted. He had prayed fervently. Yet, nothing had happened.

Yes, God was sovereign. But He was also the reason for Micah's pain. He shut the Bible and headed to his room. Collapsing on the bed, he drifted off to sleep.

* * *

Tobi closed her wardrobe. She was home. But home felt more like a prison to her. She was struggling to figure out who she was, and if possible *why* she was.

Does that even make sense?

Tobi plodded to the un-made bed. It was obvious Shola had left the house in a hurry. The bedspread was casted aside in a messy heap on her side of the bed. The white bed sheet had brown stains on it. Disgusted, she pulled everything off and whipped out fresh bed linens from the chest of drawers where they kept their towels and beddings.

She made the bed, just like she had learned years ago from a roommate back in the university. Getting rid of the dirty linens, she had a long day of fixing up the house and setting up dinner. It was no wonder Shola missed her. She was merely a maid in their home.

She went back to the bedroom, turned on the TV and tried to watch a Netflix movie but it did little to dissuade her thoughts. Her phone was the next option and she browsed up sites on the LGBTQ community. There was a particular site she had been following for quite a while and had been a support system to her.

Anonymousgirl189: *Being free with myself and who I truly am is totally liberating. I can be with who I truly love. Say yes to coming out!*

Wildchild84: *Left my wife of 10 years. It broke her heart. Cursed a lot *LOL*But hey! You've gotta make tough choices if you want to be happy.*

Tobi scrolled down to the comment section and typed:

Tgirl90: *I totally get you, but what about your family? Your parents? What if they can't understand the way you feel?*

Anonymousgirl189: *@Tgirl90 No one ever claims to understand at first. Some are totally delusional and fixated on their ideals and such. They may eventually understand, but you've got to be you girl!*

FashionGenius: *Totally @anonymousgirl189. @Tgirl90 . . . follow your heart. Life is too short to not be who you are. People may say you hit your head and all other bullocks but be you. My guy and I got married two weeks back. We are super in love and happy. Thinking of adopting in the near future!*

Tgirl90: @FashionGenius *Congratulations! Thanks for the advice.*

Tobi inhaled sharply when the bedroom door opened.

"I saw your car outside." He closed the door behind him. "I'm happy to see you home."

"You didn't try to clean up after yourself." She cleared her web tabs and closed her phone. "I came back home and had to clean the whole house. Is this why you missed me? So I could come back and do my duties as your maid?"

"Don't say that, Tobi. You know I'm very bad when it comes to house chores and such."

She glared at him. "What an excuse, Shola. You mean making the bed and picking up the broom to shove a few dust particles into the Parker is too much work for you, *abi?* "

"Okay, it's not an excuse. I was lazy. I'm sorry."

Tobi bit hard on her lip. Holding back her tongue from a nasty retort. If she had it her way, she wouldn't have returned. In one swift move, she was off the bed and standing a few inches from him. She licked her lips and took a deep breath.

"I'm going downstairs to serve dinner."

She served his food in a blue ceramic bowl. A wedding gift from his mother. She had prayed for her at the traditional wedding two years ago. Praying that her husband would continue to eat from her bosom and her pot. Tobi had been embarrassed when Shola's mother smiled at her and tapped the side of her breast for good measure to emphasize her point. Saying it would be good enough for her son.

A drop of stew fell on her finger and Tobi licked it away; the heavy taste of curry lingering on her tongue.

Shola's father gifted them with house keys on their wedding day. A beautiful home all the way in VGC that boasted of marble finishing and interiorly decorated for them to move in immediately. Tobi forced her thoughts away from how horrible their honeymoon was. A far cry from anything romantic and intimate. All she had wanted to do was to hide in a cave and remain there forever.

* * *

"I wish I could you tell you going through tests and temptations in your walk with God would be easy, but it won't." He looked at a few of the youths in the eye as a way of connecting with them. His audience was a mix of disinterested and guilt stricken people. Some muffled yawns, worn-out from a long day. A few looked like the message was somehow cutting deep into them. Pastor Wilson had taught Micah years ago that those he preached to in whatever congregation would be a mix of that.

"Temptation is something each and everyone has to face. If Jesus faced it, who are you to feel macho over the devil? Or you think you can get away easily if you had Tony's muscular look?" Ladies laughed and a guy playfully punched Tony on the back.

"Nah. It's not about physical strength but mental and spiritual endurance given to you by God's immeasurable grace. The spirit guides the soul and the body. The body will always betray you. Your mind will always try to talk you into why you can just sleep with that girl or make-out with that guy that lives down your street that's stalking you. That's why the Bible talks about us renewing our minds. Renew daily for the battle is daily. It never stops until we-", he stared at his feet, then back at the small crowd, "- until we're called home."

He walked back to the pulpit podium and glanced at his notes. "Sex. Porn. Masturbation. Homosexuality. Sexual sins have insatiable appetites. You have a taste," Micah punched his fist against his palm loudly, "and you want more. Paul said, *live as one who has died to every form of sexual sin and impurity. Live as the one who dies.*" Micah paused. "I die daily. A lot of us have rubbed Christianity in the mud by agreeing to participate in pre-marital sex. Your doing it tells non-Christians that they can do it too. But you think, *haba* Pastor, they have been doing it since *na*. You know what? At the back of their minds and somewhere in their hearts, they still look to you for affirmation. They look to you to distinguish right from wrong."

Micah mentioned a few more issues and threw the floor open for those who wanted to ask questions. A hand was raised and Micah gave room for whatever the man wanted to say. Micah recognized him as one of the singers in the choir.

"I have a friend," he began, gesticulating as he spoke, "who's sort of addicted to taking cough syrups just to get high. He claims he wants to stop. Tries his possible best, but can't seem to help it. Now he claims its best he steps aside from being a Christian because he would never get it right. What can I do to help?"

"First of all, what's your name?"

"Fimi."

Micah responded to his question and a few others before surrendering to time. They were a couple of minutes over but then, no one really complained. He took his time to get home and settled afterwards for a bowl of garri, cold water and groundnuts. Micah thought back to Fimi, hoping he wasn't talking about himself in the second person. Whatever the case, he felt the need to probably bring up a guest speaker to talk to them. Someone with experience.

But he just couldn't figure out who.

* * *

Zainab nibbled on her fingernails. "So you just stopped by to see me in the studio? All the way from Ibadan?" She queried her father, playing with little nail fragments in her mouth.

"No. I'm also here to visit my grandchildren as well." He looked around her office. Taking in the monochrome black and white walls. "Your designer did an excellent job. You know, each time I come in here, there's this calmness I feel in my spirit."

Her lips curled up in a smile. Eliana, the head designer and owner of Cre8tive Splash, had done awesome work for her office. Mixing things Zainab liked. Focusing on details to the point of painting mason jars in various colours and using them as brush holders. And filling up apothecary jars with assorted nail polishes.

It was pure genius.

Zainab had happily attended her son's naming ceremony months back.

"I know, right? Each time I come here I feel happy and excited to work. Like God is letting me know how, somehow, what I do here is important. The ladies that have shared testimonies about their lives being transformed is much more than I could ask. It feels too good to know my life counts for something to God."

"It does and don't ever forget it. I'm so happy to see you like this. I thank God every single day that you came into my life. I love you, dear."

"I love you too." She let out a breath. "Okay. What did the doctor say?"

He tapped her white desk once. "That I'm in perfect health. Gave me a couple of drugs to use and that should take care of the cough."

She blinked and narrowed her eyes. "Really?"

"Yes."

"That's great news." Smiling, she continued, "What can I offer you?"

Zainab's father looked at the time on his watch. "I've been here for fifteen minutes and it's now you ask."

She shrugged and spat her flavourless nails into a tissue and tossed it in the bin near her legs. "You know I've never been hospitable ." Then she called her assistant to bring in pack of juice and green tea.

"You've got to learn it."

She felt her face tightening as she forced a smile. "I will." *Someday. Maybe.*

Zainab wrapped her hands around her mug. She blew softly across the surface of her tea before taking a sip. Her assistant knocked once more on her door and stepped in; announcing Zainab had a guest.

Leke showed up at her door a few minutes later with his signature look of camera hanging around his neck and carrying a backpack.

"Good afternoon, sir." Leke said, bowing his head low and his fingertips touching the grey carpeted floor of her office.

"Good afternoon, young man." Her father faced her, arching his brows. *Who's this?*

"Dad, this is Leke Falola. We work together on some events. He's a photographer. I think I've mentioned him to you at some point." She looked at Leke. "Leke, this is my father, Pastor Eghosa Phillips."

Her father extended his hand to Leke and they both shook hands. "How are you, son?"

"I'm doing very well, sir. It's nice to meet you. I've heard very little about you from Zainab."

She shifted her eyes from the brochure and threw Leke a look.

"Don't mind my daughter and her ways. In fact, I was just scolding her some minutes ago. Sit down, Leke. How is the photography world in Nigeria?"

Leke dropped his backpack and sat down on the next available seat close to her father. "I can't complain. Business is fine, though it can be better."

Her father chuckled. "Isn't that the truth of life."

"What brings you here, Leke?" Zainab asked, wanting to disrupt whatever was brewing between them.

"I was around and decided to say hello. I did a photo shoot for a six-month old not too far from here and this happens to be on my way to Ikoyi so I dropped by."

"That's very kind of you, Leke."

Zainab clenched her teeth. "Daddy, aren't your grandchildren missing you?"

"I'm sure they are." He stood. "I'm also supposed to bring back sausage-rolls and meat pies. The joys of a grandfather." He extended his hand to Leke once again. "Nice meeting you, Leke. I hope that we will see each other again sometime soon and our visit would be extended."

"When are you leaving for Ibadan?"

"Next week."

"I would try and work something out."

Zainab's father nodded then jerked his thumb at her. "Don't invite this one."

Leke laughed as Zainab rolled her eyes. "Yes, sir."

"*Pele*, you look tired," Leke said to her when she returned from seeing her father off.

"I am. There are a lot of things I need to handle. I have two weddings scheduled on the same day at opposite ends of Lagos and both ladies insisted I have to be the one to do their makeup. It means I have to load up on caffeine and work extra hard. It's days like that that stress me out."

There was a comfortable silence between them until he said, "You seem very cool with your dad."

A loud cackle of laughter came from the make-up studio. "Yeah, we are cool with each other. It didn't happen overnight."

"Doesn't look like that to me. It looks like a relationship you've had all through the years." Leke got up and chose to stand close to the white canvas of an African woman stencilled to it. Her afro had a pink rose perched on it. "Is this you?"

She lifted her eyes from her phone. "No. My mother."

"It's nice. You rarely talk about her. Where is she?" He looked at the portrait once more. "You kind of look like her."

"She passed a few years ago."

"Oh, I'm sorry about that. Was she ill?"

"Yeah. Bone Cancer. I didn't find out until she had a few months to live. She kept it a secret - wanted to cherish our moment together without the further piercings of pity and sadness. It was her own way of dealing with it." Zainab could still smell the antiseptic, could still hear the beeping of the heart monitor, still see the pain in her mother's eyes and her silent plea for forgiveness.

"You guys were close?"

Zainab swallowed hard and pushed away the hurtful memories and accompanying pain encroaching on her. "In our own way, though not as much as I would have liked. I was sort of the black sheep in the family and kept to my ways even if it hurt her. We made amends later though. I only wished it was soon enough."

His eyes shifted back at her and he shoved his hands in his jeans pockets. "My dad and I hardly get along. He's just a strict man with very high morals."

"The typical Nigerian father."

"Maybe. That and the fact he was a soldier in the Nigerian army. So he always gave out his orders at home like we were all his subordinates and not his family."

Zainab paused on a message she was typing and looked at Leke. They had been colleagues for a while but had never ventured much on their personal lives. This was another side of him she was seeing.

"I'm sorry. If it's any consolation, I didn't know my father till twenty-plus years later. Long story. I wanted nothing to do with him, but he wanted everything to do with me."

Leke grinned. "Like God and us."

She nodded. Without a doubt, God had been good to her. *Too good.*

57

Her past. All the things she had done . . . God picking her up from the pits and accepting her as His child was beyond words.

I love you beyond words, Zainab. Keep believing it. A person in doubt can never get anything from Me. But you have all of Me. Rest in My love.

Zainab felt chills down her back. She still hadn't gotten used to hearing Him speak to her. Either in scriptures or the still small voice. It only made her more grateful to be worthy to hear Him.

"Yeah, at least I know God isn't like that." He took out his phone and looked at the time. "I have to take my leave. I have another appointment."

"When are you going to tell me what happened with you and Emem?"

Leke took his bag. "Can't we just leave it as we broke up?"

She shook her head.

"Let's make a deal. I tell you about Emem and you tell me about your dad."

Zainab wasn't ready to tell anyone about her past or the circumstances around meeting her dad. "No." She picked her phone once again and tapped her uneven fingertips across the screen. "See you later." She heard him chuckle as he left.

Chapter Six

He turned on his computer and imported the files from the memory card to it. He double tapped the folder and the screen came alive with over a thousand pictures of Seyi and Tosin's white wedding. As much as he loved being a photographer, he didn't look forward to the post-wedding brouhaha.

He was up till one in the morning, sorting through traditional wedding photos taken, sending a few to the bride. She was already breathing down his neck to see some of them and share with the world. Which was another thing Leke didn't like - impatient clients.

Leke started out with culling; spending not more than thirty seconds selecting the best pictures to be edited. Back when he just started, he would take a while to find the perfect picture to best describe the joys of the couple, trying his possible best to make everything perfect. But years of experience had taught him mulling over it for too long was more for his pleasure than for the clients.

His door-bell rang. Leke ignored it. Focusing more on editing a picture of the groom as he watched his bride walking down the aisle. The twinkle in his eyes and the way the corner of his lips curled when he smiled, a slight shimmer of tears in his eyes. Moments like this were priceless. Things he loved to capture through the viewfinder.

Leke cropped the picture and made it black and white, blurring parts of the image for that *Bokeh* effect.

A tingling went down his spine as he gazed at the finished work.

He had to admit how much he loved the idea of being a part of people's most precious moments. Even if the wedding was just a fanfare for some, while for others it was the start of a great journey.

The door-bell rang again and this time a phone call followed immediately after.

"Hello."

"Leke, please come and open the door." She said and ended the call.

He saved his work and shuffled to the door while pulling a shirt over his head. He opened the door and Emem's small frame breezed in, bringing with her a load of tension and emotions Leke wasn't ready to deal with.

"Why didn't you answer since?"

"I'm in the middle of editing."

"Oh okay. Sorry I interrupted you." She dropped her bag on the only table in his small living-room. "I should have guessed you would be busy after Tosin's wedding. Thanks for handling my cousin's wedding despite everything that has happened." She cleared her throat. "I just think we need to talk. Clear the air."

"There's nothing to clear. Everything is as clear as rain. You left me because you don't love me as much I do."

Her face fell. "I do, Leke, with all my heart. We just want different things."

"Yeah, you want different things with someone richer who can foot your bills," was his caustic reply.

Her lips twitched and she clasped her palms on her elbows. "I'm not here to argue with you. Believe it or not, this is hard for me too. I love you, Leke. But it's just not enough for me. Don't you appreciate me being honest with you instead of inventing one cock and bull story?" she responded, side stepping his harsh critique.

He sat on one of the two chairs and folded his arms. "Okay, so why are you here?"

"I don't want us to be enemies. I still want us to be friends."
Leke unfolded his arms and rubbed the back of his head. "I'm not
sure I can do that. Look Emem, it might be easier for you to just move
on, but not for me. It's hard. For goodness sake, we went out for two
and a half years. Here I was thinking we would get married, and then
you tell me you aren't interested in settling down with me. Please let's
be real; friendship is far from my mind."

"I'm really sorry, Leke."

He stood. He didn't want to have this conversation. "If you aren't
here to tell me you've changed your mind then there's nothing left to
say. I really have a lot to do. I have a tight deadline."

She didn't argue, just nodded and took slow steps to the door. "Be
good, Leke." She hugged him close and took a step back to look at him.
"If possible, please keep in touch."

Leke slammed the door behind her.

He rummaged through his many folders and double tapped on *L-EM*
and multiple pictures of the two of them popped up on his laptop
screen. Romantic pictures. Random pictures. Pictures of her alone.
Pictures of them being silly with funny faces. Photos of her with his
new Nixon DSLR camera.

He highlighted all the photos. A teardrop fell to the back of his hand.
He raised the hand and wiped unshed tears from his eyes.

He shifted the mouse; the cursor hovered over the *delete all* button.
Somehow, somewhere deep within, he hoped she would reconsider.
In one click, all memories he made with Emem Asuquo disappeared.

Leke inhaled deeply and went back to work.

* * *

"You are not serious!" Zainab shook her head as Korede tried to set up the barbecue grill while telling them about his trip to Abuja.

"I am."

Zainab and Adesewa looked at each other and burst into laughter. Adesewa covering her mouth to keep the diced, cube carrots in.

He continued, "My sister was embarrassed."

"I feel for her. Don't worry she would be fine."

Zainab looked at one of her favourite couples in the world. Watched as Adesewa stood tip-toes to kiss him on the cheek and whisper something into his ears. Whatever she said rewarded her with a huge grin from him. Zainab looked elsewhere, feeling like she was infringing on some sort of intimate moment between them.

"Have you told him yet?" she asked Adesewa when they were alone. It was a sunny Saturday and Adesewa had suggested a nice lunch outside. Befitting after days of non-stop outpour.

"Yes. Told him yesterday; he was surprised and started asking questions like if I was okay and not in pain. We sat down and discussed. We are going to the hospital first thing Monday so we can talk with the family doctor."

"That's good." Zainab nudged her arm. "I told you Korede was a good guy."

Adesewa smiled slightly and looked down at her fingers. The tiny diamonds on her silver band glistening in the sun. "Yes, I know. It's just that we have a lot going on. I just fully opened *Sugar and Spice* and things may be a little tight financially. I don't want to stress him. Him footing all the bills and all."

"You sound like you the old Adesewa who was totally independent. I can guess how hard this could be for you, but hey you've got to trust that God is always in control of your situation and nothing takes him by surprise. Remember when God told you to pull out from your auditing firm?"

"Yeah, and dissolve my partnership with Kobina."

"Exactly. That your Ghanian partner that was leading you to fraud. Thank God you were obedient and left in good time before EFCC pounced on them. Don't you see, Ade? Nothing takes God by surprise. He is there for you even before the storm breaks out. Who says He can't help you during your tough moments?"

Adesewa nudged her this time. "See who's talking so confidently about God. You know there was a time I wished and prayed for this day to happen. When we can freely discuss God and you wouldn't argue with me or give that disgusted look when I tell you how much smoking and drinking were totally bad for you."

Zainab pulled her leather face cap low over her eyes. Shielding her eyes from the sun rays. She remembered all too well. Looking back, she knew there were a lot of things in her life she had to be thankful for . . . irrespective of what she didn't have at the moment.

"It feels good to see you this way. Not as wild and crazy as you were. It's beautiful how God does things. Making a person transition from one way to another just by believing in a name with faith."

Zainab nodded. "I know." She watched the chicken sizzle on the grill, smoke emitting from it and imagining how good it would taste with Adesewa's peppered sauce. "Sometimes, I wonder how my life would have been if my father didn't talk to me or the wedding with IK still happened. Maybe I would have died of an overdose." Zainab stared at Adesewa. "How did you do it though?"

"Do what?"

"Put up with my excesses. How did you manage to stay even when you knew about – about other girls? Why did you stay my friend?"

"Because something in you was crying out for help. I knew you were depressed and hiding it. I saw you as a friend who I needed to pray for. But I won't lie, there were times I was afraid you would sneak up in my room and try something funny. Just for safety measures, I locked my room most nights."

63

"I would never have done that to you." Zainab knew it occurred to her once- twice. But she never ventured into it. Adesewa and Audrey were the closest people to her in her entire life. She may have proven stubborn, hard-headed. But their friendship had kept her going. Had let her know she was still being cared for.

"Thank you for being there for me."

Adesewa patted her hand, taking her eyes briefly from Korede with Seyi. "You were there for me too in so many ways. Yeah, we both made terrible decisions in the past. But we are so much better now. I love you, sis.

"Ditto."

"*Choi!* You can't say you love me back?"

"I just did."

Adesewa narrowed her eyes. "Still be acting tough and macho there. When the right guy comes, and I have a feeling it's really soon, I will see if you would still be behaving like a tom-boy."

"*Na you sabi.* He would love me for who I am if he actually exists." *From what I'm willing to share.* Zainab didn't think she could ever tell a man about her past. If she did, no one would want her. If she couldn't let go of the disgust of her past mistakes, then she didn't think any man could.

* * *

Micah fished out the flyer somewhere on the kitchen table amongst a pile of books and papers. But he didn't see her there. Not even a name. All he could recall was her message on love for God that connected to him. He decided to place a call to Pastor John who was a good friend of his.

"Hey, Micah. Good afternoon. How are you?"

"Afternoon, John. I'm good. How are your wife and kids?" When

John affirmed their wellness and they had small talk, he moved to the reason why he called. "There was a lady that preached at your church's conference earlier this year. She has a northern name that I can't remember right now."

"Are you referring to Zainab Baruwa-Phillips?"

The name struck a chord. "Possibly. Is she the one that talked about keeping the fire burning?"

"Yes, we are talking about the same person. What's up?" He could hear the curiosity in his friend's voice.

"I'm thinking of inviting her to talk to some of our youths."

"Oh."

"What happened?"

"Well, it's just that I had to plead with her to talk on that day. She isn't really into talks as such. One of the Ministers cancelled that day and I felt God telling me to reach out to her to take the person's place. It was sort of a Peter and Cornelius situation."

Micah was confused. "Please explain."

"It only took a serious confirmation from God before she agreed."

Micah didn't doubt this was what God wanted because he wouldn't have thought of her at all. "I believe this is God leading me. Can I have her phone number?"

"Let's do this instead. I'll call her and if she agrees I will text her number to you."

Micah agreed, albeit hesitantly. "I will look forward to a positive response."

"Sure. How are you, bro? Talk to me. And please, don't just tell me you're fine."

Micah chuckled. "What if that's the truth?"

"Then I want to hear what's going on with you. The youth church, your personal life. How you are coping."

"Church is great. My pastor wants me to head the youth church permanently. I'm still thinking about it. My personal life? The truth is I'm struggling. It's hard. Life seems hard. People would expect in three years I should have gotten over it and married someone else. Sometimes the thought annoys me. Like, why can't they understand? They think as a pastor, I have to be strong since I know what God's Word says about death."

"First of, congratulations on the youth church. Don't just think about it. Pray as well. Second thing is you know, people tend to have this funny belief that as a minister we don't have our own problems or don't go through massive temptations or trials. And so, if we just happen to miss it in one area, we are total failures."

Micah nodded. There were times he messed up and Kiki was there to help him pick up the pieces. She acted strong for both of them even when she didn't have to. Uttering words of encouragement to help him bounce back.

"But the truth is, God is whom we serve. He doesn't demand perfection from us by our doing but by His grace. He also expects that we trust and rely on Him every day of our existence. Persevering in moral character and never expecting efficiency in ourselves alone but in His strength. Take it a day at a time, Micah. Don't rush. Don't also linger in your pain. Take God's hands and let Him walk you out. I can't say I understand exactly how you feel, but I can boldly say God does."

The call ended not too long after that, giving Micah a lot to think about. He hadn't heard much from Kiki's parents. They refused to answer his calls. Only Solomon and Cassandra showed interest to his well-being and how much it hurt. The rest of the family believed he had killed her.

Maybe he had.

* * *

Still five years ago,

They took a train to Liverpool after a church service. He treated her to a meal at *Almost Famous*. He just couldn't bring himself to eat tiny five course meals, and besides, it was what he could afford.

Kiki teased that he was too much of an African man.

There was no need to try to catch up on each other's lives because they were already very much aware of what was happening. Ever since he returned to Lagos, they made sure they called every evening and Skyped once a week.

But there was something he was yet to tell her.

"My pastor called me into his office a few weeks ago. He said he had something really important to tell me."

Kiki paused her food midway to her mouth. Cheese from her burger dripping down her fingers onto the plate of fries. "Okay, what did pastor Wilson say? That's his name right?" She adjusted her jaw and bit into her burger. He loved how she rolled her eyes as she chewed when she was enjoying something so good.

Micah nodded, trying to keep his thoughts pure and not on the enticing curve of her lips. "He wants me to head the youth department in church."

Her eyes widened. "Wicked! I mean, that's great! Congratulations!"

"He said he wants to start training me to be a Pastor. Said I have what it takes."

"I agree, baby. I don't doubt this is what God wants for you." She wiped her hands on a tissue and held his hand; using her thumb to rub the back of his hand gently. "I'm so proud of you. Why didn't you tell me sooner?"

"I wanted to discuss it with you in person. See your reaction to it."

"You mean you wanted to make sure I wasn't pretending to be happy for you? You could have done a video call and seen my facial reaction." She tilted her head. "You still don't trust me, do you? Micah, I'm not like Blessing or whatever her name is. I'm not going to leave you just because you want to be a pastor."

"I'm the one who's bad with names here," he responded, trying quickly to lighten the mood.

"Whatever, my point is I'm not leaving you if you decide to be a pastor down the line or you change your mind and decide to be a cobbler instead. As long as God is leading you, which I don't doubt He is. I'm with you, babe. I'm not going anywhere. We're in this together."

"I appreciate that." He held her hand and pressed it a little. "Means a lot for me to hear you say that."

"Don't keep anything away from me next time, please," she admonished, her face taking on a seriousness that let him know how much his openness meant to her.

They talked a little more and after lunch, took a river cruise and bus tour around the area. He'd had Demi buy tickets two days earlier. They enjoyed the cruise, but most importantly they enjoyed the time spent together.

"When do you think we should get married?" Micah asked her as they took a tour around the Museum. Their tour guide talking in front of them.

"December is not a bad idea. What do you think?"

"Same here. I'm wondering if my parents can make it all the way here. Of course I would have to invite some other family members, but the best thing about not marrying in Nigeria is you don't get to have unwanted guests crash your wedding."

Kiki tapped him lightly on the arm.

"I'm being serious. It's just going to cost a lot."

"*Beta* soup is costly," she said wiggling her eyebrows while taking a stab at pidgin English

Micah laughed at her poor attempt.

She tapped his arm harder this time. "Hey, don't laugh at me. I really want to get this right. I've been doing research. Pretty soon, I'll be fluent, just you watch."

He threw his arms around her shoulder and kissed the side of her head. "Don't worry. I'm here for you."

"I honestly can't wait to be married to you and have you to myself," she said, circling an arm around his waist and resting her head against his chest.

"Me too, baby. Me too" was his dreamy response as her closeness sent currents through his body. A feeling he always had at moments like this. He still hadn't gotten used to it and hoped never to.

Chapter Seven

Zainab threw a groundnut at him. It bounced off his arm and landed on a bed of flowers. "Why are you looking so morose?"

Leke shrugged. "Nothing. Just not in the best of moods today." He was going through photos on his camera. They were both waiting for the couple to come out of the changing room.

She looked at him closely. His beard looked like it hadn't been shaved for a couple of days. His usual wavy, cropped hair a bit over grown. But then, that did nothing to how good he looked in his red polo and dark jeans. What was most concerning were the bags under his eyes. Zainab had noticed how unusually quiet he was when she arrived at Muri Okunola park to join him for a pre-wedding photo shoot.

"What's wrong?"

"I would rather not talk about it."

"That's usually my line." When he remained evasive, she snatched his camera from him which earned her a stern look. "If you like, look at me like that from now till tomorrow. It doesn't add or remove anything from me."

"Zainab, please."

Zainab looked at the lush green leaves, noting that the place was obviously being taken care of. Making a clear point to ignore him.

"Okay, fine. It has to do with Emem but I'll get over it."

"What did the little brat do?"

Leke raised his perfectly carved brows. Brows she thought she would love to tease a little. It would definitely not sit well with Leke.

"Sorry, that's a little harsh. What happened?" She handed him back his camera.

The serene ringtone of Hillsong's *So Will I* sang out from Zainab's phone. Putting a pause to their conversation. She offered an apology to him and excused herself. She took a couple of steps away from him to have a little privacy.

"Hi Zainab," John said. "Is this a good time to talk?"

Zainab looked back at Leke taking random pictures of the park. Still having his drab mood judging from his sunken shoulders and lackadaisical attitude. "I was actually busy with something but you can talk."

"Okay, I'll make it quick. I got a call from a co-pastor, Micah Oramah in Bethel Youth Fellowship. He wants to invite you to speak in their church. It's a youth church, growing and doing well with about a hundred members."

Zainab twisted her mouth and placed her arm under her armpit. "Why do I get the feeling you're trying to sell the idea to me?"

He laughed. "I'm not. Just want to share all the details with you."

"Uh-huh. What does he want me to speak about?" She turned to see the couple walking out, dressed in matching *ankara* material and holding hands.

"I didn't ask. But can I give him your number so you guys can talk? I remember the hard time you gave me just to get you to talk at HGC. Please, don't give this guy a hard time."

Zainab rolled her eyes. "You're making me sound like a royal witchy-witch."

He laughed again. "No o!"

She closed her eyes momentarily, thinking about it. "You can give him my number."

John thanked her.

"Whatever. I'll hear him out first. My love to your family."

Zainab ended the call just as Leke called her over. The photo shoot lasted well into the evening. Her wrists and back ached. Her tummy rumbling like her old washing machine back at home.

The couple had insisted on having a night theme as well. Zainab loved the bride's evening gown - a v-neck mauve dress with an embroidered bodice and matching purple strap sandals.

"What are your plans for this evening?" she asked. He had done a fine job of evading most of her questions and had locked up during the sessions. She wasn't willing to let him go so easily. "Is Leke finally ready to come out and play?"

Leke chuckled. He wore on his backpack, ditching the face cap he had worn all through. "What do you have in mind?"

Zainab shrugged. "I don't know. I'm actually very hungry right now for street food. Having *suya*, *puff-puff* and *akara* cravings."

"Seriously? All at once?" He nodded. "Yeah, I think I can see that working for you."

Since he didn't drive down, they got into her car and headed to the busy community of Ojuelegba. The streets were always crowded at any time of the day. Ever since she moved away from Abuja, she had tried to become accustomed to the way of life here in Lagos. The noisy commuters, the inevitable traffic and the dirtiness of inner streets.

Leke showed her where he usually got his oily take-outs and they sat in her car, enjoying the cool breeze of the AC and soft tunes of Lauren Daigle's 'Love like This', playing in the background. Zainab untied the black nylon and took out the hot newspaper-wrapped *akara* and *puff-puff*. Her fingers getting oily as she took a bite and chewed while it was hot.

She had eaten four of the fried dough balls when she noticed Leke staring at her with a dazed look.

"What?"

"You surprise me every day."

"What's that supposed to mean?" She wiped her mouth with the back of her arm.

"I always thought you were this classy babe that preferred a Chinese restaurant as the perfect meal."

Zainab shook her head. "I can eat anything, and yet the only thing I know how to do in the kitchen is boil water, soak garri and cook pasta."

Leke laughed lightly.

"What about you? Can you cook?"

"If my life depended on it, yes. I'm not perfect though. Growing up, my mum made sure we all knew how to cook. She had this quirky, feminist mentality going on for her. That a man should be able to do certain things as well as a woman and a woman should be able to change a tire or learn the specs of a generator." He took a piece of roasted yam and dipped it in peppered *ponmo* sauce and put it in his mouth. "So each time she went to the kitchen she would summon all of us to report for duty. At a point, I started taking notes but later lost interest."

"For real?" Zainab could imagine a younger version of him holding a twenty leaf notebook, struggling to pen down recipes and measurements. The image was hilarious. "I'm sure your dad would have loved that."

"We did it when he wasn't home. When he was she handled the meals herself or with my sisters."

"Your dad is that tough, huh?" She could also recall the tough times she had with her mother. Just that her mother wasn't a dictator and was really concerned about her. Zainab had all been too stubborn to accept her love and care.

"He was a terror to us all. Still is. But his bite doesn't sting as much anymore." He licked his fingers.

"So how did you end up taking pictures?"

Zainab took a long drink from her sachet of water. Trying not to notice how much his shirt accentuated his muscular frame.

"It was war. He wanted me to study Civil Engineering. I was more interested in Arts. We settled for Economics." He shifted his gaze to her. "After struggling to get my degree I followed my passion. So far, God has been good to me. I did a couple of odd jobs to put myself through photography classes. Took online courses and saved up to get a professional camera. I took small photography jobs." He looked at his hands. "God has really been faithful."

"What happened with Emem?"

"I know you've been itchy to hear that gist. Remember we have a deal, you tell me about your dad. I tell you about Emem."

"I never agreed."

Leke shrugged and bit into a sachet of water. "I'm still not telling then."

The playlist changed to 'This Girl', a story of a girl who was struggling with her pains and the troubles life was tossing her way. And probably because of that, she ventured off the path God had for her. But in the end she overcame, surrendering her heart to God once again.

Somehow, the sombre tunes gave Zainab the motivation to speak.

"I grew up with my mother in Abuja. She was the daughter of an extremist. She met my dad during his youth service and they fell in love. But like how to good to be true love stories turn out, he had to leave. I guess they figured out the daughter of a conservative Muslim couldn't possibly be with a Christian man. My grandfather was ready to kill his daughter if she defied his orders to stay away from my father."

Zainab blinked and looked out the window. She bit down hard on her lip. "Any way, he didn't know my mother was pregnant when he left. My mother had always told me my father was dead. I believed her.

Then come one terrifying day, my mother passes and leaves a letter telling me my father is alive." She could remember her mother's lawyer handing her a letter on the day of her mother's funeral. Zainab had been high when she read it. IK reasoned with her to fulfil her mother's last wishes while she had been ready to forfeit her inheritance, torn by the realisation that her mother had betrayed her once again.

"Bummer."

"Tell me about it. So I'm roped into going to see him because she bequeathed a property here in Lagos to me and the condition was see him and get the house. I went to see him. Found out he knew nothing about me. He accepted me with more than open arms. Loved me immediately. I was set in my ways. Didn't want to have anything to do with him." She chuckled. "But I can say he's been very persistent in wanting me in his life, and I'm more than grateful for it."

She didn't want to add other details leading to how her father happened to be the one who led her to Christ. How she had hit rock bottom.

"Wow. Now I get the close relationship. You guys have what a lot of people want."

Zainab laughed. "Trust me, it's not all rosy."

"But it's a good thing, right?"

She thought about her dad briefly. "Yeah, it's a good thing. Your turn."

"Emem . . . she wanted a ready-made man. The house, car, everything set up before thinking of getting married to me. So since I'm nowhere near acquiring all that, she opted out. I suspect there's another guy in the picture."

"So, just like that she leaves? Does she think money rains from the sky?"

"*Na so I see am,*" he said dryly.

She shook her head. "I told you she's a brat."

"Yeah, but when you're in love you tend to overlook some things."

"I wonder who came up with the line, 'Love is blind'. It's just –"

"Unrealistic?" Leke said.

"Nonsense."

"I guess it is."

Zainab touched his shoulder. "Are you okay? Stupid question. Of course you're not. Let me rephrase, are you going to be okay?"

He looked at her. "I'll be fine. Nothing a few days detox wouldn't solve."

They wrapped up their conversation and Zainab offered to drop him off at home. His house not too far from where they were. They said their good nights and Zainab headed home.

* * *

Tobi relished the tepid water cascading down her body. Spending as much time in the bathroom as she could. Scrubbing her body and enjoying the new body scrub she'd bought two days ago at a friend's store.

Her first day at work after her leave was gruesome. It felt like her boss just piled up work, waiting for her to return and face them. She had been working at J. Jacobs Consulting firm for a couple of years and loved what she did. The firm had worked with a lot of reputable companies despite its start-up merely five years ago. And right then, she was working with a popular beverage company that had been long in the game and were looking for ways to increase sales and reverse declining profit margins.

She had presentations to prepare and analyses to do, all dependent on her research team's findings.

Tobi let the warm water run down the length of her body. Caressing it in different corners, soothing away the stress of the day. Sometimes, she would touch herself to bring pleasure. Touching her body in ways she would get the utmost pleasure. Things Shola knew nothing about.

It was past ten, and Shola was yet to come home from work. Tobi had dinner and reclined on the bed dressed in a bum short and one of the shirts she snagged from her brother. She turned on her laptop and tried to do a background check on the company and surf the internet to dig up something on competing companies.

I wonder how Maureen is, Tobi thought diverting her attention briefly from work. Detan thought Maureen was acting strange for a while and Tobi sent her a message asking how she was. It had been a while Tobi checked Maureen's Instagram page.

There were no recent pictures of her. Just pictures with quotes which Tobi didn't bother to read. Tobi checked on her online support group - nothing much had been said since the last time she'd been online. A few people had proffered advice on her questions.; encouraging her to move forward with her life, leave her marriage and the country behind to start afresh. Tobi thought of how life would be if she decided to leave Shola. Homosexuality was a crime in Nigeria. If at all anything could happen, it would be in total secret and out of the country. There was no public freedom here. Only imprisonment, ridicule and shame.

The repercussions didn't sit well with her.

* * *

Tobi cleaned the saliva from her jaw and blinked her eyes open to see Shola standing before her.

"When did you come in?" She pushed herself up and tried to sit down.

"A few minutes ago. You were in complete darkness. Why didn't you turn on the gen?"

Tobi rubbed her eyes and closed her laptop and dropped it on the beige carpeted floor. "I must have slept off at some point. How was work?"

"Work was great. Busy as usual. How was your first day back in the office?"

"Fine. It's like I never had any holiday with the work I did today. My boss is just really lazy. Can you imagine he passed down his work to me? Something he should have finished a while back."

"He's the boss. He can delegate to whomever." Shola took off his trousers and tossed it in his wardrobe without hanging it. Tobi didn't want to imagine how untidy the small space was.

"Doesn't mean he has to take advantage of his staff. I have my work to sort out and now his as well."

"Isn't that why they pay you heavily? Besides, a lot of people don't have jobs. You do. Be happy."

Tobi wanted to tell him it didn't matter. That she was trying her best. Argue her case that she was allowed to get tired once in a while. But she decided not to. It would only build an argument and she wasn't ready for that. As a couple, they hadn't gotten to the point where they could agree to disagree.

She went under the covers and laid her head on her pillow. She felt him come under with her. She closed her eyes, knowing what was coming. There had been a certain glint in his eyes when she woke up to see him. Even blurry eyes couldn't hide his desires.

He moved close to her. Placing a hand on her shoulder and his legs resting on top of hers as she lay on her side. "It's been a while since we made love, Tobi."

"Aren't you tired?"

She felt his smile on her back. "A guy can't get tired when he wants to be with his wife." He pressed his lips against her back and she shuddered with irritation. The problem was, any time she shuddered it was an encouragement for him to continue: never that she was disgusted at his touch.

Knowing she couldn't dissuade the inevitable, she shifted on her back. She squeezed her eyes shut. Holding back tears as she allowed him fondle with her and do what he wanted to do. When he was done and had drifted off to sleep, she got up. She took another shower, allowing her tears mingle with the cold water. The generator couldn't carry the heater so she settled. It was a way of life for her now.

Settling.

* * *

He had just finished a Bible study session when he noticed Pastor Wilson sitting at the back of the church. Youths were extending their greetings to him as they walked out. Micah packed his Bible and notebook in his leather satchel and took steps to him.

"Good evening, sir."

"Micah, how are you?"

"Very well, sir."

"I came by to do some office work and was on my way out when I noticed you people were still around. I popped in some minutes before you were done." Pastor Wilson looked around the tent church. "You guys are doing very well. Your Bible study sermon was really good."

"Thank you, sir."

Pastor Wilson rose to his full height, a couple inches shorter than Micah. Micah matched his steps as they left the church. "So have you thought about what we discussed last week?"

"I've been praying."

"And what has the Lord said?"

Micah honestly hadn't put his all into it, but yet he knew what God wanted him to do. He just wasn't ready to shoulder such responsibilities. "I'm willing to try it out."

"There's nothing new to it. You've been doing this for a year and a half now. We are only about to make it official."

Micah nodded. "Yes, sir."

"So I'll announce it in the main church. You will join those being ordained and we will have a prayer and anointing service." They stopped at Pastor Wilson's black Range Rover. Limited edition. "It's been twenty-two years I've been in ministry. When I first started out, fresh from the Sunday school department, it was a huge feat for me."

He leaned against his car. Micah stood in front of him. He had heard the story before, but it couldn't hurt to hear it again. Maybe it would boost him up. "My wife didn't want to be a pastor's wife. She fought hard against me becoming a pastor to avoid this life. But like always, when it's God's will, things worked out. My first sermon sounded like a motivational speech with zero souls won. I was depressed for most of the week. It took some time for me to learn that a lot more went into preparing against Sunday service than jumping around on the pulpit and trying to act lively and pass the message to those who came. All that's needed is praying effectively and speaking God's Word to his people exactly as he wants it."

Micah agreed.

"We will discuss more. I'm happy you made the decision."

A little while later, Pastor Wilson's car drove off. Micah got out his phone and took brisk steps to his car. It was already past nine and he didn't want to get home too late.

He opened the text from John and was glad to see a phone number was in it. He decided to place a call to her soon after he sent John a thank-you message. She answered on the third ring. Her voice carrying a busy tone; female voices could be heard in the background.

"Is this Miss Zainab Baruwa-Phillips?"

"This is she."

"I'm Micah Oramah. Pastor John extended your number to me."

80

"Oh, yeah. Hi Micah. How can I help you?"

"I – er- is this a good time to talk to you?" Why was he nervous all of a sudden? He instantly felt irritated.

"Actually, no. I'm in the middle of something. Is this your number?"

"Yes."

"Great, I will call you as soon as I'm free. Have a nice night, Micah." And just like that, the call ended. He blinked and looked down at his phone.

What just happened?

Chapter Eight

"How is the research going?" Tobi asked one of the research team members at the office. "Hope you guys are gathering reasonable data."

The guy nodded. "We are trying our best. You know how it is. You literally have to beg people to answer you and give their responses."

Tobi knew all too well. She had once been in their shoes when she had to go into the field to verify some data on her own. The research team were unavoidably absent at the time.

"Just keep up at it. I need the data as soon as possible. Boss man is breathing down my neck."

"Don't worry. I'm on it."

She walked back to her office. It was small but comfortable. It had a view of the busy streets of Idumota. Sometimes, Tobi sat there staring at people haggling with shop owners over one thing or the other. And other times, she wondered if the hard glint in their faces was an indication of how hard their lives were or the blazing sun lashing out on them for leaving the convenience of their homes.

The receptionist called, informing Tobi she had a visitor. A few seconds later, a beautiful, slim woman walked in with an aura of confidence. Her lean, cocoa butter legs showed off perfectly in a grey blazer dress.

Tobi felt the woman's eyes linger on her as she did a quick scan of the documents. She felt uncomfortable. "Okay, so these are all the analysis on sales in the last two years?"

The woman nodded. "Yes."

Tobi closed the file. "Thank you. I would look into it and get back to you as soon as I have something concrete to share." The lady didn't get up, instead she settled back in her seat.

"I feel like I know you from somewhere. Did you by any chance go to…?" She mentioned the name of a popular secondary school in Lagos.

"Yes, but I'm sorry I can't place your face."

"Lola Taiwo. I was your junior. We were in the same room in boarding school. I was sleeping in the bunk bed. Two bunks from yours."

Tobi tried to remember. She raised a brow, "Shindara's sister?"

The lady nodded again.

"Oh wow. Look at you." Tobi leaned back on her seat. "You have grown *o*. I remember you were so short back then. We used to send you to run small errands for us."

"Thank God for keeping us. I kept looking at you like I've seen this face before. It's good to see you again."

"Same here. How's your sister?"

"She's fine. She's married now. Lives in Ireland with her husband and four children."

Tobi blinked. "Four kids?"

Lola laughed. "Twins and two boys."

Tobi couldn't imagine giving birth. Not anytime soon. "Good for her."

"She's very happy. I will tell her I ran into you. Are you married now?"

"Yes, I am." Tobi looked down at her fingers. She had forgotten to wear her rings that morning after her bath. She had been in too much of a hurry to leave the house and beat the morning traffic.

"That's good."

They exchanged contacts. "We should have lunch and try to catch up. It's been too long."

Tobi wasn't really interested but agreed all the same. "Yeah, sure. That would be good."

* * *

He couldn't sleep. Couldn't quit the thoughts of Pastor Wilson talking about the ordination and anointing service. Saw himself being anointed to be a full-time pastor and slowly sinking into the hole that was getting deeper by the day. As Micah thought more and more about it, he realized he wasn't sure he could go on with it. Reality was dawning on him of how far he had gone off God's path for his life. Or maybe it was the devil whispering in his ears that he wasn't good enough. Either way, Micah seemed to believe his next plan of action was for the best.

"You're what?"

"I'm taking a step back from ministry. I feel God is leading me in another direction."

At a loss for words, Pastor Wilson's mouth hung slightly open. Micah didn't think he had ever seen the old man in such a state, being that he always had a ready comeback. It made Micah feel a little bad at his decision.

"Why?" Pastor Wilson narrowed his eyes at him. "Are we talking about the same God here?"

Micah knew questions would arise. He had rehearsed his answers over and over in his head till it sounded both right and convincing in his ears. "I need to get myself together. Ever since Kiki died, I haven't been myself. In truth, my relationship with God has been a little shaky."

"This is the first I'm hearing this, Micah. Why didn't you talk to me about this?"

"I thought I could handle it myself and get over it. But the last couple of months have been hard for me, sir." Pastor Wilson still looked dumbfounded. "I'm sorry, sir. I should have spoken to you sooner. Sorry to disappoint you."

"Well, you see all sorts in ministry. I guess I just didn't expect this from you," he responded, his voice laced with disappointment. He released a deep breath. "So, what do you plan to do with yourself? Is this a temporary drawback?"

Micah had asked himself the same thing. "I'm not sure yet. I believe I will get some answers during my time alone."

Pastor Wilson leaned forward, placing his forearms on his desk. "Son, hope you're not planning on backsliding. Because this is how it starts. You have to have a plan. Would you still be attending the church?"

Micah nodded. He would attend weekly services. He just didn't want to be in any leadership position.

"I guess I have nothing else to say, since you've made up your mind. I'll be praying for you. I would put someone else as head of the department. In my heart, I believe God still wants you there and I won't put anyone else there as pastor until God says otherwise."

"I appreciate that sir. Thank you."

Pastor Wilson angled his head. Still trying to allow the news sink in. "Does your congregation know about your decision?"

"I'm announcing it to them when next we meet." Micah knew it was going to be hard for some of them. He had a lot of youths who looked up to him. Who called or sent him WhatsApp messages for counselling. People whom he was privileged to see their steady growth from baby Christians to mature young men and women with a burning desire for God. Something most of the youths in this generation were seriously lacking.

"All I can say is, it is well."

Micah sent a text to Zainab. Regretfully telling her there was no need to meet up or discuss since whatever program he had in mind was going to be cancelled.

Alright. All the best with you. Warm regards.

He knew Kiki wouldn't approve of his decision.

Micah, why are you doing this? What do you plan to achieve? The youths need you.

He squeezed his eyes shut. "I can't keep doing this. I just need a break."

You're losing yourself, love.

Micah didn't feel he had a choice in the matter. Whether he lost himself or not. All he knew was God wasn't there when he needed Him the most in his life.

* * *

Sunday service was going to be hard for Micah, but he would do what he had to do.

"I – I'm stepping back from being in this department."

The quiet room quickly filled up with murmurs and gasps. He looked at a few of them. Their shocked and confused faces staring back at him. Filled with questions. A ripple of doubt flooded his mind.

Was he doing the right thing?

He cleared his throat. "I need to take a step back. As some of you may know, I lost my wife over two years ago. It's been hard for me. Personally, I have battles I am yet to win. I felt I should let you all know."

"Is this permanent?" Fimi asked, drum sticks in hand. "Are you coming back?"

Micah looked down at his feet then back at them. "I hope not. I mean – I hope it's not permanent."

Fimi's shoulders dropped just as people groaned. He knew this wasn't what the people were prepared to hear. And yet, he knew he had no way to assure them that he would stand before them again. He wasn't sure he still even wanted to be a pastor, minister or whatever.

No man looking back at the plough is fit for the Kingdom of God, the scripture gripped hard on Micah's heart.

I'm not looking back. I'm just taking a break, Micah thought.

Service was very much low key after that. The message could have well been that delivered to a group of mourners because of everyone's solemn expression. Micah wished he could yell at them that everything was going to be okay. That it was just for a short while.

For him to get his bearings.

But he knew he was sinking in deeper into that black hole.

He blinked. For a moment, he thought he felt God speak to him. Then he heard it again:

Sin wants you. Don't yield to the call of temptation.

* * *

2014, December

He felt his heart pound in his chest as he watched her hang on to her father's arm while walking down the aisle of Kiki's church. He didn't care if the only thing she decided to wear was his mother's favourite wrapper and bathroom slippers.

All he wanted was her.

Through her veil, Micah saw her lips stretch into a smile. Her eyes were telling him how excited she was about him and their wedding. About spending the rest of their lives together. Micah had waited for this day over the last couple of months. The wedding arrangements and detailing all seemed like a blur now that it was finally here.

When she stood beside him, he could smell the scent of her perfume. Something about it made him want to pull her close and kiss her. He stopped his train of thoughts, forcing himself to focus on the service.

"I have known Kiki since she was but a child and nothing gives me greater joy than to be the one to usher her into this new journey of her life. A journey into the school of marriage. Both sweet and challenging."

The pastor, an old man with a head full of grey, spoke. He delivered a short sermon that reaffirmed God's institution of marriage for man and woman and the purpose for which He created it - for companionship, fruitfulness and purpose.

Micah and Kiki faced each other.

"I, Micah Joseph Oramah, take you, Nkiruka Rayna Nnadi, to be my wife. To have and to hold from this day forward. For better, for worse. For richer, for poorer. In sickness and in health. To love and to cherish, till death do us part." He slipped the ring on her finger.

It was her turn to recite her vows, but instead she read a sheet of paper her maid-of-honour passed to her. "I'm not going to go the conventional way and say my vows. I wrote a little something for you, to express my love." She lifted her eyes briefly at him, a twinkle in her eye, and then looked back down at her paper.

"I can remember the very first day I met you. You were the shy JJC waiting to ask me out." People laughed. Micah's lips curved up in a smile as he bowed his head. "You finally summoned the courage to walk up to me and asked to take me out. Little did you know, inside me, I was doing the whole Michael Jackson Moonwalk. The secret is, I like to think I noticed you first." He looked at her, just as she let out a shaky breath. "Micah, knowing you and having you in my life has all been orchestrated by God. Our Maker and everything. My love for you is unconditional." She used the back of a finger to swipe at a tear.

"I promise to love and cherish you. To always be by your side despite the obstacles life brings our way." She took his hand and slipped the silver band in his finger and looked him in the eye. "I take you this day as my husband, for better and for worse. In sickness and in health. To love and cherish, till only death does us part. I love you."

Micah brushed the tears from his eyes with one hand while he gently squeezed hers with the other. The pastor could have been saying German or a foreign language for all Micah cared.

All he wanted was to hear the words that gave him official permission to kiss his bride. Let the world know she was his, as he was most definitely hers to have forever.

The reception was held in a small hall at *The Castlefield Rooms* in Manchester. Only a few of Micah's family were able to attend the wedding. Their couple dance was one of Kiki's highlights. Her eyes brimming with joy and excitement as they danced to Al Green's *'Let's Stay Together'.*

"Your parents seem to have some sort of tension between them," Kiki said, her eyes focused at a certain part of the room.

Micah looked in their direction. His parents were seated opposite each other, looking anywhere but at each other. The frown and disgust on his mother's face at the woman seated beside his father. A woman his mother had grown to despise over the years. Claiming the strange woman took everything from her.

Micah was determined not to let their drama get to him on his wedding day. "I've been meaning to ask you," he whispered into her ear as he held her close. One hand on the small of her waist, the other clasping the other as they danced, "What perfume are you wearing?"

She bent his head a little low and in turn said very close to his ear, sending chills down his back, "Jo Malone. Why? You don't like it?"

He drew back and looked into her eyes. "I love it. It's just giving me very wicked thoughts."

She threw her head back and laughed as he spun her around.

* * *

But my God shall supply all your needs according to his riches in glory by Christ Jesus.

Leke tried to find solace in the words. But somehow his bank account and what Emem had done to him made him doubt.

He ran his hand over his face. "God, what can I do? What do I do?"

A scripture came to mind. Leke got out his phone and checked it out. Romans 4:20. *He never doubted that God would keep his promise, and he never stopped believing. He grew stronger in his faith and gave praise to God.*

Leke scoffed. "God, you want me to praise You?"

In all things, give thanks.

He wanted to laugh. In short, he laughed. God had to be joking. He tossed his phone on the couch.

He had jobs. Made a decent sum of money. But he had to send some back home. His mother's shop wasn't really doing well. His father was retired and living on his little pension. His siblings were not doing anything to bring in money. They were all dependent on him.

And God wanted him to give thanks?

Leke rubbed his face and sighed. He laid his head back on a worn out throw-pillow and closed his eyes. And then he began to sing. Whether he liked to admit it or not, God had been faithful. Even if he barely had enough each day. He had something.

Then he began to remember other things God had done for him. How he had gotten jobs out of favour from people he had met at weddings, who were yet to see his work. How he was called to assist on a job at a fashion show. The studio he was able to procure not too far from his home.

He uttered a sigh.

"God, You have truly been Faithful. I'm sorry if it seems I'm ungrateful. Is it bad to hope for more?"

Another scripture came to mind; *I wish above all things that thou prospereth and be in good health, even as thou soul prospereth.*

"God, when will this happen?"

In due time. I am never late to fulfil My promises, only just on time.

* * *

Zainab highlighted the scripture with purple ink. The words were screaming at her and evoking a passion deep within her soul.

He was hated and rejected by people. He had much pain and suffering. People would not even look at him. He was hated, and we didn't even notice him.

She felt her throat constrict as tears pricked her eyes. Thinking about how much pain Jesus Christ would have gone through to die for her.

Here, alone with God, was when she could be the most vulnerable. She had never been an emotional person. She could count the amount of times she had ever been moved to tears. When her mother died. When IK left her just days to their wedding.

But with God?

It was like He seemed to know every weak point she had to elicit raw emotions from her.

Like He was telling her, she was a child. Sill His little girl and would always be irrespective of how old she was and to Him, age was just a meaningless figure.

"I'm all yours, God. Do with me as you will."

John's friend, Micah, came to mind then. She felt a heavy burden for him.

"God, what do you want me to do? What would you have me do?"
Pray.

And that was what she did. She prayed in her understanding and spoke in a language unknown to her; asking God to help Micah in whatever way he needed help and before it was too late.

Chapter Nine

Lagos, Nigeria. 2015

Micah was glad to be home. The traffic on Ikorodu road building up with a lot of commuters probably heading to Lagos-Ibadan expressway. Most likely due to the usual camp meetings organized by two popular churches in Nigeria. He found Kiki in the living room - a book in hand but her eyes focused on the blank TV screen.

"What are you thinking about?"

She snapped the book shut.

"How happy I am to have you in my life," she kissed him on the lips and wound her arms around his neck, "and how much I love you."

"Or maybe you're thinking of all the stress I put you through coming all the way here with me? That maybe we should have listened to your parents and stayed over there till I could find a job."

Doubts crept up on him from time to time if he was indeed making the right decision. If he could indeed be man enough for her. The head of the home as God expected of him.

"The Bible said I should leave and cleave. That's exactly what I did. Although, I have to admit, things in this country could use a total revamping. There are just so many things wrong here."

It had been over a month since they arrived in Nigeria and Micah knew how she struggled in the first few days when the power supply had been epileptic. The first time she experienced a power outage was when she was in the bathroom. Her scream had him rushing to her within seconds.

"I know you told me the power goes out frequently, but somehow my mind was yet to get a hold of it. Did I scare you? I'm sorry. Could you please pass me my towel? I can't seem to find it."

He chuckled at the memory. He had to get an inverter installed the following week.

She stepped away from him and folded her arms across her chest. "I find it extremely irritating that I have to wait till my bin is filled to the brim before the waste management picks it up. It's all rubbish. And then there are the roads and drainage systems," Kiki pressed her hands to her lips and closed her eyes, "don't even get me started on that."

Micah went to her and rubbed her arms. Trying not to laugh. "I totally get you. You can't imagine how frustrating it is for us here."

"Then why doesn't someone just place a complaint? We should all protest, email a member of the parliament or whatever it is you do here. It's all rubbish."

He pulled her close and kissed her head. He rubbed her back in circular motions and he felt her relax a little in his arms. "Why don't we ease all this tension? You just rest and I will make something for us."

She pouted. "No. I will just sit still and keep thinking about it over and over again till I get depressed about it and my head might explode." She snapped her fingers. "I need to do something to get it off my mind." She took a deep breath, "What would you like to make?"

"Yam and plantain porridge. Garnished with pumpkin leaves and stock fish."

"Oooh, sounds scrummy. How can I be of help?"

Over the next few minutes, they worked around each other - Kiki dicing the yam slices into small cubes while he peeled the yam and cleaned up.

Micah laughed. "That's not how to cut plantain."

"Okay? So how do you do it Mr. Know it all?" She handed the plantain to him and pointed the knife in his direction. "Just for the record, that was how my big sis taught me."

"I'm sorry. What I meant to say is, it is not the *only* way to cut plantain."

She gave him the knife, bottom down. "Better."

Within two hours they finally sat at the dining area with two steaming plates of porridge in front of them.

"This is so good." She moaned as she ate.

"Stop doing that."

Her lips tilted up in a smile. "What am I doing?"

"You're making that sound again." The same sound she made when they were being intimate with each other. "It's making me think you are not really interested in eating that food at the moment." He blew on a forkful of porridge and shoved it in his mouth.

"I have no idea what you're talking about."

Thirty minutes later and the both of them were sprawled on the bed with a duvet over their naked frames. He looked into her brown eyes, brushing a strand of hair from her face. "Tell me the truth. Do you miss home? Do you wish you were back in Manchester?"

"I miss my family. I miss friends and church. But my home is with you, Micah." She rubbed the back of his head. "It may take some time to adjust, but I'm willing. More than willing to make things work for us."

"By the way, my mum said she's coming over." He saw the smile slip from her face. "I know she can be a handful-"

"I didn't say a word."

"I know. I'm talking from experience."

She raised her hand close to her face. "I solemnly swear to treat your mother with utmost love and respect and try not to get crazy mad when she intends to drive me insane."

He chuckled.

"I'm being serious."

"I didn-," he began.

She groaned. "Don't be a nutter and kiss me."

* * *

Over the next couple of months they lived their lives as newlyweds did. There were the occasional fights as they tried to understand each other and live accordingly. There was also the struggle for Kiki to adapt to her new life. But then there were also good things to praise God for.

In mid-March, Micah was browsing the channels when Kiki returned from her job search. Her eyes tired and her shoulders slouched. He dropped the remote and went to her side. Over the past few weeks, she had complained of fatigue, pains in her stomach and loss of appetite as well as vomiting.

"What's up?"

Her face filled up with a smile, "I got the job as the sales executive!"

"Wow, that's awesome. Congratulations! What about the doctor? Are we...?"

She nodded. "We're pregnant."

He hugged her tightly. "Thank You, Jesus."

"God is faithful, Micah. He always is."

Things seemed to be going fine as they tried to build a steady routine around their lives. Making family friends as a couple and Kiki functioning in the choir department at church. Then the day came when Micah walked in and found her lying on the floor and found blood seeping beneath her trousers.

"I'm sorry. It's cancer."

That was the day the hole started being dug.

Micah blinked, his forehead breaking out in sweat. "I'm sorry. I don't under- Cancer?"

"We found a tumour in her pancreas and it seems to have spread to various parts of her organs. I'm sorry," the doctor added, as if the news was disheartening to him as well.

He felt the prickle of tears in his eyes. The doctor's elderly face suddenly becoming blurry.

"Isn't there anything we can do? Chemotherapy? Radiation? Or surgery?"

The doctor shook his head. "I'm sorry, Mr. Oramah. There's nothing we can do at this point. It would only take a miracle. And these days . . . I don't see a lot of that. Any treatment we do right now would only manage the pain to improve her quality of life. There's no cure."

Micah didn't know how he dragged himself out of the doctor's office to an empty seat in the waiting room. Didn't know when the tears came in heavy cascades.

"What's wrong? Why are you looking like that?" She swallowed hard. "What did the doctor say? Is the baby okay?"

"We lost the baby."

Her sharp intake of breath and the tears that pooled her eyes broke his heart.

God, how could You let this happen?

He sat next to her on the hospital bed and looked down as he held her hands. *God, how can I be strong? Help me. Please . . .*

"Is that the only thing wrong?" He looked up to find her staring at him. "Is that all there is to it?"

"He – he said they found a tumour in your pancreas. But everything is going to be fine.

She gazed at him intently then said, "I'm dying, aren't I?"

Micah wished he could say no. Wished he could say everything was a lie. He was angry all of a sudden. "How can you say that?"

"B- Because you have this look on your face that says something's terribly wrong." She grabbed his hand. Suddenly looking like a wave of strength washed over her. "Everything is going to be alright. God willing."

He nodded. "We're in this together."

* * *

Present day

Most of his family was there. Micah saw his eight-year old niece run across the compound with her little brother in tow. He smiled to himself, remembering what it felt like to be a child. Wanting everything and needing nothing. He was the least bit bothered about life back then. He wished he could go back in time now and be like that.

But then, he was grown and this was his life.

He sighed and climbed up the stairs to the front door. He heard his sister talking in hushed tones and her husband's baritone voice chiding her softly.

They stopped talking when he walked in, and he knew they were most likely discussing him. He glanced at his mother and the smile she gave him seemed forced with an unmistakable sadness in her eyes. On the other hand, his father looked like he wanted to be anywhere but there.

Micah wondered how Belinda managed to bring the two of them together in the same room.

"Micah!" Belinda said, breaking the awkward silence. She spread her arms apart and came to hug him. "We were just talking about old times and how it used to be when we would meet every Sunday after church for lunch." She pulled back from their embrace. "How are you?"

"I'm well."

Micah greeted his parents and shook hands with his brother-in-law.
"How far *na*? Been a while since we saw. Are you losing weight?" his
brother-in-law asked, looking him over.

"No. Just been preoccupied."

"Or is it too much church activity?"

Micah shook his head. At a point in his life, he would have defended
the work he did at BYF. He would have said the work of God was
his food. But these days, he didn't know anymore. He had gone on a
hunger strike.

His mother spoke in Edo, asking him to take a seat.

"Why do I have the feeling that I'm about to be interrogated?" Micah
asked.

Belinda laughed. "Interrogated *ke*? For what? Do we look like
detectives?" She glanced at her husband and the smile slipped from
her face and was replaced with a slight frown.

His father spoke, "Micah, it has come to our notice that you are still
in mourning over your wife, Nkiruka. We understand how trying this
is for you. But enough is enough. No one would question you if you
decide to marry another woman. You are a young man. You should
think about moving on with your life. Both of you didn't have any
children."

Micah looked at his father, his jaw clenched. His father didn't look
deterred by Micah's glare.

"You shouldn't have a problem finding another woman to marry. If
you do, we can help you."

Micah had heard enough and he stood.

"I am still talking to you, Joseph."

"I can't listen to this."

"So my words have become rubbish in your ears?" his father asked.
Not just rubbish. Insensitive and annoying!

99

Belinda was near Micah, rubbing his shoulders and whispering to him to listen to their father.

"I have a few of my friends' daughters I can introduce you to. Stop all this nonsense you're doing and move on. There are plenty of fish in the sea. One woman is not the centre of your happiness and that's the plain truth."

A short, uncomfortable silence followed.

"I believe," his mother threw a frown his father's way, "what your father is trying to say is that we need you to live your life again. Besides, you are a pastor. There must be a lot of girls interested in marrying you in that your church, my son."

Micah chuckled lightly. "I'm sure it will please you to know I have stepped back from any church leadership. I'm now a free man."

Belinda gasped. "It's a lie. Since when?"

"It just happened recently."

"Why?" his sister asked.

"I'm in need of a change. That's all."

"And this has nothing to do with *Nkiruka*?"

Micah hated how her name now sounded like a taboo. He shook his head. "No. I need time to reflect on things." He took a deep breath. "That's why I have decided to take a teaching job at the University of Ibadan."

Belinda's husband quietly left the room.

His mother spoke, "Why all of this sudden changes, Micah? Aren't there any teaching jobs here in Lagos? Why all the way in Oyo state?"

"A friend of mine called some days ago." A former classmate had reached out to Micah, asking if he was interested in a temporary teaching position. Micah didn't see any reason to stay in Lagos; he decided a trip to Oyo might just be what he needed at this stage of his life.

So he had accepted.

"I will be leaving at the end of the month so-"

"So soon?" Belinda interrupted.

Micah nodded. "Yes. Before classes start so I can get a feel of it."

No one really had anything to say afterwards. His mother offered lunch and both Belinda and his father accepted. Maybe because it was something for both of them to do to get their minds off the current situation.

"You know, you can't keep running," his father said to him when they were the only ones in the room. "One day, you will have to make a deliberate decision to move on whether you like it or not, or else the pain will never go away. You may think my words are harsh, but I only care about you."

Micah nodded and thanked him. "I'm going outside for some fresh air."

* * *

Zainab just got off the phone with her sister and placed a wet palm on her head. She felt like heading over to her father's place immediately but knew acting rashly wouldn't do any good. Knowing her father could be really stubborn, he would talk his way out of Zainab's suggestion of him coming to stay with her.

She closed her eyes momentarily then opened them again. Setting her gaze on the ceiling.

How could he not tell her about his heart? About the high blood pressure?

She reached for her phone, took a deep breath and called him. No answer. Zainab tried two more times and got the same response. She ran a hand over her bob; refraining from yanking it.

Her phone rang. She was slightly disappointed at the caller ID.

"Hi Leke."

"What's up? You busy?"

She eyed the dirty dishes in her sink she had been working on before her sister called to let her know their father's hospital result. "Not really." She wiped her hands on a napkin and tossed it on the counter. It fell on the floor instead. "What's up?"

"Er- nothing much. Just checking on you. You are sounding a little off. Is everything okay?"

"Family stuff. I'll be fine. Thanks."

"You're welcome. I'm thinking of –"

She heard her phone beep and checked to see her father calling back. "Sorry, can I call you back in a few minutes? I need to quickly attend to something."

"Sure."

Her father answered on the first ring. After exchanging pleasantries, she went straight to her suggestion. "I'm thinking of you coming to stay here with me in Lagos. You can't be living in that house all by yourself."

"I will be fine. I can hire someone to come in once a week to clean and bulk cook."

Zainab was already shaking her head when he uttered the word 'hire'. "You know this world is full of crazy people who just go about killing people anyhow. You can't just hire a random person."

"I will get someone who needs the money in church."

"No."

"Zainab, you need to relax. I will be fine. I won't stress out. You have to remember I'm the parent here. It's not the other way around."

She closed her eyes and said in defeat, "I know. I- I love you."

She heard the smile in his voice as he repeated the same.

* * *

"*Oya*, tell Uncle Leke what's wrong," he said. They were out at the Palms Shopping centre.

"You're not well."

Zainab looked around at her lush surroundings. Finding the place overrated with its large parking space and expensive shops. She just needed to get out of the house. The urge to get a drink had been overwhelming. Leke had called back, asking if they could hang out. It felt like a divine intervention. A door God was opening for her to escape the jaws of temptation.

She shoved her hands in her sweatshirt pockets and crossed her legs at the knee.

"Seriously, talk to me."

She explained her father's situation and how she wanted him to move in with her and the conversation that followed.

"I can see why you're frustrated. But then, you also have to understand that change isn't easy. He's been there his whole life. What do you expect?"

"That he would see reason to being near his daughters and grand-children."

Leke folded his arms. "As if it were that easy. Sometimes, people can't force your hand on what they believe is necessary. Even if they might be right." He gave a soft punch on her shoulder. "He'll be fine."

"I know. I've already told God about it."

"Can I ask you something? How did you become a Christian? I mean, I see you and think of how *worldly* you must have been back then." He raised his hands. "No offence."

"My dad. Spoke to me about Jesus and the rest is just story."

She felt his eyes on her when she stared down at her sneakers. Then he got up and stretched his hand out to her, "Let's go somewhere. I want to show you something."

She eyed his hand wearily. "Should I be afraid?"

"Only if you want to. Don't worry. I won't take you to a ritualist, not yet anyway."

"That's very comforting." She twisted her mouth sardonically, and then took his big, cold hands in hers.

They chatted about their individual works and the evening breeze caressing both their faces. Zainab always felt Sundays were the best time to go out in Lagos. It was free of traffic and silly obstructions of some traffic wardens and police officers who were hungry for a payout.

The car slowed at the bridge overlooking a huge sparse of water. The sun was going down. The lights on the huge boats on the sea made the atmosphere appear romantic and beautiful. Funny, but it was the kind of place Zainab could imagine being proposed to.

"What are we doing here?"

"This is one of my best places in Lagos. This and Lekki-Ikoyi link bridge. That bridge sort of reminds me of the Eiffel Tower in Paris. That's when there's light *sha*." He hung his camera around his neck. "Sometimes, when I'm driving back home in traffic, I like looking at this place. It would be a miracle when Nigeria has lights all over the place without the sounds of generators humming in the air."

Zainab looked left and right. "Are you sure people won't think we are trying to commit suicide or worse, the police would come looking for us?"

"I don't think so." He came to stand beside her and they both leaned on the car. Watching the view.

"Tell me what you see."

"All I see is the sun going down and lights in boats."

Leke laughed. "Seriously? Try harder."

Zainab looked intently. "Still nothing. What do you see?"

"I see orange, yellow, purple... as the sun is setting." He raised his camera and took a couple of pictures. "There is something about natural beauty that points to God. It's good to take a break from the craziness of life and look at the good things."

He turned to stare at her. She felt him look at her lips and shift his eyes back to her face.

Zainab looked away.

"Poetic."

"I used to write poetry way back."

"You don't anymore?"

He looked at the pictures. "No. It's been a while."

"Tell me something from the top of your head."

He raised a brow. "Now?"

She nodded.

He seemed in thought for a few seconds before saying, "If love was a river, I want to drown in it. If love was fire, I want to burn in it. And if God is love, then I want to drown and burn in Him."

Zainab let the words run through her mind again. "Deep."

"Thanks." He stood up straight. "Let's go. I'm hungry. I know a nice *bukka.*"

"You want to take me to a *bukka*? You're really a broke ass boy."

"Enter the car, *jor.*"

* * *

Glad to be home, Micah took off his shirt and dropped it on the bed. He padded to the wardrobe and took out her perfume. The same perfume she wore on their wedding day. The bottle still a quarter filled.

Micah sniffed it. Then he laughed.

"If only Belinda could see me now. She would think I've finally lost it."

Haven't you? she whispered.

"Maybe I have."

He closed his eyes and thought of the months following the news of her diagnosis. How he delayed breaking the news to their family, determined to pray for a miracle. But as the weeks went by, he had no choice.

Especially after they lost the baby.

"Why does God take the good ones?" Demi had said, crying over the phone, lamenting over Kiki's diagnosis.

Micah recalled how her face was etched with pain. How everyday he kept praying and his faith kept slipping when he saw no change in her. How the tempo of those in the prayer department had waned considerably and had begun to pray for God's will to be done and no longer for a miracle.

He remembered a lot of things. Things he wanted to forget and things he wanted to always remember.

How did anyone expect it to be easy to forget?

Slowly, he sank to the floor and wept.

* * *

Like her friends, Maureen was still in shock at Pastor Micah leaving. They had filled her in on the tragic loss of his wife. How she passed on from cancer. The disease took her life despite the prayer vigils held on Pastor Micah and Sister Nkiruka's behalf.

Maureen wrapped her hands around herself and rubbed her arms. It was a little chilly and she wished she took a sweater with her to the cinemas. A small group of youths had decided to hang-out that Saturday and settled for the cinemas and a late dinner at one of their homes.

"Maureen, do you want popcorn or a hotdog?" one of her friends asked. The cashier was also staring at her with an impatient look on his face.

"Popcorn."

"*Oya*, two medium popcorns, one hotdog and two bottles of water. Please, add ketchup and mayonnaise to my hotdog. I hate mustard," she dished out to the cashier who was already loading up medium sized boxes with caramel popcorn in a hurried manner.

Maureen and a few of the youths from church settled down in their seats. The movie was set to start in five minutes and they had hurried in to get good seats. According to Detan, the best seats were up in a corner where he could hold her hand and plant a kiss or two in the dark.

After the movie, they said their goodbyes and Maureen headed home using a cab.

Her thoughts drifted to Detan and Pastor Micah's advice to her. She had avoided seeing Detan for the last week. Wondering how she was going to break the news to him. She hated breakups. Hated when everyone would ask questions about him and she had to keep saying how they had broken up.

Better a broken relationship than a broken marriage, was the usual saying.

But who would mend her broken heart?

But I warned you right from the start. Walk with Me, Maureen, and you will not fulfil the lust of the flesh. Walk with Me.

Chapter Ten

"I told Dara I ran into you. She sends her regards," Lola took a sip of the pink coloured Cocktail she ordered. A name Tobi couldn't remember.

"Greet her for me."

"That's a lovely ring." Lola gestured at Tobi's blue-stoned ring. "How long have you guys been married?"

"Five years."

"Wow. You should have like two kids now, right?"

Tobi was starting to get uncomfortable. *Why did I agree to have lunch with her?* "No kids."

Lola looked taken aback. She blinked a few times. "Why? Do you guys have any issues? Like you've been trying to get pregnant and nothing has happened?"

"I don't think that's any business of yours."

Lola nodded. "True. I'm sorry I asked. I was simply concerned. I guess that's the irony of life. Some people who don't want to get pregnant give birth by the dozens and those who desperately need a child find it difficult. The universe is playing tricks on us."

"The universe?"

"Yes. What?"

"Nothing. I – I find what you're saying interesting." *And silly.*

Their meals arrived shortly after and they ate as they spoke; Lola doing most of the talking. She had schooled in America after secondary school. The culture shock disturbed her for a month or so. She kept calculating how much things were back in Nigeria in comparison to how much things were there. It got so bad that she almost always felt guilty for buying certain things. Then she talked about her friends. She met various people from different countries. Kenyans, Zambians, South Africans; the list went on. Tasted different foods. Experimented with different things.

"I didn't just pass through University, I let it pass through me. Both the mundane and the crazy stuff."

Lola winked at her.

Tobi tried to remember how Lola was back in school. Her geeky glasses came to mind. She was shy. An introvert who was more interested in observing the usual siesta and reading her books. She hardly had any friends.

So her transformation was a little disconcerting to Tobi. A little.

"Let me guess. You're wondering how I changed from the little mousy girl to this? I got tired of not experiencing life. It was tiring being seen as the geek in class with no social life. One day, I just made the decision to live a little."

Tobi understood. She even admired Lola's boldness to step out and live. *If only I can live my life the way I want.*

In Me is life.

"Did you say something?"

"Yes. I asked if you enjoyed your days in uni."

Tobi knew she didn't do anything as exciting as Lola. "I did to an extent. University of Lagos has its perks."

"Ah . . .Unilag. Good for you."

Tobi looked at the time. Her lunch break was almost over and she needed to get back to the office in good time.

"It was fun. Our short hangout. We should do it again," Lola said as they stood by Tobi's car. "Maybe next time we could go to the beach?

Since I moved back here, I haven't really made many friends that are like-minded. So what do you say to this weekend?"

"Er – I'll be in touch. The work with your company is really keeping me busy. I also have a thing with my husband's family. I will let you know when."

As Tobi drove back to J. Jacobs Consulting, she couldn't help but think of Lola and how she had stared at her when she suggested they hang out again. The way her eyes seemed to caress her face.

Probably Tobi had imagined it, but she thought she saw Lola's eyes flicker to her lips. It was brief, almost like it didn't happen. Tobi shook her head. Accepting she had only imagined it.

* * *

"How do you know when someone likes you?" Zainab asked casually. She tried her best not to look or sound weird as she munched on a slice of bread and slathered some peanut butter on two more. Seyi was asleep and they were both in the living room. The beautiful smell of baked pastries drifted from the kitchen enclosing all around them. Adesewa was currently working on new recipes for her bakery, *Sugar and Spice.*

"Why? Is there a guy you like or someone you think likes you?"

Zainab rolled her eyes. "Answer the question. How did you know Korede was the guy for you?"

"Well, I prayed about it. Told God if it wasn't even going to end in marriage, I was not interested in being in the relationship. I guess I can say I knew deep within that Korede was the guy for me. I was happy that I could discuss spiritual matters with him. I was free with him. Could share my lowest times with him."

She bit into her sandwich. "You told him about Daniel? How I gave you the stupid idea to try and seduce him on his wedding day as a form of punishment to him?" One of the many things Zainab had done in her past was encourage her best-friend to put on a short black dress and try to woo her ex by having sex with him on his wedding day. It was the same day he was getting married to Zainab's half-sister, Efe..

Zainab hadn't thought of the emotional implications of her advice or how crazy stupid it was at the time. How she had hurt not only her best-friend but also her half-sister whom she didn't see eye to eye with at the time.

"Yeah, but I didn't say it was you. Mind you, I made my own decision in following your advice, so don't take the blame for it. I also know you wouldn't say something you yourself won't be able to do." Adesewa headed to the kitchen and Zainab followed suit. "Anyways, he didn't judge me. Instead, he told me we all have our own mistakes."

"That's interesting."

"*Oya*, tell me. Who's the guy?"

Zainab gave a mirthless laugh. "Who said there's a guy? I was just asking."

Adesewa threw a wet napkin at her. "Liar. Tell me *na.*"

"There is no guy in my life. Well, except my father."

"Don't be difficult. There has to be a reason why you want to know."

Zainab dusted the crumbs off her hands. "What if I'm asking so I can know at the right time?"

Adesewa arched a brow.

"His name is Leke. We work together on some jobs. He's a photographer. He just broke up with his girlfriend."

"Sounds like a perfect match. Invite him over for lunch."

"No." Zainab shook her head. "N-O."

"Why? I want to meet this guy. Zainab, this is the first person you will really talk about since IK. I want to meet him."

"That's why I didn't want to tell you. I know you just want to drill him with questions. I am not going to let you embarrass me."

Adesewa pouted. *"Ahn-ahn.* I'm a very supportive friend. I want to make sure he's a good guy. I care about you."

Zainab slammed her palms on the counter as she stood. "We are not even dating."

"But you want to?"

Zainab groaned and gazed heavenwards. "God, please deliver me from this woman."

"I promise not to ask him embarrassing questions. I promise not to embarrass you. I promise to behave myself. We would all have a good time. I can use my spiritual radar to check him out for you."

"My spiritual antenna is working well, madam."

"People always tend to get biased when they are in love or really like a guy."

Zainab gave her a stern look. "Seriously?"

"Just invite him."

"I've heard. Can we please talk about something else?"

"No. Text him now."

"Why now? I will do it when I see him. No need to waste credit."

Adesewa nodded. She brought out a tray of hot, golden brown chicken pies from her double oven and placed them in front of Zainab. "What's his surname?"

"Falola."

Her best-friend placed a pie on a plate and slid it across Zainab and passed her a fork. "I'm going to check on Seyi." Then, she turned and walked out.

Zainab stared down at the plate. Everything seemed strange to her. But then the pie looked so good. Zainab decided to take a picture and tag her friend on Instagram.

"Where's my phone?" she said. It wasn't where she left it to charge. Seyi was asleep in his cot. Then it dawned on her. "Adesewa!"

"Shhh! Do you want to wake him up?"

112

"Give me my phone." Zainab snatched it from her. Adesewa hadn't even bothered to wipe away the evidence.

Hi Leke. You up for lunch at a friend's place this Saturday? She cooks a mean fried-rice with barbecue chicken.

Zainab glared at Adesewa. "That's not fair."

She gave a cheeky grin. "I was helping."

Zainab raised a brow. "Okay *nau*.. I will tell him you are making pounded yam as well. Not poundo yam. *Pounded* yam. With *egusi* soup and all the assorted meat. And I don't care if your back pains you."

"Vengeance is of the Lord *o*..."

"*Gerrout!*"

* * *

Leke had no idea why he had stared at Zainab the other day. Especially in that manner. It wasn't like he was completely over Emem.

He sighed and rubbed his eyes. How quickly she had looked away from him and downplayed it. Ever since they met a few years back, Leke had been captivated by her and her tomboyish ways. Her mocha skin tone, slim body and height could pass her off as a model.

He couldn't imagine how wild or crazy she might have been before she gave her life to Christ. Her multiple ear-piercings, though she often used one or two at a time. Her current hairstyle with blue streaks was a bold move.

He could remember her mohawk style. Laughed when he recalled the look of disdain on the mother of the bride's face when she walked into the room to see Zainab making up her daughter. But she kept working. Not the least bit moved by the unwanted stares.

Leke glanced at his phone when it vibrated. He read the text twice. Then he sent a reply:

Leke:

Sure, what time?

Zainab:

It's actually pounded yam. 3pm fine?

Leke checked his calendar to make sure he had nothing planned then. It was only a family photo shoot and that was at 10am. He sent a text saying he would be there and she could text the address to him.

He had never thought of Zainab as anything more than a friend. Could this possibly be a new direction God was leading him on?

* * *

That Saturday afternoon, Leke was surprised to learn that Zainab's best-friend was the complete opposite of her. She was extremely girly. Army green jump-suit, manicured nails painted in white and beige stripes. Her weave long and curly, cascading down her shoulders.

She was definitely not like Zainab.

"Hi Leke. I'm Adesewa Williams. Nice to meet you. Come in." She stepped aside and the smell of freshly cooked *egusi* soup greeted him. His stomach let out a little growl. He hadn't eaten much in the morning; saving himself for the big meal.

"This is for you." He extended the gift bag he had brought with two bottles of non-alcoholic wine.

"Awww, that's so sweet of you. Thank you so much. Zainab is in the backyard."

Leke took in the interior of the living room. The floor to ceiling walls were painted white, and the sofas and accent chairs a mix of colours that complemented each other in a beautiful way. It gave the room a cozy feel. Outside was a different look entirely.

"Baby, this is Leke," Adesewa said, moving to stand by a tall man who held a phone. "Leke, this is Korede."

They shook hands. Leke's eyes went to Zainab who held a baby against her chest while the other hand pressed a phone to her ear. Leke guessed he was not less than six months old. His head, full of hair and his mouth slightly open as he drooled down Zainab's arm.

"That's our son, Seyi," Adesewa proffered.

"You have a beautiful home and family," Leke said.

"Thank you."

Zainab moved towards them; her tall, lean frame dressed in her usual tomboy garb; jeans, sneakers and an oversized black tee shirt that had the words *Radical for Christ* written vertically across the front. Her hair colour, a mix of green and black.

They greeted each other and she handed Seyi over to his mother.

"How did you end up with a friend like Adesewa? I was half-expecting to see another girl-guy," Leke whispered to her.

"Ha-ha. Our friendship goes way back. She's like grown-up Barbie."

Leke laughed.

They spent a little time outdoors talking - Leke laughing at Adesewa recalling how Zainab was and how she shaved off all her hair when her mum passed. Leke had tears in his eyes, hearing about Zainab's escapades.

"It's interesting how you work with someone and barely know much about them," Leke said while they all ate at the dining table; Seyi in a high stool being fed pap.

"So Leke, tell us more about yourself. Have you stayed in Lagos for long?" Korede asked.

"I don't know if six years counts as long. Left IB after school and came to Lagos for greener pastures."

"And how has that been?"

They conversed some more over dessert. Adesewa had served a chocolate cake with ice-cream. Leke had to leave an hour later.

"Your friends are cool. You're really blessed. Thanks for inviting me."

"You're welcome."

"I think this is the first time I have really had fun in Lagos."

"Asides with Emem, you mean?"

Leke tried to think back to the times he'd had with his ex. They had fun, but most of the time she complained about how life was treating her badly and how she wished she had money to do what she wanted. "Even with Emem, I didn't have this much fun."

Zainab folded her arms across her chest. "If you say so."

"We should do this again. This time maybe just the two of us."

"Are you asking me out?"

Am I? "Yeah, we can hang out as friends. There's nothing wrong with that."

Zainab nodded. "Sure."

* * *

Tobi watched her husband conversing with his cousin. Shola looked nice in his black, guinea brocade and round vintage sunglasses. With one hand in his pocket, he held up a glass of juice to his lips. It stopped midway as he said something, laughed then finally took a sip. Looking at him from a distance and his easy manner brought back memories of why she took a liking to him in the first place.

She had frequented Purple Lake with her friends back then. The club always had this foreign feel to it. The DJ was experienced in flipping jams and keeping the mood high. The drinks were also on point. In all, it was a place where every big boy and girl wanted to be. It was a typical day for Tobi and her friends as they ordered their usual drinks and danced hard under sparkling lights.

"That guy has been staring at you for a while now," her friend, Mimi, *yelled over the music.*

"Are you sure it's me and you're not drunk?" It was no hidden news that

116

Mimi was the finest between both of them. Even if she decided to wear a flour sack as a gown, she would still look good with her amazing figure.

Her friend wagged her index finger at her. "I'm not that drunk, dear." She nudged her chin behind Tobi. "Take a look."

Tobi turned her gaze to the man seated at the bar. His eyes were on her. He smiled and raised his half empty glass to her in greeting. His pink lips seemed too pink to Tobi and she wondered if he rubbed lipstick on them.

Tobi looked away, not the least bit interested. She needed to burn the energy in her; feeling slightly dizzy from the two cocktail drinks she downed minutes earlier. She raised her hands in the air as the music switched to something old school. Tobi didn't know how long they were on the dance floor but they were both parched and made their way to the bar to get a drink.

"Can we get two more of that deliciousness?" Mimi told the bartender.

"Hi. How are you?" They both turned to see Pink lips by Tobi's side.

"She's fine," Mimi said. "You?"

"Couldn't be better." His eyes were on Tobi. "I see you girls are totally kicking it this night. What are you celebrating?"

"Nothing! It's Friday night, duh!"

Pink lips chuckled. "Yeah, TGIF right?"

Mimi nodded.

"I'm Omashola. And you are?"

Mimi handed Tobi her drink. "I'm Mimi. This is Tobi."

"Does Tobi talk?" He tilted his head, eyes intently on her as though trying to study her.

Mimi laughed out loud. Tobi guessed the girl was seriously drunk. Either that or she was totally smitten. Tobi looked at the guy. "Is there anything in particular you want me to say?"

His pink lips spread in a smile. "No. I just wanted to hear your voice."

Mimi rolled her eyes and murmured, "Such a bad pick up line." Tobi didn't have time to agree with her when a guy approached Mimi and she

117

was engrossed in conversation with him.

"Do you want another drink?"

Tobi shook her head. The rotating lights in the club making her dizzy. "I think I've had too many. So why are you here?"

"My guy is getting married. Today is his bachelor party." He tipped his glass to the group of men in the VIP lounge surrounded by girls.

"Aren't you supposed to be with them?"

"I'm good where I am. Your crazy dance moves caught my attention. You twerk really well."

Tobi raised a brow.

"I kid you not. You also have beautiful cat eyes." He glanced up at his friends and back at her. "Can we step outside to talk? Probably get to know each other better?"

"I don't think so. I barely know you."

"That's more reason why we should talk." He paused. "I'm not a serial killer or anything. I won't kidnap you."

"The mere fact that you would mention something like that is enough to run away from you." Tobi turned around to look for Mimi only to discover she wasn't there. Her eyes found her on the dance floor, dancing with a guy to a slow number.

"At least your friend knows how to have fun," Omashola said. "Come on."

"Okay. But I'm going to take a picture of us together and send it to my contacts so if anything happens to me, they will find you."

He laughed. "Go ahead."

"Can I ask a question?" she asked when they were outside.. "Are your lips really pink or did you use lipstick?"

Omashola burst out in laughter.

Tobi shook the memory away. After she had recovered from her embarrassment and he had stopped laughing, they stood outside for the next couple of minutes. Conversations revealed how much they had in common. She knew why she was at the club in the first instance

- to get her mind off her job and the feelings she had for her soon-to-be former colleague, Mimi.

It was ironic how she wanted to get Mimi off her mind and had agreed to party with her that night. Maybe as a final hurrah before submitting her resignation letter. At times, Tobi wondered if meeting Shola had been a sign. A sign to discard every silly thought she had entertained of being with someone of the same sex. So she hadn't pushed away Shola's advances, but had agreed to go out with him date after date, saying yes when he finally popped the question.

Then, very quickly, she realized how unhappy she was.

A commotion at the entrance chased away Tobi's thoughts and she looked at the people who came in dressed in matching *aso-ebi* for Shola's cousin's wedding reception. The party was already in full swing. The smell of party jollof-rice wafted to her nostrils. It hurt that she couldn't eat anything. She hissed at the sweaty bottle of water a server had placed in front of her a while back.

Ever since her outing with Lola two days ago, Tobi had been on a purging spree. Maybe it was the universe telling her to keep away from Lola.

"Hey, how are you feeling?" Shola asked, pulling out the seat beside her. "Hope the purging has stopped."

Her hand instinctively went to her stomach. "I haven't gone since we got here."

"That's good. Momsi was asking after you. Aunty Gbemi wanted you to help supervise the serving but mum spoke for you." Shola dropped his phones and car keys on the table. The glint of his silver cuff-links catching her eyes. "Mum actually thinks you're pregnant, that's why."

Tobi snapped her eyes at him. "Pregnant *ke*? Why would she think that?"

He shrugged. "I don't know for her *jor*. But then it's not a bad thing *nau*. If we get pregnant, everyone will be happy."

Except me. She pressed her lips shut.

"Gosh, I'm hungry. Can you manage to get something for me?"

Tobi rolled her eyes. "But you could have gotten something for yourself before you came here."

Shola gave a poor imitation of a pout. "Please."

She didn't say a word as she got up and went to do his bidding. There were four different caterers at different sections of the hall and Tobi strolled down to the nearest. An assorted array of dishes greeted her. She settled for *ofada* rice wrapped in local leaves and its peppery sauce. Tobi placed the food on the table and was settling down herself when a waiter brought a bowl of pepper soup to Shola. Just a little whiff of it, the sight of the fish head and its black dotted eyes staring at her, sent Tobi looking for the nearest toilet. Praying there was an empty stall.

She knelt on the tiled floors and opened her mouth, waiting for the pile to come out. Nothing came. She heard Shola's voice outside, asking if anyone had seen a petite woman dressed in green running into the toilet. Just when she was about to call to him she threw up.

God, please don't let me pregnant!

Chapter Eleven

Being in that environment reminded Micah of his university days and brought memories of his time in London. The hurried steps of students as they made their way for their lectures, and those who lingered in hallways; talking while waiting for the next lecture or whiling away time. He was trying to settle in his friend's two bedroom apartment. He also wasn't eager to stay on campus with the rest of the lecturers in their assigned quarters.

His bedroom was smaller than his toilet back in Lagos but it didn't matter to him. He was determined to make the most of his stay in Ibadan. He gazed at the framed picture of him and Kiki holding a glass at the engagement party Solomon threw for them.

"I still can't believe you are here," Chinedu, his friend and roommate, said to him when they were having a dinner bought from an *amala* joint in town. "Especially when you told me you wanted to be a pastor and not use your degree. You know you were the best in our class. A lot of people were shocked when they heard you are now a pastor. We all expected that you would be working for UNICEF or WHO and be one top shot."

"Life has unexpected twists and turns, my brother. One never knows what to expect."

Chinedu nodded and smacked his lips; a sound that vaguely irritated Micah. "True that. Why did you decide to give it all up?"

"I didn't give it up." **Didn't you?** Micah knew that harsh whisper anywhere. He ignored it. "I'm on a small break. Wanted something different."

"Lucky you. To be able to make a smooth transition."

Micah wished the guy would just stop talking and finish his food.

"I – er, I heard about your wife." Micah had lost his appetite. "It must be very painful for you. Sorry, man. Do you mind me asking what happened?"

"Yes, I mind. It's not something I want to discuss."

Chinedu pursed his lips. "I understand bro. If you need anything let me know." He rose with his two empty bowls in his hands. ". I'm just a knock away." With that, he shuffled out of the room.

Micah stayed there for a few minutes, enjoying the silence. He finished off his food and did the dishes. Laying his head on his pillow and deciding to call it an early night, the sudden sounds of music playing disrupted him.

He groaned and threw a pillow over his head. It was going to be a long night.

* * *

He didn't want to wait for Chinedu, deciding to take a shared taxi to the university not to miss his lectures and get acquainted with his surroundings. He was to meet with the Dean of the faculty after his first class. Micah wondered how his life would have turned out if he did his Master's degree in Ibadan and not London. Studying abroad had been a wish and it was at the last minute when everything clicked. He got his study visa and money for late registration, and his school fees came with ease.

There was no way he would have doubted God didn't want him there.

The morning lecture went by smoothly. Standing in front of a hundred plus, year one students who didn't look as excited and young-eyed when they first entered. After his meeting with the Dean, and instructions on what to do and what was expected from him, Micah headed to the library to do a little work before going to get some food.

Chinedu was home. But he wasn't alone judging from the two empty glasses on the centre-table and the female shoes at the entrance of his bedroom. A couple of minutes later Chinedu came out bare-chested and in his boxers. "Oh, you're back. When did you arrive?"

"Some minutes ago."

His roommate gestured his thumb at his back. "I have a guest."

"I figured."

Chinedu opened his mouth to say something, then changed his mind and walked into the kitchen. Micah focused on his food and minutes later, Chinedu was going back to his room with a tray. There were hushed voices, then Chinedu came back out. He looked at Micah's food and went back into his room. This time, one voice was a little raised. Micah almost laughed. He took a swig of his bottled water and went back to eating.

"Actually, she's my girlfriend."

Micah raised a brow. *Where's this going?*

"She's a little shy," Chinedu whispered. "Could you please go to your bedroom? I'll call you when she's gone so you can come back out and do what you want."

Micah only threw him a quizzical look. He packed his food and walked into his bedroom. Not up to a minute later, he heard hurried footsteps and a door slam shut. Micah was done eating and was sitting on his bed, doing research online with his laptop when Chinedu knocked on his door.

"I'm sorry about all that. She's just too shy and has issues relating with people." He had thrown on a t-shirt.

"It's fine."

"I mean, she would like to meet you but not now. I don't know for her *jor,* she has too many issues."

Micah nodded. "I understand Chinedu. No need to explain. Just give me a heads up if you want me to stay out for a while. And if my staying here bothers you, I can look for another place."

"No. For what *nau?* It's cool. Like you said I will let you know earlier. How was your first day?"

"It was okay. Nothing dramatic happened."

His roommates tilted his lips up to a smile. "A lot of dramatic things happen on campus."

Tell me about it. "I will prepare myself. I have to do some work against the next class so-"

"Yeah. Yeah, I will let you work. See you later, bro."

As Micah worked, he couldn't help but think about Chinedu's actions and what he was hiding. Because one thing was sure, he was definitely hiding something.

* * *

"I'm sorry, Detan. I can't continue with this relationship," Maureen said aloud, sitting on her bed; willing her voice to sound convincing mostly to herself. She blew out a breath and scratched her brow. Maybe she shouldn't break up with him. He was a nice guy. A lot of her friends had attested to that. Probably he would change down the line.

And what if he doesn't? Don't settle. Walk in the Spirit and you won't fulfil the lust of the flesh.

Maureen mulled over the thought. But it wouldn't be nice to break up with a guy like that. They wouldn't be able to talk freely. She wouldn't be able to explain herself fully. She needed to talk to him privately. Not giving it an extra thought, she sent him a text saying she would drop by. Afterwards, she rummaged through her wardrobe and selected a collared shift dress with flat sandals.

"Hi." They were in the living room. She was surprised to find the space clean unlike times when she usually had to pick up after him. The grey carpet looking like it had been scrubbed extensively. He, on the other hand, looked like he needed to shave. His chin filled with stubble.

"Hello. Nice seeing you," he said with eyes running over her till he looked her in the eye once again. "Are you ready to tell me why you've been avoiding me?"

"I've been busy. Work. Church."

Detan was nodding as she listed them. Like he didn't believe a word she was saying. "You have been too busy to text or reply my messages? Please, come up with a better lie."

Maureen folded her arms. "I'm –"

"Is there another guy in the picture?"

She jerked back. "What? No, I'm not cheating on you. I'm not that kind of person, Detan."

"Okay. Good to know."

"I have been busy and I have also been thinking about us." She ran her hand through her hair. "I've missed you."

His laughter lacked its usual mirth. "Wash. Maureen, say what you want to say."

"I don't think we should go on with this relationship." He raised a brow. It was obviously not what he had been expecting. *God, give me words.* "I love you. I really do. But I'm really concerned about how nonchalant you are about God and church. I hate that you keep pushing me around when I invite you for a program or you act like having God in your life is not much of a big deal. It is to me. And so, if you aren't willing to get close to God, then I can't go on with this relationship."

She released a breath. She had finally said it, but it didn't make her feel good.

He scratched his neck. The sound of his nails coming in contact with shave bumps crossed her ears. "Let me get this straight. You are breaking up with me because I'm not taking God seriously?"

She nodded slowly.

Detan stood, his tall, lanky frame towering over her. "This is the craziest thing I've heard. Baby," he took both of her hands in his, bending a little so he could look her in the eye, "I love you. You know I've never been much of a religious person. But if it will make you happy I can change. I will follow you to church. I will even fast on some days."

Maureen shook her head. "This isn't a business deal, Detan. If it's not from your heart and something you really want to do for God, then it isn't real."

"It would be real if I start doing it and get the hang of it." He kissed her on the lips softly. "I will learn." He lifted her knuckles to his lips and stroked her cheek gently. "I will."

She searched his eyes. She wanted to believe him, but deep down she knew the truth. That a person can act saved but true change was from within. Only the Holy Spirit could be about a lasting change. She withdrew her hands and sat on the armrest of the nearest sofa.

He came to kneel beside her. His warm breath on her cheek sent tingles down her back. "Baby, you know I love you right? I didn't know this was so important to you. I promise to take God seriously."

"De-"

"*Shh.*" He placed a finger on her lips.

Go home! The warning clanged in her ears.

She looped her arms around his neck as he kissed her, enjoying the feel of his cold lips against hers. His palms rubbing her back and pulling her closer to him. Maureen felt the sudden urgency to be with him. She returned to her senses briefly when his hands went up her thighs. Just briefly, because she couldn't caution herself. Too weak to tell him to stop. The warning reducing to a faint whisper.

When they finally pulled away from each other, under sheets, Detan had pressed lips against her sweaty back, telling her how good she was. In return, Maureen shed silent tears, her palm pressed across her mouth as she gulped back sobs. Feeling disgusted with herself.

God, I'm sorry. I'm so sorry.

Silence.

* * *

"I hate rainy weddings," Zainab said. "I wonder why people are jumping on this Thursday wedding wagon."

"What's wrong with a rainy wedding? You're not the one wearing white." Leke adjusted his camera on his neck. He caught a glimpse of one of the groomsmen sticking a finger up his nose. Leke was deeply tempted to take a picture of that for laughs. To print it and hand it over to the girl he was trying to toast at his table. He turned and saw a lady staring at him. She maintained eye-contact for just a few seconds, then looked away. The faint hint of a smile was on her face.

"I know. It just makes me feel weird. Dull." She released a deep breath. "I had a rough night and when I eventually went to sleep, woke up late and didn't make my green tea 'cause I had to rush down here."

He watched as she applied a thin layer of black pencil under her eye lid. He loved it when she wore makeup. It made her more feminine and appealing.

"Yeah, why do you like taking that stuff? You are slim enough."

She licked her lips and for a second he thought she was nervous. "I just like the earthy, bittersweet taste of it. It invigorates me."

"Really? Emem used to take it a lot. The thing still makes little sense to me."

"You men can't understand much about us. Why you bother trying is funny 'cause you end up more confused than ever."

"At least we try." He managed a glance back at where the lady was sitting and found her laughing at something someone said. His eyes ran over her face and elaborate head-tie. He usually didn't like to mix work with pleasure. Besides that, he wasn't new to ladies checking him out while he worked. Some of them crude and only interested in a one night stand.

Leke was disgusted and politely turned them down.

"Are we still on for dinner? I'll stop by and pick you up. Hope you don't mind my rickety car."

Zainab twitched her mouth. "Has that ever been a problem?"

He smiled back. She was done with her job and heading back to the studio. Leke, on the other hand, had to stay till the party was almost over before he could call it a day.

* * *

Zainab allowed herself a peek into her ex's life. His relationship status on Facebook was recently updated. *Married to Onyekachi Asiegbu.* Zainab didn't allow herself feel any emotions as she went through his posts. Photos of his wedding were uploaded for public consumption. Her eyes drank in the luscious woman who was his wife. An arm was on his shoulder and the other placed against his chest, showing off her big diamond ring. She looked directly at the camera. Her red coated lips spread apart, exposing pearly white teeth. Her long, straight hair finding their limit at her chest.

Zainab stared at IK - his eyebrows still bushy and his beard now fully grown, making him look older and more mature. Attractive. She could remember times when she had jokingly combed his eyebrows and shaped them to perfection. His soft, smooth skin, a pleasure to touch. The musky scent of him, always calming to her and turning her on.

If she closed her eyes, she could recall their most intimate times, but she didn't yield to the temptation.

Instead, she remembered the funny way they met years ago at a *suya* spot in Abuja. The two of them were busy haggling over the last two sticks of *suya* much to the vendor's amusement. She had won, and had earned IK's respect. Captivated by her tough exterior. They exchanged phone numbers and he asked her out. He introduced her to his world as the owner of a club and the life that came with it. Especially the drugs.

She snapped her eyes shut, willing the memories to go away. A moment later, she gave in to laughter with tears streaming down her cheeks. Telling herself IK had probably married a woman who was totally girly and was sure she was not a lesbian. Zainab wiped the tears away. Sober, she stared at the picture again and then exited Facebook.

Zainab flopped on her back.

God, is there any hope for me? I want to get married. I want a family of my own. Children. Am I worth it? Being someone's wife and being called a mother?

You are a new person in Christ. Old things are passed away.

Zainab shut her eyes. She desperately wanted to believe the Words, but was also afraid to hope she could have anything as good as what Adesewa had. Which man would want a former lesbian as a wife and mother to his children?

A man who knows everyone has sinned and fallen short of My standard. I have set apart a man for you, Zainab. But in My own time.

She literally felt her heart skip a beat. Just then, her phone buzzed with Leke telling her he was outside waiting.

Could Leke be the man for her?

She chuckled at what Adesewa had said after meeting him, *The guy is fine! Don't mess this up o.*

The air was cool from the rain so Zainab had opted for something warm. Jeans, tee-shirt and a cardigan. It wasn't exactly date material but the last place Zainab thought they would go to was a classy restaurant. But after one look at Leke, dressed in a grey blazer and black pants with a navy blue shirt, she dashed back into the house and texted Adesewa on what she could wear.

"What do you mean you have nothing to wear?" Adesewa accosted her. "We seriously need to take you shopping."

"Shush *jor* and tell me what I can wear."

"What do you have?"

Zainab stared at her wardrobe. A range of colours of jeans, a few ripped, along with hooded sweatshirts, camisoles, scarves, black skinnies, a lot of graphic tees and jackets stared back at her dauntlessly.

"I don't have anything."

"What do you mean you don't have anything? What about what you wore at the conference earlier in the year? The high-waist skirt and *ankara* jacket?"

"I forgot to have it washed since I got back from Jos."

Her friend groaned and Zainab could imagine her eyes closed, pinching the bridge of her nose. "Wear one of your *ankara* gowns with a nice pair of sandals and first thing Monday, we are going shopping."

"Thank you, Mummy."

"Have a nice date."

Zainab quickly got dressed and dashed out to meet Leke leaning on his car, phone in hand.

"I was beginning to think you were no longer interested." His eyes took in her appearance. "You look good. Why did you change?"

She shrugged. "I didn't want to look too informal."

He chuckled. "One thing about you is even if you dress in a worn-out wrapper, you are confident in how you look. So I'm not bothered. But yeah, I kind of like the new look. C'mon, let's go."

Chapter Twelve

They ended up at a beautiful restaurant located in the highbrow area of Ikoyi, and Zainab was happy she changed her outfit. The place had an African theme going on, with hushed conversations and aroma of good food all around them.

To the corner of the room was where a band setup and a man sitting on a high stool with a mic few inches from his mouth. His eyes were closed as he spoke passionately..

. . . Yes . . . I believe

I believe in the words I speak

I believe they have the ability to take you to the peak

Because words are not merely spoken to preach or to teach

But they are combinations of letters to make you produce better and be a go-getter

These words . . .

Sometimes, I feel so sad and mad when I hear people talk and call you names

And I'm like, "Hey, don't you realize she's a dame?"

And then they stare at me like I don't have a clue of what I mean

Like her actions and behaviour are a mirror of her being

But then I know, yes I know, that when I speak it would make her weak

And somehow, yes somehow, our future won't be so bleak

These words . . . I know I believe

Applauses erupted across the room when he finished his rendition, and the band kicked off with a jazzy tune. Zainab would never have pictured Leke as the sort of guy who liked jazz. She found it amazing - how long they had worked together and how little she knew of him.

"How often do you come here?" she asked when their orders were taken.

"Once a month. Maybe two."

"Ever done one of your poetry things up there?" she nudged her head at the mini stage.

"Once. Stage fright. I think I would rather write than speak."

"Did you bring Emem here as well?"

Leke's eyes widened. *"For where? She will just be insisting we come here often."*

She was too baffled to laugh. "Chill, if you knew she was a high maintenance chic, why did you keep going out with her?"

"Is it bad to like good things? You know *better* soup *cost*."

"Not when it has to drain a hole in your pocket. What is wrong with you men, anyways?"

Leke laughed. "Well, I come here whenever I want to relax and when I have the money to splurge a little on myself. Just loving up on me." He placed an arm on the batik table cloth and cupped his chin. "Tell me more about you, Zainab."

She felt that tiny flutter in her tummy again. Here she was with a guy, on a first date. Something she hadn't done in over four years. She kept telling herself to be cool about it.

It's just a date.

"Like?"

"I dunno. Anything. What do you love to do? What do you hate?"

"I hate it when Christians say; I don't want to sound cliché. If you are a Christian and you say Christianese," Leke chuckled. "Then you aren't sounding like a broken record. You're simply being who you are. We speak a different language which people of the world don't understand so don't apologise for speaking your language. Especially if you are speaking to another Christian."

"Maybe you should give me an example."

"Like if someone says prayer works or fasting works then has to apologise for proffering that response because it sounds too ordinary a response. Do you understand?"

"I do. And what do you love?"

"God," she said without a doubt.

"*Whoa.*" He sat back and gazed at her. "I get the whole Christian thing and I'm not attesting to it, but asides that, what do you like?"

"I don't have a different answer. You don't get it, Leke. I have come a long way from my past. God's love, His Person, is the air I breathe. Without Him, I was just a girl with no moral obligation or meaning. But with Him in my life, I feel like a larvae going through metamorphosis."

"Hmm...You should go do a spoken word poem with that."

Zainab chuckled. Her heart was racing at the mere thought of God and how good He had been to and with her. Their food was brought and the aroma of fresh fish caused her tummy to rumble.

"What about you? What do you hate?"

"Dishonesty."

Her mouth went dry. "Why?"

"Let's just say I've had my fair share of betrayal and not looking for more. Everything has to be in the open. That's how a relationship works."

"True." The barbecue fish had a peppery tang to it. Looking back, Zainab knew she lied to IK but not to his face. She had simply hidden certain parts of her life from him. She was uncertain if he would stop loving her. But the truth had blown out when her cousin told him.

Two hours went by quickly till it was time to head home.

"I had a lovely time."

"Me too." Zainab smiled at him. *The best.* Yet she knew if things were ever going to move forward between them, she had to tell him the truth.

All of it.

* * *

Tobi found herself sitting cross-legged at a hospital, and consistently checking the time. She was waiting for a nurse to announce her turn to see a doctor.

She thought back to the party. After spending close to twenty-minutes in the tiny cubicle, to make sure she was free, she rinsed her mouth and joined Shola at their table. Both plates were already empty. There and then, he had asked her to get a pregnancy test done.

"It's just food poisoning. It would clear after a few days."

"Since when did you become a doctor?"

"I understand my body."

"It won't cost you anything."

"I am not pregnant, Shola."

Shola had sighed. "You are too stubborn for your own good. And if I didn't know any better, I would think you are happy with us not getting pregnant."

Tobi had kept quiet, knowing how close to the truth he was and she was too chicken to admit it.

She drifted back to the present when a nurse beckoned her to see the doctor. A couple of minutes later, after a visit to the toilet to pee into a cup, she was back in the doctor's cubicle of an office. On the table were a stack of patients' files with varying thickness and other medical paraphernalia.

There and then, the doctor dipped a test strip in the small cup of urine and stared at it. Tobi felt that was the longest moment of her life.

The doctor turned her gaze on Tobi, and then smiled.

"Congratulations madam. You are pregnant."

Tobi didn't want to believe it. "No. it's not possible. I use contraception."

The doctor pulled off her gloves to reveal powdered hands and perfectly manicured nails on slender fingers. "What contraceptives do you use?" She tossed them in an aluminium bin behind her.

"Oral contraceptives."

She nodded. "And you haven't missed a dose?"

"I – I don't recall missing one."

The doctor looked at Tobi with a bored look. Like she had seen and heard it all. "How long have you been on the pills?"

"Erm –"

"When last did you see your period?"

"I haven't seen it extensively. Just minimal – bleeding. That can't mean anything, *abi*?"

"Actually, it can. Missing it consecutively for two days increases your likelihood of getting pregnant. Didn't your doctor explain it to you?"

"Oh my god." Tobi felt like she would throw up. The air in the room seemed to be thinning out. She grabbed the arms of the chair tightly and took small, deep breaths. How had it happened? How had she forgotten? Then she remembered the night she had returned home late from work and had neglected to take the pills. She had expected Shola to be out of the state, due to his work, only to find him at home.

"Madam, are you okay?"

Tobi looked at her briefly, then at the table. She blinked.

"Madam?"

Tobi said the first words her brain was prompting at. "I want an abortion."

* * *

Tobi couldn't go back to work immediately. Still feeling disoriented at the test result. She scanned the rowdy room and Lola waved at her. Tobi walked briskly to her and dumped her bag on the table and practically slumped on the seat.

Lola arched her perfectly pencilled brow. "What's wrong with you?"

"I'm pregnant." Tobi didn't know why she said it.

"Oh, wow. That's good news. Congratulations."

"No." Tobi pressed her lips firmly together. "I don't want the baby." She laughed. "I don't even know why I'm telling you this."

Lola reached out across the table and held her hand. Tobi looked at the hands and back up at Lola. "You need someone to talk to. That's fine." She withdrew her hand. "Why don't you want the baby?"

"It's a long story."

Tobi closed her eyes. She couldn't afford to tell Shola, or any close relative for that matter. Everyone would want her to keep the baby. *How could I be so stupid to get pregnant?*

Lola snapped fingers in front of her. "Babe, are you here?"

"I'm sorry. It's just overwhelming."

"Talk to me."

"I'll be fine. Nothing a glass of water and good food can't solve." Tobi ordered her food and when it was placed in front of her, the last thing she wanted to do was eat.

"Tobi. Are you sure you're okay? Usually married people tend to be overjoyed when they haven't had a child in say –"

"Five. Five freaking years of my life."

"But you look horrible. Why don't you want the baby, Tobi?"

Tobi shifted the food aside. "The truth is I want out of my marriage. I'm tired of being married to a man. The sloppy way he leaves the toilet. Throws his shoes from one side of the room to the other. Leaves tiny hairs in the bathroom sink after shaving." Lola cringed at that. "He also eats a lot. He doesn't really understand me. There are some days he does and then some where he frustrates me that I pick up my bags and run away from the house for a couple of days. Marriage has not been the easiest thing for me."

Lola cocked her head to the side. "I understand. You know, you never asked me why I haven't married. And it's not that I haven't had toasters come my way."

"Then why?"

"Almost for all the reasons you gave. Men don't just understand my emotions. And in a way I feel they never would. I once dated a man who told me women are just a necessary evil. Can you imagine? And the worst part about men is they don't understand personal hygiene. At least majority of them. There was one time I kissed a guy and it felt like I was making out with someone's armpit!"

Despite her sour mood, Tobi couldn't help the laughter that bubbled from within. "That's so disgusting."

"*Abi nau.* I'm happy you're laughing. You really have a nice laugh."

"Er - Thank you. So, do you ever plan on getting married someday?"

Lola shrugged. "Maybe. Maybe not. It all depends. . ."

"On?"

"The right person." Lola winked at her.

* * *

Zainab wagged a finger at her "No. I'm not wearing that."

"Why? It's so beautiful." Adesewa ran a hand over the dress. The sequinned part was a complete turn-off to Zainab. "You know, you have to explain how you would wear clothes and not wash them for a month. That's just very bad, Zee. You need to change this nasty habit of yours."

Adesewa parked the car.

"Please, don't start." She yawned shoved her phone in her front pocket. She was dreading the next couple of hours with her friend's idea of shopping under the brunt of Lagos' sun.

"There are some essential things a woman must have in her wardrobe and you lack most of them. You need to do away with the baggy jeans and unflattering tops. I don't even think I've ever seen your real shape *sef.*"

"Very funny."

"*Ahan nau,* you need to do away with the old and embrace the new." Adesewa selected a blouse from an array and placed it against herself. "What about this? The colour goes well with your skin tone."

Zainab almost gagged at the bright hues of pink and yellow. "No."

"Okay." Adesewa picked another top made of silk. "This one *nko?*"

"No."

Her friend muttered under her breath as she replaced the clothes and went through more sections.

"And this?" It was a beautiful pleated skirt in black and white.

"God forbid."

Adesewa sighed and went through the tedious task of showing her outfit after outfit and all failing to get Zainab's pass mark.

"You're stressing me *o*! We don't have that much time and I have to pick Seyi from crèche."

"Fine. Could you just choose something that's less like you and more like me? I like neutral colours. Probably purple as well. Just don't go overboard and try to make me wear pink, baby blue, red, orange, lilac or something –"

"Feminine?"

"Just do."

Adesewa threw a pleading look at the weary sales girl. "Let's start again, please."

Two and a half hours later, and three shops down, they had shopping bags filled with clothes.

"You will need a leather skirt to embrace your feminine side."

Zainab hissed.

"A high-waist black and blue jeans, a poncho, a maxi dress, a lace dress-"

"Why do I need a lace dress for goodness sake? And please, don't say it has something to do with my feminine side."

"I was going to say girly. It brings the girl child out of you." Adesewa maintained her gaze on the road. "You need a bodycon cocktail dress just in case for events."

Zainab rolled her eyes.

"Also, two blazers, a jumpsuit to wear on a *date* and a waist blouse – I still don't know why you fought against the leopard striped blouse. It would have looked so nice on you."

Zainab was no longer in the mood to argue. "Just buy me lunch and take me home."

Zainab dumped her purchases on the floor and sat at the edge of the bed. The only thing she had really liked were the shoes and few accessories they purchased to match her outfits. She flopped back on her bed. Not the least bit bothered by the clothes strewn on her bed earlier in the morning as she rushed out.

I wonder if Leke would like the clothes on me.

Somehow she couldn't get Leke out of her mind.

"God, You have to tell me. Is this the real deal or not? I'm not going to expose my heart and emotions if it's not worth it. And I don't want to choose. I like Leke. I really do. He's funny. Considerate. Caring. Of course he has his negatives, but then no one's perfect and it really isn't too big a deal for me. Is he the one?"

I will show you the way to walk. In the meantime, clear your room and wash your clothes.

Zainab's mouth fell open. "God, seriously?"
Then pay your dad a visit.

Chapter Thirteen

Early 2016

She took off the pink headscarf. "How do I look?" she asked, wincing a little. For the briefest moment, she also looked nervous. "My mum bought like five different head wears. I like them, but they aren't me."

On Kiki's lap were different colours of turbans. Some funny looking.

Micah stared at her head. The smooth curves at the back and the slight discolouration at the top of her head, distinct against her brown caramel skin. In addition to that change, she had lost a considerable amount of weight. "One word. Beautiful." He pressed his lips against her forehead.

"Somehow, I don't believe you."

"Well, hope you believe I love you."

She brought his knuckles to her lips and kissed it. "I know." He held her close and fought back tears. Praying silently as Micah had been doing for the last two months that God would do a miracle. They had made the decision to resume treatment in the UK after much pleading from Kiki's mother and the fear of Nigerian hospitals.

"Can I tell you something and you won't take it personal?"

"Sure."

"Your mouth smells."

"What?" He raised his palm to his mouth and blew then muttered, "Oh my goodness."

She was laughing, her hand pressed against her tummy. Micah joined in, glad to hear the echo of her laughter around the room.

"I should brush."

"No. I'm not concerned about your whiffy breath."

She snuggled closer to him.

"Weirdly, this doesn't feel like home anymore. Being here."

"So you miss Nigeria and the power supply and *grimy* potholes?"

"God, no. I mean, I miss us. I miss our little routine and being alone in the house and cuddling up. The sheer thought of just us. I miss that."

Micah squeezed his eyes shut. *God, please. Do something! But not death . . . I can't take it.*

My grace is sufficient for you.

No, God. I don't want Your grace. I want my wife to be healed!

She drew lines on his arm. "I hate that I can't do much of anything these days because I get so tired and everything seems to hurt."

"Then rest."

"Why would God do this to us?" A weak cough escaped her lips. "Why would He do this to me? Why when we just got married? Why did we have to lose our baby? Micah, what did I do to deserve this?"

He swallowed hard. Trying to hold back his tears. Trying to be strong for both of them but quickly losing the battle. "I don't know, Kiki. I have asked the same questions. I've tried to reason it out but I can't come to any conclusion," he sadly responded, struggling to remember lessons from Bible college on God's will. He pressed his lips to her head, feeling her silky fabric of her turban - a now permanent feature of her wardrobe. He wanted to offer more comfort, let her know that this wasn't a fault of hers but couldn't get the words out past the lump in his throat.

"Is it wrong to feel abandoned by God in my moment of need? It feels like he doesn't care," Kiki continued, despair cloaking her entire being.

God, do You hear her? Where are You?! Micah yelled internally, raising his eyes to the ceiling.

Kiki continued, "You know, when we took our vows, in sickness and in health till death do us part? I never would have imagined this - that death would come so soon," her ironic chuckle, low and raspy.

He released her and watched her face as she reclined on the bed. Her eyes had lost their shine and had a yellow hue to them. The chemo-radiation was prolonging her life but it didn't necessarily reduce her pain. Her eyes were closed and he was heading out of the room.

"Micah, you'll be fine."

He spun around. "I'm fine."

She smiled. "Okay." Then she drifted off to sleep. Peace etched in her features. Her mouth parting slightly.

Micah closed the door gently and felt tears on his cheeks. He stood there for a few minutes. Then stepped out to the kitchen. His father-in-law was seated, facing the windows which dominated the room. The sun pouring in bringing in some much needed light to the dimly lit room.

"Good morning, sir."

"Micah." Kiki's father simply said, not sparing a glance his way. Gone were the cordial greetings and warm handshakes. All Micah got from the old man was a cold stare and an unfriendly demeanour. But Micah took everything in stride. If Kiki was happy to see her parents, then he would be happy as well.

"Hope you slept well."

"How is my daughter?"

"Kiki is resting now."

An uncomfortable silence stretched between them.

"What about mum?"

Kiki's father raised his mug to his lips, took a sip and dropped it back on the table. "Sit down, Micah."

Micah pulled out a chair and sat. Pushing aside his slight irritation. "Do you know why I left Nigeria?"

"No, sir. That information was not volunteered to me."

"I came from a polygamous family. My father had three wives and twelve children. I grew up amongst the wives' anger, hatred and rivalry for each other. The need to watch your back when you're sleeping at night. The push to become a better person. I suffered a lot in that country." The old man rubbed his forehead and Micah was suddenly aware of how much he had aged in the past month. "Struggling to make a good life for myself and when the opportunity came for me to leave I was married with two children. I didn't mind if I had to do odd jobs or be a houseboy for my family to have a better life and escape the monitoring eyes of my step-brothers and sisters. I just had to be away."

"I'm sorry about that, sir."

"Life got better. My wife became an ardent Christian, attending church frequently and praying fervently. I always believed her prayers have kept this family standing till this moment. And when Kiki announced she had met a man, and he was Nigerian... I was deeply concerned. When she told me you were a pastor I assumed she would be safe. But I was wrong."

"I don't quite understand."

"Then let me make it simpler. What were you doing when my daughter got cancer?"

Micah blinked. "I'm sorry, you think it's my fault Kiki is sick?"

Kiki's father held a pained expression.

Micah chuckled. Dazed. "I can't believe this."

"She was fine all the while she was here in the U.K. She hardly gets sick. She was in perfect health until you took her away from us!"

Micah was speechless.

"How do I know you didn't just come here to get permanent residency and use my daughter? How do I know you are not the one who brought this cancer to my daughter's body?"

Micah clenched his hands and got up. Mixed emotions coursing through his body and the most identifiable was anger. *God, what is this man saying? What sort of useless attack is this?*

Be still. I am God.

"I don't know what to say to all these false accusations. I'm in pain. My wife is in there fighting for her life and we are all praying for her to get better." Micah looked at him, dispelling the hatred creeping up on him. "I know you are in deep pain as well. But please, it would be very wrong of us to talk about this. Mr. Nnadi, I *love* my wife. I would willingly take the sickness off her body and put it on mine. If it were possible I would give her my own pancreas. I – I would give my life for her. We are praying. I have a team of prayer warriors in Nigeria praying."

"But you can't give your life for her. Your words are meaningless. I wish that I had never allowed you take her out of the country. I wish I never gave her to you."

Micah felt like he had just been punched in the gut. But that wasn't the end of it. Kiki's father left the room, delivering his punch line.

"If you say you are a pastor, then you are a failure."

* * *

Present Day.

The air in Ibadan seemed a lot better than that of Lagos. It was fresher, cleaner. And the traffic lighter. Or maybe he was glad to get away from things that constantly reminded him of the pain. So far, Micah had enjoyed his stay in Ibadan and once in a while Kiki would pop up in his mind and heart. *She would have loved this place.* He shifted

146

his thoughts to BYF. Thinking about the youths and how they were faring with the new pastor. Fimi had called during a lecture and Micah finally returned it when he was done.

"Pastor M? Good afternoon, Pastor M."

"Fimi, good afternoon. Nice hearing from you. How's everything?"

"It's not the same without you," he had said, not mincing words.

"Okay? What's happening?"

"A lot of people have stopped coming to church. And it's not bad weather or anything. They have just stopped coming."

Micah expected it but didn't say that to Fimi. "Maybe they are busy. Or they are trying to adjust to the changes."

"I don't think so. The atmosphere feels different. The Word is good, but flat. Even me, I'm considering leaving."

"*Haba*, Fimi. Don't do that. You go to church for God. Not for man or anything."

Fimi sighed. "I know. But- it's not just God we love to see and experience in church. We also want to feel loved and enjoy communing with youths as well as having learning about God. The new pastor just goes on and on about how music videos are demonic and how we need to live protected from the madness of the outside world. Pastor M, does he even realize we live in this world and it's not like we are living in a bubble?"

Micah smiled. He had never heard Fimi speak this long on anything.

"Then him going on and on about it is irritating. Telling us to vote wisely during the upcoming elections and to think about our Christian leaders. Talking about hip-hop artistes and how we should not listen to such tunes. I speak for a few of us when I say what he preaches has no relevance to our lives. The church is getting boring. You don't preach at us, Pastor M. You make us experience Jesus for ourselves."

Micah let out a long sigh once Fimi was done. "I'm sorry to hear that. There's not much I can do from my end. Fimi, but keep holding on. Keep in touch with other youths. Create a WhatsApp group or something. Let God lead you."

Hypocrite!

The word seared Micah's heart.

"I'll try. But we miss you, Pastor M."

"I miss you guys too."

Micah ended the call. He dumped his car keys on the table and was going to his room when he saw the shoes at Chinedu's door. He heard a female voice and then Chinedu's. Then laughter followed. Micah shook his head and went into his room. Chinedu's shy girlfriend had been coming over for the last three weeks and secretly leaving during the day and a few times at night. At first, Micah had found it funny and strange but he was getting concerned.

Why would she leave like that? And why was Chinedu spending the night with a woman who wasn't his wife?

But it was the least of his worries.

He was concerned about the youths at BYF. In truth, he knew a couple of them might leave. There were some he had purposely followed up to ensure they were in church on Sundays. But Micah never considered they would stop.

Strike the shepherd and the sheep will be scattered, the scripture came to Micah.

God, I haven't done anything wrong. I left them in good hands.

Whose hands?

The question shook him and he swallowed past the lump in this throat. Micah didn't understand. He had told Pastor Wilson to replace him, expected the Senior Pastor to choose someone who was spiritually upright to do the work. What then happened?

He who puts his hands to the plough, and looks back, is not fit for the Kingdom of God. This isn't where I called you, Micah.

He sat on his bed. He couldn't go back. Didn't want to. "God, when

I placed my wife's life in *Your* hands, where were You?"

No answer was whispered across his heart.

No Scripture came to mind.

The silence all around him was heavy.

* * *

He refused to discuss what happened with her father. Didn't want to upset her. "Are you angry with God? Because of everything that has happened."

"I was. When I was at the hospital, I screamed into the pillow. I cried. I said a lot of things. I asked Him why. Why now? Why cancer? Why me? But now, I've thought a lot about it. Prayed, and I choose to believe it's all for good. No matter the outcome."

"I don't think I have that same level of faith."

He wasn't sure he ever could.

"Remember the three Hebrew boys who were thrown in the fire? They believed in God even if they were not going to be delivered. I'm choosing to do so. If God doesn't heal me. . . I can't stop believing in Him. I'm nothing without Him. Dead or alive."

"But we want Him to heal you, right?"

"Yes. Come on, let's dance."

"What? Dance *ke?*"

She threw her head back, her laughter a familiar tune in his heart. Then she looked at him, pleading him as though she knew their time together was limited. "Dance with me, Micah. Please."

"You're too tired. You should rest."

"Please." She reached out to her iPhone on the bed and ran through the playlist and settled for a Steffany Gretzinger's song, *We Dance*. Then she stretched her hand to him. "Please."

"You steady me . . . slow and sweet, we sway, take the lead and I will follow," she sang. Her eyes locked on his. Her sweet smile, causing him to sway along with her.

"But why this song though?" He disliked that it was slow. Almost depressing. "Can't you choose something upbeat?"

"Because . . . because this is life, Micah. Ups and downs. But together, we will ride over them. Together with God. Let's remember the happy memories, Micah. We won't let this shake us."

Micah placed her arms around his neck and gently brought her close to him. Both of them swaying to the song. He buried his nose in her neck, breathing in the scent of her hair. Listening to the lyrics of the song. His heart breaking as each sentence took root in his heart. His soul.

When my faith gets tired
And my hope seems lost
You spin me round and round
And remind me of that song
The one You wrote for me
And we dance
And we dance

"God, I love you so much Kiki," he whispered against her ear. The smell of her drugs lingering on her neck.

"I love you too."

God, please heal her. Micah prayed desperately in his heart as the music played on.

Give her to Me, My son.

He squeezed his eyes shut, his heart screaming no.

* * *

She stared at the soft green hues that coated the walls in her bedroom. The warm, vibrant colour, a far cry from what she felt at the moment.

Her mind was playing the make-out scene over and over again. She wanted to forget, but her mind and body betrayed her. She kept thinking of Detan's touch and kisses. The way he made her feel loved during the process and at the end she thought herself dirty, stupid. The pain of her lost purity poking at her heart.

Isolation was fast becoming her closest friend.

Maureen couldn't help but notice how Detan was acting differently since the other day. He called less often. He refused to pick her calls. She sent text messages, inviting him to church and he never responded. The guilt only grew larger. The sudden void looming over her was increasing.

She had failed God.

She had failed herself.

Her eyes filled with tears. Why had she gone to his house? Why didn't she listen to God? The condemnation from her actions was becoming too much to bear. There was no one she could talk to. What would she say? That she willingly went to her boyfriend's house, knowing full well he would be alone?

Her phone buzzed and her heart jumped at the sight. Detan was calling back.

"What happened to you? I have been calling you since!"

"Did you come to my place?"

She was confused. "No. After what happened, I didn't think it was wise to do that."

"Anyways, my phone got stolen last week and I recently just retrieved my line. I also had to travel for work so . . . I've been quite busy. How are you?"

"Oh, I'm sorry about your phone." She was relieved it wasn't that he had used and dumped her. "I'm not doing so well."

"Why?"

She raised one leg on the bed and rested an arm on it. "Detan, what happened the other day should not have happened. It can never happen again. You don't know how bad I feel." She rested a palm on her face. "I'm ashamed to go to church."

"Baby, take it easy. It was just one night."

She hated how casual he sounded.

"It's not like we aren't getting married. We didn't sin. We will marry and all this sin or no sin would be no problem."

"It's not as easy as that, Detan. How would you know when you don't go to church?"

"*Shebi* if you confess your sins there's no problem? Then do that and forget about all this. We are still getting married?"

She kept quiet. Waiting for a scripture to drop in her heart. Any confirmation if she should go ahead with the wedding.

"Maureen?"

"Y-yes." She shut her eyes. "We are still getting married."

* * *

The Lord your God is in the midst of you, a Mighty One, a Savior [Who saves]! He will rejoice over you with joy; He will rest [in silent satisfaction] and in His love He will be silent and make no mention [of past sins, or even recall them]; He will exult over you singing.

Zainab prostrated at the altar. Letting the words play out in her head. Worshipping and praising God in the Spirit. A tingling sensation washed all over her and she felt her whole body shake. Tears pricked her eyes.

Minutes later, Zainab stood. The voices of the back-up singers reducing. "Thank You, Lord. God wants someone here to know that He will rejoice over you. He will sing a song of praise. A song the both of you will dance to in this crazy dance of life."

'Amens' resounded over the room.

"Today, I believe God wants me to share about His Silent Love. I must say when I first heard Him, I thought I was mistaken, but He said it again. Tell them about My love in their pain. Tell them I will refresh their life with My love." She raised her hand. "Thank You, Jesus. Thank You. Oh, thank You. The love of God is deeper, higher, and wider than you can ever imagine. You need a renewed thinking to understand this love."

Zainab told them about her past. Her mix with drugs, sex, lesbianism. The pull to end her life. "But God said no. I have more in store for your life. I am going to rejoice over you and I will look at you with new eyes. Like you never committed a sin. Like a husband is enthralled by his new bride. You are beautiful to me. Let's read Zephaniah chapter three verse seventeen. Let's read it together." They did. "Let it soak in. God loves you enough to show up at your darkest trials and your deepest needs. In the previous verse, you see people rejoicing to God for destroying their enemies and in the last verse, God is rejoicing over them.

"When you are in pain, run to God. Run to the One who will quiet you with His love. He would whisper words of comfort to you as He holds you in His arms. You may think He isn't there for you 'cause you can't see or feel Him, but He shows up physically using the hands and voices of those closest to us. Even strangers. He would tell you everything is going to be okay. I have plans for your life that you still know nothing about. Just come to Me and let Me love up on you. You, My beloved."

Zainab heard weeping in different corners of the room. She also had tears in her eyes. But she knew she had delivered the message. She dropped the mic on the podium and found her way to her father's side. He had two hands pressed to his lips, eyes up. When she came to Ibadan, she had expected only to check up on her father and leave in a day or two.

"I think you have something to share with us in my church."

Zainab shook her head. "Nope. I just came to see you."

"I think you do. Pray about it."

She had prayed and God had indeed given her a message, and she prayed for whoever it was. That they would listen and they would heal.

Chapter Fourteen

"Have I told you how well you preach?"

"Like zero times," Zainab teased. In actuality she had learned from her father; sitting in on sermons and watching him unravel the Word so skilfully, bringing out great insights and helping you gain new perspective. "Thank you, dad." She was still in awe at the testimonies of healing that took place after her fifteen minutes ministration. The Presence of God's Spirit had been heavy in the room. Almost like she could touch it.

Zainab felt goosebumps rise up her arms at the thought.

"You should come and preach more often."

"No. I'm not going to be tied down to a church. Don't look at me like that. I've explained that I believe there are a lot of places to go to. To share the Good News."

"But you also have to be churched," he stated.

"I know. I attend Adesewa's church."

"Okay. How's Leke?"

"He's fine."

"Just fine?"

"*Ahn-ahn*, what do you want me to say?"

Her father smiled. "Nothing. You just have this certain bounce in your steps and I'm wondering if Leke is the cause of it or perhaps there's another man in the picture. You know he still hasn't come to see me."

"Dad, you're the only physical man in my life right now."

"But I don't want to be."

Zainab rolled her eyes.

"And I'm not going to push for you to marry. I already made that mistake with your sister. It's not something I would repeat. But I have faith that one day you will walk in and introduce your man to me."

"Truth is, I like Leke."

His smile widened. "But?"

"But I'm yet to find out if he's God's will for my life. I know what God wants me to do. To be an evangelist. To preach the Gospel. But if I'm to get married, then it has to be with someone who can run with me to fulfil God's vision for my life. Someone that won't hinder me and force me to be a stay at home mum and submit to him because he's the man of the house."

Her father laughed. "I wonder how submission will work for you."

"I will submit *na*."

"Would you?"

"Yes. God will help me." Zainab knew it was something she would definitely struggle with. Having always been headstrong.

"Can I let you in on a secret?"

"Most def." She set aside her cup and leaned forward, placing her hands under her thighs. She had missed moments like this with her dad. Times when they could chill and talk about the Word of God. Lovingly argue on certain things and learn as much as she could.

"The Holy Spirit is your best partner and teacher when it comes to marriage. Every attitude or action you would take if you choose to submit yourself to the Holy Spirit, would help you. Efe's mother," He smiled a little, "she was a very spirit-filled woman. She used to tell me, there's nothing she wouldn't do without the Holy Spirit; which should be the truth for all of us Christians. There's this Scripture she loved, *for when you live controlled by the flesh, you are about to die. But if the life of the Spirit puts to death the corrupt ways of the flesh, we then taste his abundant life.*

"What passage is that?"

"Romans. That's the only clue I'm going to give you."

She groaned. "I thought you had stopped doing that. Just tell me exactly where it is."

"Why would I stop? You need to keep searching the scriptures. You aren't a baby . . . I won't spoon feed you."

"Okay, fine. I'll check it out. What else should I know?"

"The Holy Spirit enables and empowers healthy living. He helps fight against sin and gives you the power to be Christ-like."

"And also to bear the fruit of the Spirit."

"Exactly. There's nothing you want to achieve that you cannot achieve with the power of the Spirit of God. And so for marriage, the Holy Spirit would help you be the kind of wife your husband needs and likewise for your husband."

"That's a lot to chew."

"Then take it a bite at a time and savour as much as you can. The Word of God is like Honey in our mouths."

"Psalm 119 verse 103."

"Good girl."

Zaianb was deep in thought for a couple of minutes. "I think God wants me in some kind of revival ministry. I've been praying about it for the last few weeks. Like He wants me to wake the sleeping Christians up and tell them, hey! Jesus is coming soon and you've got to get your A-game together and start moving with the Spirit in being an end time warrior who will bring more souls into the Kingdom and be a light for God."

Revival of the Saints.

Zainab blinked. *God what are you asking of me?*

Tell My people it's time to wake up and begin to work in My name. The harvest is ripe. My Spirit is available.

She allowed the words sink in. *I yield myself to You, God. Use me. How do I go about it?*

Tell them to walk in the Spirit. I will pour out my Spirit on all flesh.

* * *

Tobi applied a nude shade of lipstick and smacked her lips for even distribution. She used the edge of a tissue paper to clean the sides of her mouth and under her lips.

"Someone looks good today. What's the occasion?"

"Must there be something up for me to dress well?"

"I know it's not my birthday. And it's not yours. Neither is it our anniversary. So what's up?"

Tobi ran her sweaty palms over her beige bodycon dress. "I have a presentation today and I am hoping this would put me in my *oga's* good books. So sorry, it's nothing over dramatic."

He bent low and whispered in her ear, "Pity. I wished you said it was for me." He nibbled at her ear and she waved him off.

"Go away, *jor*."

"But baby, you look so good. Come on." He kissed her neck. "Let's play around a little before you got to work. Sex would give you a level of confidence."

"Says who?" She stared at him in the mirror.

"Me."

"Uh-uh. Sex is not relaxing for me. It's work."

"That's a lie from the pit of hell."

Tobi closed her eyes as his fingers dug into her shoulders gently. Letting a moan slip from her lips as his touch loosened knots and bolts.

Relieving the stress of the past week and the tension building up at work because of their latest project.

"So, do I get something in return for this kind gesture?"

Tobi slapped his hands away and stood. "No." She packed her make-up bag and walked to the bed where her handbag was. Faraway from Shola and his raging hormones. "Don't you have to get to work?"

"I do. But I have time to kill with my baby."

"I don't."

He sat on the edge of the bed; watching as she gave one last look at her make-up in the compact mirror.

"I'm beginning to think you don't love me."

Her hand stopped mid-way to adjusting her hair. She looked at him. "Why would you say that?"

He shrugged. "Your behaviour. The way you act all numb when we are having sex. The way you behave sometimes . . . like you would rather we didn't marry. Plus the fact that you are cool with us not even having a child. Normal women would be panicky and fidgety about it, but you? You take it in stride like it's not a big deal."

"I'm not like other women, Shola."

"Could have fooled me," he muttered.

Tobi felt uncomfortable with the silence that followed as she got on her shoes. The need to leave the house heavy on her.

"Do you still love me, Tobi?"

"Are you really going to ask me this?"

"Yes. I am."

"I love you, Shola."

"Then prove it."

"How? By having sex with you now when I have an important presentation this morning? No. I can't."

"Fair enough. Then when you get back home, we can celebrate your job well done." He stood and came to her. "I love you, Tobi. I may not say it often and my actions may speak otherwise. But I do."

"Noted." She stood on peep toes and placed a kiss on his cheek. "Bye."

Guilt filled the car as she drove to work on the busy roads of Lagos. Knowing she had made an appointment with the doctor to terminate the baby just after work hours. Knowing she was the only one keeping Shola from being a father.

Did she feel bad about it?

No, she felt horrible.

* * *

His mind lingered on what he had discussed with Fimi. Two days after they spoke, Fimi had created a WhatsApp group comprising of thirty youths. Micah wasn't interested in joining the group and told Fimi as much. Not wanting to be dragged into such responsibility.

He placed a call to Pastor Wilson, raising his concerns about the youths.

"I'm well aware of what's happening. Numbers declining. Offering at its lowest. The Pastor-in-Charge is trying his best."

"But the youths don't seem to be getting along with him."

"I realise that. But then, remember I was going to announce you as the new pastor there till you turned it down. There was little notice to put someone there."

"I understand. I'm just concerned about them."

"As I am. Micah, the offer still stands. I still feel God wants you here. But realise this, the work of God won't and cannot be static. It won't suffer. He would always ensure that. So in as much as I want you here, don't take too long. I understand things have been difficult since your wife, but hand your pains to God and let Him use you, son. The finances of BYF are fast declining and we are pumping more in than what is coming out. It looks like a profitless investment."

Micah was slightly irritated at Pastor Wilson's major concern. Were the finances all that mattered to him?

"I'm heading out."

Chinedu looked up from his papers, a red pen in hand. "Where to?"

"Just around town. I haven't had the chance to look around much."

"It's my fault too. I haven't been a good host." He tossed his papers and the pen on the coffee table. "Let's go out together and I can show you some really nice places in town."

"I thought you were busy."

"I will come back to it when we return. Besides, I'm hungry and man must chop."

For the next hour, they went to different spots. As many as Chinedu remembered and as many as Micah could drove them to. Chinedu did majority of the talking about his time in Ibadan and his travails as a lecturer. They had a nice dinner of *amala* and *ewedu* in a *bukka* before heading back to their apartment.

"Micah, ever since you came here I've not heard you pick up the phone to call a babe once. Are you still in mourning?"

Micah didn't know how to react at his forthrightness.

"I don't mean any disrespect or anything. I'm just asking."

"It's fine."

"Does that mean you won't answer?"

"Chinedu, I'm not ready for any relationship." *Plus even if I am ready, I don't think I can find anyone as perfect as she. I'm not even willing to find any.*

"How long has it been now?" Chinedu asked, removing the toothpick from his mouth.

"Three years."

Chinedu whistled. "That's a while. Sorry, bro. Sexual healing helps as well. If you want, I can introduce you to a pretty girl that would do anything for an A."

Micah hissed.

Chinedu laughed.

A young lady crossed the road and came to stand by his car when the traffic was a little slow. She knocked on his window. Chinedu made a passing comment on how good she looked.

"Good evening sir. Sorry to disturb you." She handed him a rectangular flyer. "I want to invite you for a program. It's a three day revival program in our church."

A car honked loudly behind them and the lady looked behind them, an apology on her face. Micah noted there was a little gap between him and the car in front. "Thank you." He waved her off and moved forward. A second later she was knocking on his window again.

"Yes?" he asked when he wound down.

"I hope you will come ,sir."

"I can't promise anything."

She nodded. "Thank you, sir. I look forward to seeing you." Then she crossed the road and went to join a group of other ladies who were most likely waiting for her.

"See all these girls. Just parading the place and shoving flyers in people's faces. I know you are a pastor and all. But I'm just saying it as I see it."

Micah should have said something in their defence. But he didn't.

"I mean, it's not compulsory we all be Christians. We all serve God *na*. What's the issue?"

Micah still said nothing and Chinedu probably took that as his cue to keep quiet. Micah knew he was wrong. But somehow, he felt a little good about what he did. About not saying anything.

* * *

March, 2016

"I love this." Kiki took a long sip of her chocolate milk-shake. "Do you ever think there's chocolate in Heaven?"

"Stop talking like this."

She looked away from him and down at her cup. "How should I talk, Micah? We both know that time is running out. What better thing to talk about than the greatest place to be? I have accepted my fate. I know it's hard for you and my family, but this is just the way the story will be."

Micah only stared at her.

"I'm thankful to God for allowing me have these few more months. I'm thankful for knowing you and being your wife."

He reached out and held her hand. Cold and moist in his. "I'm grateful you said I do. I – I just can't wrap my head around everything. Sometimes, I wake up and hope to see you healthy, full of hair and having light in your eyes as I see now." He shook his head. "I don't know how you can have so much faith and hope with this useless cancer. We should be travelling the world, eating beautiful things, h-having babies."

His voice broke and he heard her drop her foam cup and envelop him in her arms. Cooing and rocking him back and forth as though he were a child. Whispering softly that everything was going to be all right.

"I love you, Micah." He adjusted so he could face her. "These last few months you have proved your love for me in so many ways. You have kept to our vows." She placed a palm against his cheek. "I need to say this, even if it's hard for me. After I'm gone, don't mourn too much. Live your life."

"Why are you saying this?"

"Because I know you. I mean, it would obviously hurt now to think of you with another woman. Touching her and kissing her. Your hands doing wonders on her as you've done to me. But it would be selfish of me not to tell you to move on. Don't hold on to me for too long."

He kissed her. "Stop talking."

"Mica-"

"Stop." He pleaded and wrapped his arms around her frail frame, crushing his lips against hers. Kissing her with as much passion as he could. He was careful not to hurt her as well as he expressed every emotion running through him - desperation, anger, pain, hurt and love.

Please, don't let her go.

Silence.

* * *

Tobi offered to take Lola to lunch after the success of the presentation and her boss' promise of great things coming her way. Tobi hoped it was an increase in her salary and a chance to handle higher accounts for J. Jacobs Consulting.

"I haven't mentioned how much I like what you're wearing."

"Thank you."

"Are you sure you're up to this?" Lola asked. Tobi knew what she was referring to.

"Yes, I am."

Lola nodded. "I'm happy you're making this decision for yourself. Enough of all that man must be the head of his home nonsense. You have to do what you have to do. If you feel getting pregnant would tie you down in the marriage, then get the abortion." She took Tobi's hand and caressed the back of it with her thumb.

"Thanks for your support. I really need someone who can understand me."

"Oh dear, I understand you plenty."

They ate lunch and Lola promised to be with her when she went to the hospital.

Hours later, the pain was indescribable. Lola rubbed her back and told her the worst was over. Tobis phone rang but she didn't answer. She knew it would be Shola calling, asking where she was and why she wasn't home.

Tobi didn't want to go home just yet and mentioned it to Lola. They both sat in Tobi's car. Tobi's chair reclined so she could rest her back.

"How do you feel?"

"*One kind.*"

"Sorry dear. It's one of those things."

"Have you had an abortion before?"

Lola nodded. "Yes. Back in university. A bad experience with a guy that I should never have been with. It's part of my reasons why I decided to be who I am."

"What happened?" The pain killers were taking effect.

"I met a guy I thought would be my Prince Charming and everything I would need. Well, things didn't end that way. He was very abusive. Both verbally and physically." Lola looked down at her hands. "And also sexually. Anyway, I got brain and left the relationship as fast as I could. I didn't let myself buy into the idea of his sick love. It wasn't love. It was a demonic act."

"I'm sorry." Even though Tobi didn't like sex, Shola was no beast in bed. He was gentle with her.

"It's fine. Life always offers lemons."

Tobi stretched a hand to Lola. They linked fingers and then Tobi let Lola kiss her on the lips.

Chapter Fifteen

Tobi thought it was the effect of the drugs the hospital had dispensed, or she probably dreamt it. But when she woke in the morning, the lower part of her body was not aching as much as last night; it all came to her.

Lola had indeed kissed her.

Tobi's hand flew to her lips as though he was still expecting it to feel the warmth from the kiss. The taste of Lola's lips on hers, lingering in her mind.

"Where did you go yesterday?"

Her head snapped up to see Shola leaning against the bathroom door, arms crossed and his eyes on her. His expression unreadable.

"I was at work. Sorry, we stayed back late to celebrate."

"Why didn't you pick my calls or send me a message? Don't I at least deserve that?"

She nodded. "I'm sorry." Her phone buzzed and she picked it up.

Lola:

Hey you. Feeling any better?

Tobi dropped the phone back on the side table. "What time is it? Can I make you breakfast?"

The corner of his lips tilted to a smile. "Are you trying to bribe me?"

She stood, careful not to flinch from the slight pain in her tummy. "Yes." She ambled over to his side. "Should I make yam and egg or something?

"That's not the kind of breakfast I want." He looked her over. "But I will settle for physical food for now." He stood up straight and went into the bathroom. "I have to get to my mom's place."

Relieved, she sighed inwardly and followed him. "What's happening there? Hope she's okay."

"She's fine. She invited some pastors to pray and wanted us there so they could pray for us. Told her you would be at work so I would come in since my time is more flexible."

"I appreciate that. You considering me."

He brushed a strand of hair from her face. "Let me bath."

* * *

"I missed you while you were away," Leke said.

"Awww, I sort of missed you too," Zainab teased and he laughed. "But yeah, I missed you."

"How's your dad?"

"He's great. Sends his greetings."

"Gist me about your ministration. One of these days, I should come hear you."

And hear me say I was a former lesbian? "That won't be necessary."

"*Ahn-ahn*, why? I have to hear you at some point. Especially, if we want to explore what's going on between us. We both don't know if this will head anywhere yet, but I would really like to hear you."

"That's kind of you."

"Unless there's something you're hiding."

Zainab looked down at her hand then back at him. "Everyone has a past right?"

Leke nodded. They were at the famous Ikeja City Mall that was brimming with people that Saturday afternoon; mostly teenagers who were strolling around in their little cliques.

"Well, I have one. And it's something I feel ashamed of even though God keeps telling me He loves me and all is forgotten."

Leke stared. Waiting.

"I was a former lesbian."

He sat back. "Wow."

"Shocking right?"

"Kind of, yes. I mean, it explains the tomboyishness you have going on. I just would never have thought to that side."

She grabbed the warm foam cup filled with hot-chocolate as some kind of distraction from hiding her face behind her purse or running out of the building. She took a sip. The rich smell of chocolate calming her nerves. The dark, sweet taste resting on her tongue before going down her throat. She looked at him, a frown on his face.

God, what is he thinking?

"What else?" he asked.

"You haven't responded to what I said yet."

"You might as well lay it all on the table so I know and respond to it all."

She opened her mouth to speak but felt the nudge to hold back. "That's all there is to tell right now."

"Seriously?"

"Yes."

"Well, I don't know what to say. I mean, it's all in the past now. You have been delivered from it."

She took it as a question. "100% sure."

"Then there's nothing to say." Zainab remembered what Adesewa had said about all of them having their own pasts and not being perfect. There and then, Zainab settled in her heart that if Leke wasn't going to be in tune with her in spite of her flaws and past mistakes, then God should just let whatever emotions were slowly developing end abruptly. And if possible, their friendship would remain intact.

* * *

Tobi texted Lola to meet her for lunch at their usual place and now that she sat at the table, waiting for her, she was nervous. They hadn't spoken much after yesterday and Tobi wanted to know what was happening.

"Hey you," Lola greeted. The scent of her perfume enveloping them. Tobi acknowledged how good she looked in her red blazer dress. "Thank you, dear. How are you?"

"I'm good. Better."

"And the pain? Hope it's subsided."

Tobi nodded.

"That's great. What of your husband? Did he suspect anything?"

"No, I told him my staying out late was work related. I didn't give anything away."

"That's good. All is well?"

Tobi bit her lip. How was she going to broach the subject? Lola had to quickly take a call and it bought Tobi another couple of minutes to compose her thoughts.

"Sorry," Lola apologised once she ended the call. "I had to attend to my colleagues. Someone can't go for lunch again without them disturbing you."

"Was I imagining it or you kissed me?" Tobi blurted.

Lola eyes flickered to Tobi's lips briefly. "Yes. I did."

"Oh -" Tobi blinked. Her heart beating wildly. "Why?"

"I thought that was what you needed. I may be wrong; I just assumed we were like-minds. If it isn't something you want, it's totally fine and we would act like it never happened and move forward with our friendship; that is, if you still want us to be friends."

Tobi slumped back on her seat. Amazed and a little perturbed at the same time. She leaned forward and whispered, "Are you – are you a lesbian?"

Lola laughed. "I'm a high femme."

"What?"

"It means a queer woman who's extremely feminine."

Tobi's mouth formed a small 'o'.

"I see you are quite unfamiliar with our world." She cocked her head to the side. "How long have you known?"

Tobi felt like a child under Lola's scrutiny. "That?"

"That you are queer. A lesbian."

"I - I don't know." Tobi's eyes scanning the room to see if people could hear their conversation. "It's something I'm still trying to understand. Truth is, I don't really know who I am. It sounds stupid that a grown woman like myself can't figure out who she is."

"Don't beat yourself over it. I like to tell myself this life is an adventure that has to be explored with all measures. And if it helps, I didn't discover until my bad episode abroad."

Tobi checked the time. Her lunch break was over and they hadn't eaten anything yet.

"Let me get us something to eat." Lola rose and took quick strides to the order point, not aware of the men who stared. She returned a few minutes later with two white nylons of take-outs. Tobi raised a brow at her.

"Let's eat in your car instead. It gives us room to talk freely."

* * *

"My first girlfriend was my roommate. Things were fun until we had to part ways. She wasn't satisfied with just me."

"Ouch," Tobi said.

"It hurt but then a girl's gotta move on."

Tobi chewed on her spicy porridge. "Guess cheating is no respecter of relationship or gender."

"Girl, it happens everywhere. It just carries its nasty self all around."

They ate in comfortable silence for the next few minutes.

"I've always felt different when I'm with girls. A good feeling."

Lola nodded in understanding.

"But the thing is, in this part of the world, being gay is heavily frowned upon."

"And where I come from, I can hold a woman's hand and hold my head up high as I'm walking down the street. Nigeria is just backward in everything. They are a bunch of homophobes who believe we are all going to hell and would burn in an unquenchable fire. They need to read their Bibles more to understand God isn't opposed to homosexuality."

"Yeah, I've seen some articles about that online. How the seven scriptures that talk about homosexuality aren't actually talking about it being a sin. I know, but I kind of feel bad when I think of another girl. Like it's wrong."

"Don't buy into the lies, Tobi. Accept yourself for who you are."

Tobi glanced at the time on the dashboard. "I have to go back to work."

"Look, I'm free this evening. We can meet up. If it's not possible, then we can choose another day."

"I'll let you know."

Lola smiled. "This was fun. I enjoy spending time with you."

"Same here."

"Let me quickly call an Uber. I hate driving in this Lagos. Those *danfo* drivers drive me crazy."

Back at the office and settled at her table, reminiscing at her time with Lola and brimming with excitement at the possibility of starting something new with her. Whatever it was.

Why do you reject Me, Tobi?

"Who are you?" she said out loud, looking about the room for a tiny speaker or someone hiding under her table, wondering if she was going mad. Wasn't this how mental cases started?

I am the One who created and loves you. Yet, you want to exchange the knowledge of Me for something abominable. To give your love to what I created and not to Me.

Tobi jerked back. Her breathing heavy as she blinked severally. "W-what do you want from me?"

I want you to know Me.

*   *   *

The old man stared at him. "How can I help you?'

"I'm here for the service. I thought this was the entrance."

"No, it's actually the other hall to the right. This room is too small to contain them."

Micah nodded. "Thank you, sir."

Micah chose a good place to sit at the back after locating the hall. He still questioned why he drove all the way here. Why he was in a church building for a program all because the flier was given to him. But the topic for discussion had piqued his interest.

Dancing with God.

Micah only spoke when he was spoken to and responded to greetings. The service kicked off at the appointed time and the worship session was ordinary. He knew his youths back at BYF could do better. He was considering sneaking out when the older man he saw earlier walked out and stood by the chair and table set up for him.

"Permit me to sit. I'm having leg pains due to the cool weather. Let's just worship God for the next few minutes." He picked a tune and there was no backup singer. There was none needed for his deep baritone voice that carried a tune so well. Micah found himself syncing to the worship. Feeling like the prodigal son who had returned home.

Minutes later, they all took their seats.

"What I have to share this evening is a peculiar topic. I also have a lot to learn from it. A dance could be slow or fast depending on the music played. It could be sweet or sad. But in this life there's only one dance partner you need; and that's God. Let His Words be the music singing over us as we dance through this life. I take my Bible reading from Psalm 17 verse 4 and 5 in the Amplified Classic version which says, *Concerning the works of men, by the word of Your lips I have avoided the ways of the violent (the paths of the destroyer). My steps have held closely to Your paths [to the tracks of the One who has gone on before]; my feet have not slipped.* Powerful stuff.

"Dancing with God means following His steps in every way and through every situation. Even if it means you have to close your eyes as you follow Him, you are confident He won't lead you in the wrong path. And even if things don't go the way you planned or want them to, you still trust him. One way to dance with God is to be enveloped by the Spirit of God. Dancing with God is following Him as He leads us, but it also entails following the lead of His Spirit. And when I say dance with God, I mean spiritually and not literally dancing with Him; although that could happen. You can't box God."

Micah felt like the words were for him alone. The old man went on to explain how Samuel anointed David and the Spirit took control of him from that day forward. How the Holy Spirit enabled him to do certain things.

"How much room are you giving the Holy Spirit to be in control of your life? Are you still struggling or giving Him a free hand?

"My daughter was here and ministered to us on Sunday, talking about those who have gone through one pain or the other and God wanting to comfort you. Don't hold yourself back from receiving His love and touch. You will only hurt further. Let God's Spirit envelope you today. Galatians 5 verse 16 and 25 says, *But I say, walk by the Spirit, and you will not gratify the desires of the flesh. If we live by the Spirit, let us also keep in step with the Spirit.*

When the message was over, Micah felt it had been too short. Hungering for more of what the soft spoken man had to say on God and comfort. About the Spirit of God.

Micah felt like he was doing a waltz at this point in his life and all the emotions he had been through. He considered waiting to speak with the man after the benediction.

"Good evening, sir."

"Ah, how are you? You were the one that missed your way last time?"

"Yes, sir."

"I guess that's not the only way you've missed."

"Pardon me?"

"Let's go over to my office. I have a few minutes to spare before my doctor's appointment."

* * *

"What's your name son?" The older man asked when they were finally in the nicely decorated office. A large picture frame of a girl and boy smiling at something.

"Micah Oramah, please have your seat."

"I'm Eghosa Phillips. Now," He placed his arms on his table, "how can I help you?"

"I was really – your message touched me. And I guess I felt the need to speak with you. If that makes any sense."

"If you are led by the Spirit, it would definitely make sense."

"I have questions. You mentioned something about it not being the only way I have missed. What did you mean?"

"I don't know the details, but I know you have strayed from your First Love. Or am I wrong?"

Micah didn't deny it.

"What do you do Micah?"

"I teach in a university. University of Ibadan. I am – was a pastor."

"Was? Why?"

Micah cleaned the sides of his mouth. A trail of saliva on his thumb and forefinger. "I faced certain challenges in my life that led to it."

"Can I ask what those challenges were?"

"It's not something I want to talk about."

Eghosa Phillips nodded. "Of course. Well, when you are ready, I'm here." The old man rose and Micah did similar.

Micah didn't want to leave yet so when they both went out and noticed the old man trying to hail a taxi, he spoke up. "Can I take you for your appointment?"

"You don't have anything better to do this evening than be with an old man?"

Micah smiled. "I'm free."

"Okay then. Let's go."

* * *

While the hours went by in the hospital, the old man opened up to Micah about his knee problem and high blood pressure. His two daughters. His time in ministry and ups and downs he faced.

Micah wondered why the old man would divulge this much to a stranger.

"People think us pastors can't make mistakes. They forget we are humans. My daughter faced a terrible blow after she got pregnant outside wedlock. It's surprising how much persecution comes from the church. The same people who are meant to love you, judge you."

"I guess we can say not everyone in church is really who they say they are and the devil sometimes uses those closest to us to give the deadliest blows."

"Spoken like one who's matured."

It was funny that it took two hours to see the doctor and the old man barely spent twenty minutes there. Micah offered to take him home. A two-storey building in a spacious compound. An old Mercedes parked.

Micah followed the old man silently, half-expecting the place to smell old and funky but was surprised at how tastefully decorated it was. Wooden finishing, quarter turn staircase and a medium sized chandelier at the centre. The living room was left out of the exquisite touches. Black leather settee and a marble centre table occupying the space. Walls painted in soft tones of beige and white. A rectangular wall mirror just above the three seater couch.

"You have a beautiful home, sir."

"Thank you."

Micah was tempted to ask why he didn't have a car. He wanted to ask how Pastor Eghosa could trust a stranger with private details of his life and family. But Micah didn't.

"Sit down, Micah. You have earned my respect for sitting for so long with an old man boring you with his life history."

"You didn't bore me sir."

"You don't have to be polite."

Micah laughed. "I'm not."

"So are you ready to talk to me? Or would like to eat something?"

Micah raised his hands. "I'm fine sir."

"Well, I'm hungry but I don't want to keep you waiting. Let's talk."

Pastor Philips stared at him. Waiting.

"I lost my wife three years ago to pancreatic cancer."

"I'm sorry to hear that."

Micah wondered how much he could say.

"You blame God."

"I do." It was a relief to finally say the words out loud. Keeping them in for so long was hard. "I blame God."

"Why?" the man asked. He didn't look at Micah as though he were judging him, only trying to understand. "Why do you blame God?"

Micah looked down at his brown sandals. A birthday gift from Kiki. "Because I prayed. I cried out to Him for healing. I fasted. I had prayer warriors in church praying for her. But God still denied her healing."

"You also felt betrayed?"

Micah eyes came to Pastor Eghosa once more. He bobbed his head. "Yes. I have served Him. I did everything the Bible said to do; I prayed. I had faith that was probably as big as a watermelon. I confessed His Word; *by His stripes we are healed*! I did all that. And yet God asked me to let her go."

"I'm not belittling your pain, Micah. But do you believe in the sovereignty of God?"

Micah nodded.

"And do you also believe God has the best in mind for you? Irrespective of what evil the devil has in mind?"

Micah nodded again.

"Then let me ask you this, would you still love and have faith in God if He took everything you had?"

* * *

Maureen shoved aside the gnawing feeling. The same feeling she got each time she stole a piece of meat from her mother's large pot of soup many years ago. It had suddenly taken up space in her life. Finding a way to taunt her.

"What time did he say he was coming?" her mother asked.

"Ten."

"It's five past ten and he isn't here."

"Maybe it's traffic, Mummy."

Her mother nodded. "This early morning? I hope so." She dabbed gently as the sweat beads on her forehead. Careful not to mar her makeup. Her mother hardly ever used cosmetics. She disliked them. But today, she applied some, in a bid to look good and impress Detan's mother.

The doorbell rang, the security guard informing them they had visitors.

"Let them in!" her mother instructed.

Minutes later, the living room oozed with a range of expensive perfumes. Detan, Tobi and their parents were settled in their spacious living room.

The two mothers were busy assessing each other as they spoke and laying high praises on their children.

"My daughter, I can see you brought home a good catch," Maureen's mother said. "He's a very respectful boy."

Maureen forced a smile. "Yes, Mummy."

"My son has nothing but good things to say about Maureen. You raised her up very well."

"My sister, God had been faithful *o*. Ever since I lost my husband all those years ago, God has been helping me look after her and her younger brother. He's now in his second year in the university."

Detan's mother nodded sympathetically, her hand falling on her husband's lap as though to mark her territory. "*E pele,* Ma. God will continue to watch over them."

Maureen shifted in her chair. Her eyes settled on Detan briefly and the weary look on his face. They both wanted it to be over. Maureen, a lot more.

Chapter Sixteen

"I finally told Leke."

"So, what did he say?" Adesewa was rummaging through her wardrobe. She picked one of Zainab's small bottles of expensive perfume and sprayed a little on her wrist, raising her hand to her head to sniff it.

"He didn't have anything to say. Like the whole thing baffled him." Zainab watched as her friend took out one of her leather jackets. "Maybe disgusted him *sef.*"

"*Haba*, don't say that. Give it time. A relationship requires patience."

"Yeah, but I have a feeling he's not going to stick around much. No. You can't take that jacket."

"But I like it *nau.*" Adesewa took off her floral print kimono and wore the jacket. Her tummy had started protruding. After the pregnancy and abortion talk with her friend, she often thought about what her mother might have gone through being pregnant and alone. Fighting off abortion and submitting to her father's demands. Zainab slowly developed compassion for her mother, easing out the pain and hurt over not having known her father sooner.

"Doesn't it look fab on me?" Adesewa brought Zainab back to the present.

"No. It makes you look fat."

"Liar." Adesewa folded the jacket, kept it on the bed and went back to looking through her things.

"I still don't know why you take my clothes. You are the fashionista. All I have are dark colours which are not my thing."

"You have *expensive* dark colours."

Zainab was silent for a moment. "How's pregnancy like? Does it hurt?"

Adesewa chuckled. "No. Not at first, probably towards the end. But then every woman's pregnancy is different. Some people have terrible morning sickness, their faces swell and they get terrible acne."

"Didn't you have eczema when you were pregnant with Seyi?"

"Yup."

Zainab rubbed her eyes, seating up.

"What's wrong? There's something up with you and you aren't telling."

"I can't stop thinking I probably shouldn't have told him. What's the point? It's not like I do it anymore. The past is the past. So why do I have to share?"

Adesewa sat on a nearby chair. "You really like this guy."

Zainab pursed her lips. "I like him. Not really like him. I'm still getting to know him, but I was – *am* hoping, that he would be the guy." She flopped back onto the bed. "I hate all this emotional stuff."

Her friend giggled. "That's because you have always been wired to be a woman. You may dress like a tomboy, behave tough, but deep down you are still the woman God created you to be. Not like those people who believe God made them to be gay. It's just ridiculous."

"You have a point. I didn't even think God made me like that. I just flowed with it because my cousin introduced me to it when I was small. Probably ten or so, and it became a norm for me."

Zainab could still remember that day.

"Have you ever kissed a girl?" Sonia asked out of the blue.

"What?" Zainab stopped kicking at stones and glanced up at Sonia. She

was curling a strand of her hair around her finger.

"Would you like to?"

"No. It sounds weird."

"It's actually not. I do it all the time. I have this friend in school who likes to kiss a lot. Both guys and girls."

Zainab thought Sonia was joking until she said, "Do you want to try it out?"

Zainab stared at her cousin's lips, always harboured the thought of them being too pink to be natural. Her face flawless albeit a pimple which decided to show up whenever she was in her period. Then Zainab found herself thinking it wouldn't be a bad idea to kiss her.

As if Sonia could tell what Zainab was thinking, with a knowing smile she jumped to her feet and walked towards Zainab. Zainab's gaze now fixated on a small stone coated with sand.

"Are you scared?" Sonia asked.

Zainab shrugged. "No. What's there?"

Sonia's pink lips spread into a smile and she leaned close while Zainab momentarily snapped her eyes shut.

Zainab shooed the thoughts away. A part of her wondered if Sonia was still into it or had finally surrendered to God.

"A lot of people in the world are embracing homosexuality. Movies and cartoons. Children." Adesewa visibly shuddered. "It makes me worried about the culture change my children are going to put up with. How much they would have to stand for the truth despite what their friends or what the world says. Thank God, Nigeria isn't like that."

"Yet," Zainab added. "It would get to that if we Christians slack or keep living in a bubble that we in this part of the world are exempted from such things. These things still come in one way or the other. Even as Christians there is no one immune to sexual struggles."

"Audrey was still gisting me the other day about how a girl came up to her and asked if she wanted to hang out."

Zainab was slightly amused, knowing the Audrey she knew would most definitely freak out.

"Audrey quickly stated that she liked men."

"I can imagine."

"Zainab, it's not funny."

"Yeah, I know but picturing Audrey in that situation is laughable."

"You know I heard of a pastor's daughter who's also gay."

"Like I said, it's bound to happen."

"So, what can we do?"

Zainab had no idea. Then she remembered what God had said to her about reviving the saints. But what had that got to do with it?

Preach the message of Salvation to all. Love and Preach.

Zainab in turn told Adesewa.

"So we just keep on preaching? Would that solve much? Churches that are meant to speak against it are embracing the nonsense."

"Calm down."

Adesewa let out a breath.

"Remember, we hate what they do but still love them because God loves them."

Adesewa opened her mouth to speak, and then closed it. "I have an idea. Let's go watch a movie. I'm in the mood for something action."

Zainab raised her brow and said jokingly, "It's like this pregnancy is messing with you."

"I just want to get my mind off this."

A thought came to Zainab's mind. "Did you hate me back then?"

"What?"

"When I was the old me, did you hate me or what I did?"

"I didn't hate you. I was very much concerned. I didn't want you getting married to IK based on a lie. I wanted you to change. Give your life to Christ. But no, I never hated you."

"Thank you.

* * *

"My mum wants us to have lunch with her on Sunday after service."

Tobi watched Shola as he flipped through the channels late Saturday evening. "Why are you just telling me? What if I have plans?"

"Sorry, you went out for your brother's intro early in the morning so there was no time to discuss it. And what are you doing on Sunday that we can't pay Momsi a visit?"

"Nothing." Tobi had told Lola they could meet up Sunday afternoon. "I wanted to rest. It's been a long week." Her mother had worn her out with street gossip and talk on Maureen's mother.

Maureen.

Funny how Tobi had long since sailed from that ship. She saw her future sister-in-law and no longer felt a twinge of jealousy. Ever since Lola had come into Tobi's life, being there for her, Tobi had shifted her focus to something more promising. But then there was the incident at her office. The soft voice that had whispered to her. Telling her he wanted to know her. Tobi didn't want to think she was going mental, accepting it was –

She shook her head. God couldn't be talking to her. Like Shola liked to say, when she was still clubbing way back when he had stopped, what did light have to do with darkness? God wouldn't want to have anything to do with her.

Or maybe it isn't even God talking to me. There are gay Christians right?

She also didn't want to believe it was the devil talking to her. Tobi knew she hadn't done anything wrong yet.

"Babe, are you good?"

"Huh?" Tobi saw her husband watching her. "What?"

"You seem faraway. What's up?"

"Nothing. Just thinking. It's not important. I'm going to take a shower."

"Chill, I want to talk to you about something."

The tone of his voice revealed it was probably serious. He muted the TV and turned his gaze on her. It was then she noticed the worried look on his face.

"Sure."

"When I went to my mum's place and the pastors came to pray. One of them mentioned something about you."

Tobi hated it when Shola paused midway of making his point. "So?"

"He said you need to be careful and that you had blood on your hands."

She blinked. "Blood?"

Did they mention the abortion to him?

"He also said you are about to do something and if you do, there's no going back." Shola stared at her, as though hoping whatever secret she had would jump out like a rabbit in a magic hat. "What are you planning to do?"

"The pastor is probably fake because I haven't done anything and there is no blood on my hands." She opened her palms for him to see. "See? No blood."

"I think what he means is blood somewhere in your past or some-where in your life."

"Nothing has happened, Shola. I'm fine. Your mother should stop allowing fake pastors into her house before they case everything she has and rob her in the middle of the night."

"What about the other thing I said?"

She looked confused.

He sighed. "About you at the verge of doing what you shouldn't do."

"Oh, that. The only thing I want to do is be promoted at work. Maybe he doesn't want me to prosper. And which pastor in their right mind would say I shouldn't prosper?"

"Something doesn't add up."

"Exactly what I'm telling you. Your mother should be careful of people she looks up to as pastors. These days many are in wolves' clothing pretending to be sheep."

Shola placed a hand against his forehead.

"Do you have a headache?"

"I'm fine. You can have your bath." He picked up the remote and the resumed watching his TV show. Tobi hurried up the stairs, two steps at a time. She closed her eyes and leaned against the bedroom door, her heart racing like masquerades were actively chasing it.

She had no doubt about it now; God was involved in her matter. But she had no idea why.

* * *

Would you still love and have faith in God if He took everything you had?

Micah blinked his eyes open. His time with Pastor Eghosa heavy on his mind. His deep questions lingering and prodding him for answers. The truth was he didn't know how to answer. He had already turned his back on God. It had taken him three years to do that.

Slowly drifting from His Presence.

He got out of bed and went to take a shower. Pastor Eghosa had invited Micah to church. But Micah had declined. He was to meet with Pastor Eghosa after service at his home. But Micah wasn't sure he wanted to go back. Probably he didn't want to hear he was fighting a lost battle.

Still, he had questions that maybe the soft spoken man could answer.

Micah arrived just a few minutes past two. Pastor Eghosa welcomed him into his home once again, and this time, he had the dining area set up with food.

"I have church members who come in once in a while to help me with domestic duties. On Sunday, they buy me lunch."

"So it's not all bad."

"We thank God for that."

The smell of *moi-moi* drifted to Micah, waking up hunger pangs.

"Hope you don't mind joining me for lunch."

"Er-"

"Of course we can eat and talk."

Micah nodded.

"How was service, sir?"

"It was fine. Five souls won today, another reason for heaven to rejoice and make my life more meaningful." Pastor Eghosa's hand shook a little as he dished white rice into his plate and Micah offered to help him. "Thank you. When I tell my girls I'm getting old they always laugh it off. It is well."

"How come they can't live with you or you move over to where they are?"

"One is married and building life with her husband. I don't want to be a third wheel. The other one is an evangelist. Single. She has suggested it but I'm not interested in leaving my home. My wife and I had wonderful years in this house. She passed when my second daughter was fifteen. Road accident. I miss her still." Pastor Eghosa smiled. "So you see, we have a lot in common."

"You asked me if I would still love God and have faith in Him if he took everything I had. Can I ask you the same question?"

"Without a doubt, I would choose God. Because I know God's character and I trust Him. I know God is just. Faithful. True. It would hurt, but I choose to glorify Him in spite of the pain and see the good He chooses to bring out of it. In other words, I choose to still dance with Him. Sad as it may be, my pains don't change Him but He changes my pain. He turns my mourning into dancing."

Micah glanced at his plate and the half-eaten food. Tears forming in his eyes. "When I lost Kiki, I began asking myself why a good God would cause His saints pain."

Pastor Eghosa smiled a little. "Why would Jesus endure the pain of the cross? Why would God send Jesus, His beloved Son, to die for our sins? Was it to spite Him? Or to purposely make Him suffer?"

"No. But what about scriptures that say, *a thousand shall fall by your side and ten thousand by your left, no harm would come near you?* What happens to using such scriptures if God is still going to do whatever He wants with our lives? We might as well live in fear of dying all the days of our lives."

"The devil has really dealt with you. Filling your head with doubts."

Micah blinked at the jab.

"I talk to you like this because you have been a pastor for a few years and have attended Bible College. David said, *He set a table for me in the midst of mine enemies.* Did he say in the midst of well wishers or loved ones? No. He said with enemies. So it means they can sneer at me as I'm cracking my delicious chicken bones and drinking my cold drink. It means, even in the midst of these ones, still look up to God. Still trust Him that He wants what's good for you. God doesn't want us in pain. The enemy does. But what the enemy planned for evil, God will turn it around for good."

"So what good came out of losing your wife?" Micah asked stubbornly, refusing to see reason.

"For one thing, it made me able to talk to you and a whole lot of other people going through one pain or the other."

"That's all? Surely, God won't make you go through all that pain for just me or someone else."

Pastor Eghosa lips tilted up to a small smile again. "But isn't that what Jesus did?"

For once since Micah had stepped into Pastor Eghosa's home that afternoon, he was stunned.

"Let God in, Micah. Let Him take your pain. Let Him sing over you."

Chapter Seventeen

Leke couldn't forget what Zainab said at the mall. He knew she dressed macho but never linked it to being gay. He tried not to imagine her with another girl or anything crazy.

But he had to admit she made a bold move.

He asked himself what he would do if he were in her shoes; how he would feel if he had to 'fess up to his past mistakes just to build trust. He would be worried if any woman would be comfortable with him.

Probably how Zainab felt.

Leke cracked his knuckles and stared at his computer screen. His neck ached from poring over the images. The past two days being hectic. A wedding one day and a bridal party the next . Sometimes, Leke felt being around women all day was no longer a pleasure with all their gossip and demands.

He stared at one of the girls in the pictures. She looked a lot like someone he knew. His eyes were starting to close and he stood and sprawled himself on his bed. He had told Zainab he didn't like dishonesty and she had willingly told him about her sins.

How am I supposed to deal with this?

Leke thought about Emem. Last he heard, she was seeing someone new. Most likely someone with a bigger bank account. There were days he still missed her. Days he wished he could be the man she needed. But he kept telling himself it was all over and it was best he moved on.

He groaned. "God, what do I do?"

* * *

Tobi should have guessed why her mother-in-law was interested in seeing her. Tobi wished she had followed Lola's advice to fake a headache and body pains so they could meet up.

"Mummy, she said she hasn't done anything. Please, leave her alone."

"But you were here *nau*. You heard what the pastor said."

"Maybe he's a fake pastor."

"*Dake enu re*! You don't talk like that about a man of God."

Shola sighed in defeat and faced his phone. His mother faced her once more. "Tobi, my dear. You can talk to me. *Abi*, you want Shola to excuse us? We can have a mother and daughter talk."

"No, Mummy. Maybe Shola is right. There's nothing that I'm doing or have done that would warrant the pastor pronouncing such things."

"Ah, don't talk like that. They are prophets. They told me I should not travel one time like that and that plane crashed! Another time, they told me not to eat a particular meal but give the dog; the dog ate it and died. Many times, they have helped me and many testimonies have resulted from heeding to their visions." She adjusted the crooked *gele* on her head. Somehow Shola's mother reminded Tobi of the boisterous actress in the Nigerian movie, *The Wedding Party*.

"Mummy, I understand. Maybe they are wrong in this case. Did they mention which blood?"

Her mother-in-law said no. "But sometimes they don't have all the details. You have to be the one to think and find out what exactly they are talking about. After all, it's your life not theirs. We don't know, maybe they are seeing something or someone that is blocking the both of you from having your own children. Shola, the both of you have to be careful *o*. This world is very wicked and full of devilish people. The both of you need to be more prayerful! Hope you do night devotions."

"We would start."

"Ah! The both of you are not serious. You should be doing a lot of prayer and fasting. Tighten your spiritual belt and fight every evil force. *So gbo mi?*"

Shola answered for them. "Yes, ma. But please encourage Tobi for me. She is not the churchy type."

"Not the churchy type? *M gbo* Tobi? You still aren't going to church? The only way to get answers is through prayers. I don't want to hear this talk again about you not going to church, or do you want me to die without being a grandmother?"

Tobi almost bobbed her head. Almost. "No, Mummy. Don't say things like that."

"Then please, start attending church with your husband." She clapped her hands together. "*Oya*, let's eat. There's pounded yam and *efo elegusi*. Tobi, go and serve your husband."

"Aren't you eating, Mummy."

"No. I'm on a seven days fast."

"Mum, you're fasting again?" Shola asked. "You just finished one the day before."

"Fasting cannot be too much."

Tobi excused mother and son as they went on a banting spree and plodded to the large kitchen. The cool breeze from the A.C cloaked her bare shoulders, making her wish she had worn something warmer. Shola's mother hated heat and had installed A.C's almost everywhere in the house. Only the toilets had been spared the niceties. Tobi remembered the first time she came to Magodo and saw the beautiful home that was Shola's parents'. The beautiful garden in the compound and the details from the entrance hall, the two living rooms, toilet and state of the art kitchen.

Everything screamed of wealth.

Tobi rinsed a plate and a small bowl, and served her husband's food. All the way in the kitchen, she couldn't tell what was going on in the large living room. Pausing what she was doing, Tobi quickly placed a call to Lola.

"I'm sorry I cancelled. I was really looking forward to hanging out with you."

"It's fine. I decided to use the opportunity to rest. You are still there?"

"Yes. And you won't believe what's going on."

"What?"

Tobi glanced at the door. "It's a long story. Would gist you when we see."

"Tomorrow during lunch then?"

Tobi nodded. "Yes."

"Alright, dear."

Tobi carried the food out on a tray and placed it on a stool in front of Shola. He disliked sitting at the dining area. Felt it too large and informal with its polished brass chairs with cushions too hard to sit on and the Italian mahogany table top that you always had to be careful of not spilling anything on it.

"Well done, my daughter. You are doing a good job. If only your womb will begin to follow suit. I know it's God that gives children. He will give you yours soon."

"Amen."

The guilt came. She recalled the words whispered to her in her office, and also what the so called pastors had said, and she ignored them.

* * *

She was surprised when Leke asked to meet with her. There they were, outside her late mother's home and sitting on the boot of his car. The clouds dark with tell-tale signs of rain heading in their direction. Zainab pulled her jumper tighter and curled her fingers into her sleeves.

"I'm sorry I've been AWOL. I had two jobs back to back over the weekend. Didn't get home till ten pm on Sunday and I slept in the whole of yesterday."

"It's fine." She had bitten off her nails from nervousness and painted her nails twice. Her hands too shaky to get the polish on right after he had called earlier in the morning. "I understand the job." She also understood that he needed time to process everything.

"How have you been?"

"Fine. Fine. I got an invitation to minister in Abuja. I also have a wedding over there around the same time."

"Nice."

They lapsed into a round of silence with Zainab thinking he should get what he wanted to say over with.

"I've been thinking about what you said. I don't hold anything against you, Zainab. Your past is your past. You are done with that. I see no reason why I have to hold it against you."

Her mouth fell open and she inhaled sharply. "Seriously?"

He got down. "Of course. What kind of person would I be to push you away because of what happened years ago."

"Three to be exact."

"Exactly." He faced her. Hands at his back. "I care about you. I'm willing to make things work between us if you're willing."

She was at a loss for words. Her throat felt as if it was clogged with lumps of bread she had for breakfast.

"Say something." Leke was close now. Close enough for her to capture the uneven hairs of his beard and the small birthmark on his earlobe. Something she hadn't noticed before then. His leg brushing against hers; unimposing. The hint of a smile on his pink, full lips and for a moment she wondered what it would be like to kiss him.

"I-I'm also willing."

"Great. So we are going to do this, the first thing is you go up and change and meet back here so we can go out."

"Okay? What's the second thing?"

"You tell me the other things you want to."

Zainab still didn't feel the nudge to tell him. "What if I'm not ready yet?"

"Then I will wait till you're ready."

There were not a lot of fun places to hang out in Lagos. To Zainab, it was either the cinema, beach, food joints or creating something fun for yourself. Leke chose the cinema. They were ten minutes late for the movie and ended up sitting two rows to the screen.

Zainab didn't care much for that. She was just happy that Leke was by her side.

Chapter Eighteen

These days, Maureen seemed to be coasting along with life. She wasn't attending BYF as much as she did before. Giving excuses as to why she couldn't make Bible Study and Sunday services. She was told about the group on WhatsApp and had joined at some point. But the interactions and the spiritual high made her feel like she didn't belong there anymore.

She couldn't even query Detan about not going to church. After sleeping with him the second time – a time when she had been vulnerable - she decided she was in no position to demand that of him.

Who are you to question his way of life when you are no different? You just profess Jesus but don't live the Christian lifestyle. You are a failure. You are nothing but a hypocrite.

She didn't shake the lies away anymore. Letting them settle in her heart.

"Are you living here now?"

Maureen looked up to see Tobi standing before her. *When did she come in?* She adjusted herself on the chair. "No. I was-"

"Lil sis!" Detan's voice boomed from behind and both ladies turned in his direction.

"Detan, what did you do to Maureen?"

"I didn't do anything to her. Why?"

"She's not looking her usual self."

"I'm fine, Tobi. I'm just tired."

"*Pele.* You should rest." Tobi turned her gaze to her brother once more. "But then how can she rest when this whole place is dirty and she has to clean. Detan, you have to get a maid when you guys marry *o*. You can't stress Maureen like this."

"*Abeg*, leave me *jor*."

Maureen grabbed her things and took that as an opportunity to leave. Tobi offered to drop her at home.

"I'm heading home and only came here to pick my i-Pod. Forgot it the last time I was here and Detan forgot to bring it with him on the day of the Intro." Tobi smoothly navigated her way onto the express. She spared Maureen a quick glance. "Are you sure you're okay?"

"Yes."

"How's your church?"

"Fine."

Maureen wasn't in the mood for chatting. Sandfield was just around the corner. "Can I please get down here?"

"Why? I thought you were heading home."

"I am. I remembered I wanted to get something at the Mall. Sorry."

"Okay. Let me clear from the road."

The car slowed to a stop as Tobi found somewhere to park close to the bus stop. A few people bent low to peer through the window; calling out their destinations. They stopped when Tobi shook her head and waved them off.

"Thank you." Maureen got down and waved her away.

Maureen took the foot bridge to the other side of the road then boarded a tricycle to *The Palms*. She took a walk around the mall, feeling hugely uncomfortable at not brushing her teeth before leaving Detan's. It had been a long day at work and her mother hadn't thrown a fit at Maureen spending the night at her fiancé's place instead of returning home late.

If Pastor Micah was around, this might not have happened. He would have followed up with and made sure I made the right decisions.

She walked into the popular supermarket there and purchased a pack of mint and a bottle of water. The overpowering mint taste improving her self-esteem for the time being. She went to the food court and occupied an empty seat. Watching as people walked in. Quietly observing them.

Maureen was in no hurry to leave. Didn't want to go home and hear her mother talk about the wedding and the necessary plans to be made. Or the relatives they should invite and those who had a lot of money to 'spray' them at the wedding. She just wanted to be left to her thoughts and believe she was still the upbeat Christian single girl, even if it was just for a few hours.

* * *

It had been a long time Zainab felt the way she did. Even her girls at work noticed a change in her.

"It's not like you aren't always happy o," said one.

"It's just that you are happier. Like you are super happy," said another.

Super happy.

Zainab guessed that was a good way to describe how she felt. Ever since Leke thought her worthy enough to date. She knew God might have put in a Word in her favour.

You are beautiful in My sight. A precious bride to behold.

"God, You are making me blush."

I love you with an everlasting love. From the east to the west, that is how faraway your sins are to Me.

She silently said a thank you. It was strange for her, but she felt her heart flutter each time she thought about Leke. Her joy knowing no bounds when he showed up at Abuja, taking the night bus so he could make her meeting. Only he had been too proud to allow her pay for his flight back.

"God, is he the one for me?"

My plans for you are good and not evil. Wait on Me.

"You've lost me. Now I don't know what to expect."

What if I told you I had someone better for you?

Like a toothpick popping a balloon, she felt her joy deflate. *Someone better than Leke?*

Trust Me.

* * *

"I have a wedding I want us to attend together," Lola started. Tobi hurriedly cleaned off whatever lipstick stains Lola left on her cheeks as Shola walked into the house. His eyes moved from one woman to the other, then back on Tobi. His brow raised.

Who's this?

"Shola, this is my secondary school friend, Lola. Lola this is my husband."

"Pleased to meet you. Tobi, you didn't mention your husband is better looking in person than in the pictures you showed me the two of you."

Tobi forced a laugh and stared at Lola. *What are you doing?!*

"Nice meeting you too," Shola said. "How come I'm just hearing about you?" He posed the question at Lola.

"Life brought us together again when we ran into each other at work a few weeks back."

"Oh."

Tobi knew the look on Shola's face. He didn't really care much for Lola. Tobi was sure he would relay that information to her when he got back home from hanging out with the boys.

"Alright. I came back to get my phone charger. Forgot it in the bedroom."

Tobi offered to get it for him.

"No. I'll get it. Thanks."

Once Shola had finally left the house Tobi gave a sigh of relief, settling down once again beside Lola.

"Your husband is fine."

"Yeah. Thank God he didn't catch us."

Lola shifted closer to Tobi. "What? We were just kissing. In fact, we should move our relationship to the next level."

"We are in a relationship?"

"Yes *ke*. Or do you want me to ask you to make it official?"

"You don't mind that I'm married?"

"Not at all. It's even a better cover for us. No one would suspect a thing. What time is hubby coming back?"

Tobi told Lola he usually returned late in the evening.

"Good. I know how we can use the time." She winked at Tobi.

If you will not walk with Me, you would only dance to the tunes of Satan.

Tobi turned up the volume of the speakers, hoping the song would tune out the voice.

* * *

Micah thanked him. "You know, I've learnt a lot from you in the last one week than in the last two years of my life."

"Shows you haven't been reading your Bible much."

Micah gave that to him. "I haven't. Kiki's death knocked me. You know her father said something to me that hasn't left me. He told me if I was a pastor then I had failed because his daughter was dying. That my prayers weren't being heard by God."

"You believed him."

"At a point in my life, yes."

"And now?"

"I know better."

Pastor Eghosa smiled. "Spoken like a true believer. Test and trials don't mar you, they make you. It took me a while to learn that."

"I'm still in training wheels."

In truth, Micah had begun his Bible reading again, and this time, he started with the book of Job. A man who had lost everything he had but still trusted God. A man who believed he was justified enough for God not to hurt him. And for God to show Job how much he trusted in himself to save his family and not God who always had the final say. And that Job could trust God.

In the end, Job had come out stronger and better.

Something Micah was also hoping to happen to him.

"I'm thinking of going back to Lagos. Back to my former church."

"Ah, I was hoping you would say that. I sense those youths need you more than before, judging from what you told me."

"I'm hoping the Senior Pastor would take me back."

"I'm sure he would, but I have certain concerns. How do you plan to move on, Micah?"

"What do you mean?"

"I know you love your wife. I understand the pains. But how would you move forward with your life without letting it affect you and other plans God has for you?"

"I would try my best. I will let go of more of her belongings; my sister would be happy with that." When Pastor Eghosa still looked at him expectantly Micah asked, "What do you suggest?"

"That you move out of the house."

Micah blinked hard.

"You heard me properly. Healing doesn't take place how you see best. You think you can handle seeing her pictures. Walking down the same corridors she did. Cooking in the same kitchen. I know it's hard, Micah. I know. But to heal, you just have to let go and believe you would see her again. Do you ever plan to remarry?"

"I haven't given it much thought."

"Think about it."

* * *

He was sitting in a beautiful garden with a small fountain at the centre. There were diamonds, stones, precious jewels beyond what Micah had ever and would ever likely see in his life. He picked one up, examining its beauty, dropping it when startled by an old man walking in, holding what appeared to be a sack. The old man smiled at him and sat down at the fountain, laying his bag at his foot. Micah watched as he took out what looked like a mould of dirt.

"Do you want one?"

Micah shook his head. Not knowing what it was but disgusted. "No, thank you."

"Why?"

Micah decided to be honest. "It looks bad. Like mud and dirt."

The old man chuckled and dipped the mould into the water, cleaning it. He then raised his hand, what Micah saw left him stunned. It was a red stone.

"What's that?"

"Ruby." The old man smiled. "You didn't want it because it looked bad, dirty and disgusting. But I have washed those dirt particles away and now it looks attractive. Do you want it now?"

Micah felt too sheepish to respond.

"What has been freed of impurity need no longer be called impure."

Micah woke up. It was two in the morning. But the dream had felt so real. The gemstones and what the old man said. And suddenly, a calm feeling washed over him.

* * *

Leke took shelter under the small shed that was the bus stop. He wasn't the only one there, a few other people also trying to dodge the rain. He drew his backpack closer to him. It was a bad time for his car to refuse to start and he had to take a bus down to meet potential clients in Lekki. Fortunately for him, he arrived before them and they agreed for him to take photos at their mother's 60th birthday party.

He looked down the road, hoping an empty bus would come his way so he could head home, have a warm bath and chat Zainab up. He was glad he was able to surprise her at the meeting she had in Abuja. Amazed at the level of authority she exuded when she spoke and the unmistakable presence of God in their midst. It had been wonderful.

Someone sneezed close to him and Leke noticed the lady standing under a transparent umbrella. Shivering. Her *ankara* gown hanging loosely on her body. Her eyes fixed on the wet road as cars drove by, splashing water on the curbs.

A white bus soon stopped in front of them and they all made a beehive for it. A lot of pushing and shoving in the process. Leke knew better than to join them. Having suffered a stolen phone in the process years back. The bus left, leaving him and a bunch of other people there. The lady there as well. She sneezed again. Her teeth chattering and her body trembling.

Leke remembered he had a material in his bag. A gift from another client he had forgotten to take out in his hurry to make his appointment. He took it out and offered it to her. She eyed him suspiciously. He explained its purpose and she took it from him.

"You haven't even sewn it yet. What if you can't wear it again?"

"I'm not a native person. I highly doubt I would miss it."

"Thank you," she said and he held the umbrella while she opened it just enough to wrap it around her shoulders.

"Forgive my manners. I'm Leke."

She stared at his cold, wet hands then back at him. Leke retracted his hand, embarrassed.

Another bus slowed to a stop in front of them and this time they all went in. Leke ended up sitting next to her. As soon as the driver passed the toll gate there was a long line of cars. Leke hoped the traffic would be light. He gazed at Maureen. She was staring out the window. Not that there was much to look at than an advert for a new Nigerian movie on a billboard.

"I don't know why there always seem to be traffic when it rains," she said.

"I know, right. Let's just hope it doesn't drag for long."

They both settled into silence. The bus driver shifting from one gear to another as he tried to manoeuvre his way out of his lane. His approach unruly as was the custom of most *danfo* drivers in Lagos.

"So what do you do?"

"Customer care in a bank." She mentioned the name of a reputable bank in Nigeria. "And you?"

"Photographer."

"That's nice." The bus jerked forward and she grabbed the rusted metal of the front seat. They both stared at the bus driver yelling in Yoruba at a woman to give him room to enter.

"You came to take pictures in Lekki?"

"No. Came to see clients."

She nodded. "Oh okay. You enjoy what you do?"

"Very much so."

They did small talk. Conversing on trivial things. Leke had the feeling she was doing him a favour responding because of his kind gesture back at the bus stop. Maureen was nearing her stop and on impulse Leke did something he had never done before. He asked for her number.

"What can I store your number as?" Hoping she would finally proffer a name to the face with sad eyes.

"Maureen."

After she alighted the bus, he had a strange feeling he would see her again.

This one, beloved.

Leke didn't understand.

Chapter Nineteen

This one, beloved . . .

Leke thought about it over and over again. When he slept, he dreamt of her, and when he got up in the morning, the thought picked up again. He wondered if it had anything to do with the dream he had a few weeks ago.

The old man in the dream had proffered him a ruby after washing the dirt off it. Then Leke had thought he heard Maureen was his ruby. So what was the dirt about? Why was he surrounded by other gemstones? Was Zainab among the gemstones?

"God, help me out here because I'm officially confused."

He busied himself with making breakfast and doing a video call with Zainab. Yet, Maureen remained in his thoughts.

Leke:

Hey. Good morning. How are you doing? Thought to check up on you and say hi.

He scratched his beard. He was due for a shave. Leke went about his day; went for a jog, editing photos, getting a haircut and his beard trimmed. He had his bath and was having a late dinner of fried chicken and garri in his living room when his phone beeped with a message from Maureen.

Maureen: *Hello. Good evening. Sorry I'm just replying to our message. I'm fine and you? Thanks for checking in.*

Leke typed.

Leke: *I'm great. How was your day?*

Maureen: *It was okay. Busy with wedding arrangements.*

Leke: *Oh. Congratulations.*

Maureen: *Thanks.*

Leke: *When is the D-day?*

Maureen: *Three months away.*

Leke: *November wedding. That's cool.*

Maureen: *Yh.*

He stared down at his food absentmindedly. *Was I wrong? Did I interpret the dream wrongly?* Leke sighed and was going to end the conversation with a good night when he had an impression in his heart. He had asked Zainab how she was able to hear from God so fluently. How she could know certain things. Word of Knowledge she had said, and any believer could pray to receive that gift of the Holy Spirit. Leke wanted it.

God, what am I doing? I don't even know if she's a Christian or talking about You is a touchy subject.

Despite the lack of an audible response, Leke felt the urge to type.

Leke: *God loves you, Maureen. I just felt the need to say it. He loves you very, very much.*

A scripture came to heart, but Leke had to search it out before sending it to her. It made little sense to him, but it might to her.

Leke: *I think you should read Hosea 12:6.*

Some minutes later, she responded.

Maureen: *Why are you telling me this? Are you a pastor?*

Leke: *Pastor ke? No. But I'm a Christian. Are you?*

Maureen: *. . .*

I am/was. Maybe. I don't know.

Leke: *Sounds complicated. You want to talk about it?*

Maureen: *Not necessarily. It's not something I would like to share.*

Leke: *Then talk to God about it.*

Maureen: *I don't think God wants to hear from me. I've disappointed Him.*

Leke: *Doesn't mean He no longer loves you. Try talking to God. Have you read the passage yet?*

Maureen replied a few seconds later.

Maureen: *Just did. Thank you. I'll try to talk to God. I have to go now. Have an early day tomorrow. Good night.*

Leke: *Okay. I'll chat you up again. Sort of like a follow up. Remember there's no sin God can't forgive. Good night.*

Leke dropped his phone, glad he obeyed the urge to talk to her. Clearly, she needed to hear the message. He said a prayer for her then, that God would help her through whatever situation she was in, and then he dug into his meal.

* * *

Micah looked up to see a slim woman approach him. Her black, branded t-shirt with the words Disciple boldly written across it in red. Her long legs clad in grey joggers.

"You must be the famous Micah Oramah," she said.

He stood. "And you must be Pastor Eghosa's eldest daughter, Zainab."

"Guilty. Please, sit. My father will be down in a few minutes. The cold weather must have gotten to his bones."

"The arthritis?"

"Yup."

Zainab sat opposite him and crossed her legs at the ankle. She produced a phone and tapped away. Micah used the opportunity to check the notifications on his phone, but from time to time, he found his gaze shifting back to the woman a few feet away from him. Her braids in a loose knot around her face and her thick long lashes moving up and down as she stared down at her phone. There was also the distinguished hollow of her cheekbones deepening and her lips curling up as she smiled at something.

Then it dawned on him.

"I'm sorry. You're Zainab Baruwa-Philips?"

She shifted her eyes from her phone screen to him. A questioning look on her face. "Yes."

Micah almost laughed. "I don't believe this," he muttered to himself then said to her, "We spoke earlier. Months ago, actually. You might not remember but John, Pastor John, gave me your phone number. I wanted you to minister at our church."

"Oh, yeah. You're the guy that wanted me to speak at his church. I remember. Wow. I would have said you were stalking me but that's impossible." Her brows drew together. "How did you meet my father?"

"It's kind of a long story."

"I'm totally interested."

Micah shared how he went to the church and heard her father preaching a message Micah had desperately needed. The meeting at her father's office. The hospital trip and meetings in his house.

"You mean he let you into this house without knowing you?"

Micah gave a slight nod and her eyes widened.

This woman is beautiful.

He couldn't help but notice her brown eyes and full lips. The dimple at the side of her mouth. Her uneven eyelashes. He wondered if she was seeing someone. Micah blinked. He dismissed the thought immediately.

"I can't believe my father. No offence to you, but I think it's wrong for him to let you in."

"I perfectly understand. But I assure you, I never brought any harm to your father. I was also sceptical about him inviting me over."

She seemed to consider that for a moment.

Micah also noticed the smooth curve of her nose and the protruding of her lips when she pouted. He looked away, rudely discontinuing his line of thoughts. Thoughts he had no right to.

"Your dad said you're an evangelist."

"I am. I go where God sends me. Sometimes, it's a place I would never see myself setting foot in, other times it's where I can't seem to get enough of. I guess that's how it is though; everyone needs to hear the Gospel irrespective of who you are or where you stay."

"You definitely took after your dad."

"But she is very poor in hospitality," her father chipped in, leaning against the corridor. A certain glint in his eyes.

Micah stood. Zainab laughed.

"How are you feeling, sir?"

Pastor Eghosa strolled into the room, a slight limp to his gait. "I'm fine. Micah, sit down. Zainab, why didn't you offer this man something to drink or eat?"

She set aside her phone, adjusting her hair. "It skipped my mind. I'm sorry." She directed her attention to Micah. It was then he noticed her ear piercings. "What can I get you, Mr. Oramah?"

"Nothing, I'm fine actually."

"You see, Daddy. Sometimes, nothing is fine." She settled back on the sofa.

"Well, I want breakfast. Bread and tea."

Zainab groaned. She stood, shoved her phone in her pocket then trudged off to the kitchen.

"I assumed you would leave for Lagos first thing in the morning. There's always traffic on that Lagos-Ibadan expressway."

"I wanted to see you before I left. Give a proper good-bye."

"Hopefully, this isn't the last we would see. Maybe when next I'm in Lagos I would give you a call."

Zainab returned with a tray, with steam rising from the tall mug.

"Here you go. Bread and tea. Thank God you didn't ask for more."

"Or else it won't only be my leg paining me."

Micah bowed his head and smiled.

"Ha-ha. Very funny. Do you want me to excuse both of you?"

"No. Sit. I believe you and Micah have become acquainted."

"Yes." She plopped herself down on her previous seat. "He let me know how you let in a perfect stranger into your home. Efe and I have been chatting about it. She's also not pleased."

"I'm sorry. It won't happen like that the next time."

"Good."

"Next time, I'll ask for full credentials about the person and have the police investigate him thoroughly before I bring him home."

Micah laughed.

Zainab didn't even smile.

Micah was there for another hour till he finally had to take his leave. He enjoyed the easy comrade between father and daughter. The love they shared. Pastor Eghosa had casually mentioned all the travails his eldest daughter had been through during one of their conversations.

Lesbianism, smoking weed, fornication.

Micah didn't see them as the worst sin someone could commit. Only saw them as the most prevalent ones trending in the world right now. And yet she had come out stronger and better. Pastor Eghosa's voice tinged with pride as he spoke about Zainab. Now more than ever, Micah was interested in her ministering at BYF.

* * *

Tobi felt like she was finally free to live the life she wanted. Yes, she was still a married woman. But she could enjoy the best of both worlds.

It was that simple.

She searched through her wardrobe for a nice blue lace she could

209

wear for the wedding Lola had invited her to. She couldn't decide which head-tie would fit it. Lola wanted to buy the *gele* for her, but upon hearing the ridiculous price for it Tobi had agreed to wear one of hers instead. After all, Tobi didn't even know the couple. She would rather put the cash in an envelope and give them than let the material take up much needed wardrobe space.

"Where are you headed?"

"A wedding. I told you last night."

Shola's face contorted into a confused frown. "You did? When?"

Tobi gave him a look.

He winked. "Oh yeah. When you finally agreed to please your husband."

"You're just a clown," she responded, smiling openly at him.

He walked over to their bed and sat. "What's with you these days? You're very happy. You have this spark in your eyes. Did I miss something? Because I feel like I'm being left out of the picture."

"Everything doesn't have to revolve around you, Shola," was her quick response.

"Ouch."

He was a silent observer as she packed two pairs of shoes and wore her accessories.

"Tobi, are you cheating on me?"

She froze midway to wearing her lace-wig. Just in case she decided not to wear any head-tie. "You have come again with your self-doubt. I'm not cheating on you with any man."

"Then maybe a woman?" his joking response, hitting the truth more closely than he could have imagined.

Shola laughed. "Don't mind me. Who are you going with to this wedding? Because I know you don't like to go alone to these things and you didn't invite me, nor do you have that many friends. In fact, you have zero friends."

"I'm going with Lola."

"Oh, the weird chick."

As expected, when Shola returned that day, he had asked questions about Lola. Where she was from, what she did and other questions parents asked their children when they were trying to decide reasons their children couldn't be friends with them.

"I thought I explicitly told you I don't like her."

"You didn't say why."

"Must I give you a reason? Isn't my no good enough."

"For this situation? No." Tobi applied a perfume, the one Lola liked. "You know I don't have that many friends and you want me to drive away the only one person I decide to be friends with."

"Maybe you don't have friends because the people you refuse to be friends with are too normal for you."

She tossed her phone in her purse. "Are you saying I'm abnormal?"

"No. I'm saying your friend is the abnormal one. Did you see the way she was staring at me like I was a cockroach but a good looking one?"

Tobi noticed Lola had probably been too obvious with her disdain for men. "You are exaggerating."

He paused, his head bowed and arms crossed over his bare chest. "I'm not going to argue with you, but you have got to start respecting me and my decisions. I want you back in this house not later than seven pm."

Tobi glared at him. "Are you now going to turn me into a prisoner?"

"A prisoner is impounded. You are just on parole."

"What the hell does that mean?"

"It means I'm going to protect you from yourself." He walked to the bathroom, "See you at seven." Then he slammed the door.

* * *

"I ran into a guy back at my father's place. He's very interesting."

"Interesting like how?"

"Cool. Easy going. Very handsome."

Adesewa shrieked and threw popcorn at her. "Spill!" Zainab found it too appropriate that her friend had a large zip-lock of buttery popcorn with her when she had stopped by for a manicure and pedicure at *Artzee's World*; blaming it on the pregnancy. Saying she Googled the best foods for her to eat and popcorn was one of them.

And now, sitting on the sofa in Zainab's office, she began eating.

"Don't you ever stop having itchy ears for gist?"

"No."

"Sha don't let me have cockroaches in my office." Zainab narrated the story, starting from John linking Micah with her down to how he ended up at her father's home and the seamless flow of conversation between them.

"Do you have a picture of him?"

Zainab stared at Adesewa like she had just said she was having twenty kids. "Are you okay? How do you expect me to have a picture of him?"

"Very simple *nau*. You raise your phone in his direction and act like you're using your phone or taking a selfie and then you take his picture."

"I have now confirmed that you're not alright."

"Tell me more. Do you find him attractive? Is he finer than Leke?"

Zainab thought about it. They both were muscular. No, Leke was more muscular. They both had broad shoulders. Leke had a head full of hair. Micah was practically bald but his full beard made up for it. Micah was calm and matured. Leke was jovial and fun.

"Oh my goodness! You're actually thinking about it."

"You asked me. Was I not supposed to?"

"I actually thought you would ignore me."

Zainab threw her hands in the air. "There's no need for comparison.

We are barely friends. We are not even acquaintances."

"It's fine. I was teasing you anyway. How's Leke?"

Zainab smiled. "He's fine. We are meeting up later in the day."

"I'm so happy you now have a love life."

"Thing is, I'm not sure Leke is God's will for me."

"*Ehn?* Why?" Adesewa said, confusion written all over her face

Zainab explained her conversation with God. "That's why."

"Hmm, then we keep praying."

* * *

Zainab applied mascara on the lady's face. A certain nudge in her heart to know the petite woman seated. The lady had walked in and specifically asked for Zainab to do her make-up. Willing to pay double the amount. Usually, Zainab assured her clients her girls were equal to the task because she had trained them, but Zainab felt a pull to her.

A heavy nudge for her to start a conversation with her.

"Your dress is lovely," Zainab complimented.

"Thank you."

I'm just going to go with this.

"Sometimes we meet different people in life who could make or mar our destinies. I've been in that position before."

The lady stared at her with a puzzled look.

"Do you believe nothing happens except for a reason?" Zainab asked.

The lady looked sideways, if perhaps other people could hear their conversation. There were no other customers and the girls were chatting at the far end. Zainab had specifically asked for privacy.

"I don't know. Maybe."

"Maybe?"

"Yes. I guess I believe the universe brings certain people together for a reason." She smiled a little as though recalling a memory.

"Do you mind if I share a story with you? I'm Zainab and you are?"

"Tobi. As long as you don't mention anything about religion and it doesn't slow down what you're doing 'cause I'm already late for the wedding."

Ah, God. I see where this is going.

Share your testimony.

"Well, it has nothing to do with religion. More about a relationship. I didn't give two cents about religion. I did different things with my life. My life, because I believed it was mine to do as I pleased. I was wrong. God gave me this life," the lady snorted and Zainab wasn't the least bit bothered, "I smoked weed. I once used to be attracted to women. One woman in particular which spiralled into other minor relationships."

"You were a lesbian?"

Zainab nodded. "Yup." She used her forefinger and dabbed brown eye shadow on the eyelids. "I didn't realize how wrong it was until God opened my eyes."

"So you are a Christian now?"

"Yes. Proudly so."

"But you Christians are reading the Bible wrong. God never condemned homosexuality and there are scriptures to prove it. You guys aren't reading it in context," Tobi said defensively.

"Like Leviticus, Genesis, Sodom and Gomorrah and Romans?"

"Yes."

"Why do you think they even searched out the Bible? I think it's because they are seeking God too. But we can't get God to accept our sinful ways and look for ways to justify it. The Bible is to help us correct our ways, not for us to find ways to make our sins acceptable to us. Let me put it this way." Zainab applied some blush to her cheekbones not once breaking her concentration. "God made man and woman. When married, they reflect the image of God because together, as man and woman, they reflect the image of God in totality. Woman to woman and man to man, doesn't reflect that image. It's against His design and blessing to mankind."

Tobi said nothing. Only stared at her through beautiful smokey eyes.

"The issue here isn't about being religious, homosexual or straight. A straight person can also go to hell, right?"

Tobi relaxed a little "I guess so."

"The issue here is if you are alive to Christ and dead to sin."

"What if I don't want to give my life to Christ? I see a lot of hypocrisy in the church and I think it's best one just does his or her own thing."

"Then you are missing out on the best relationship in the world. Remember I said relationship, not religion. God loves you, Tobi. I believe He has extensively made known to you. The air you breathe, the job you have, Jesus dying for you and so much more." Zainab smiled at Tobi through the mirror. "I'm done with your make-up."

"Thank you. Do I give the money to you or your cashier?"

"Is this your first time here?"

Tobi nodded.

"Then it's on the house. Paid for by your relationship seeking friend, Jesus Christ. Hope I'll see you again."

Tobi shrugged, thanked her and walked out. Zainab made a mental note to add her to her prayer list.

* * *

It was good to be back. He first went to Pastor Wilson's home to announce his presence and ask if he could return to BYF. The older man had been elated at the news. Gushing he would introduce Micah to the congregation and the youths.

That's if they are willing to take me back.

On Sunday, Micah stared at what was left of the youth church. Barely forty youths in an auditorium which had the capacity to take two hundred. He had left about a hundred plus behind.

"It's good to be back."

Fimi hooted and people stood and clapped their hands. A few shouted 'Thank You, Jesus!'

Micah chuckled. "Okay. Settle down."

Welcome back, son.

Micah heard the still small voice whisper against his heart. It was the best welcome ever. "It's good to be back. Really. First thing I want to do is share my pains for the past years and all that's happened to me since losing my wife. My struggles, and how my faith was shaken. How I almost trailed off God's path for my life. But I'll start with this; no matter how much your faith is tried and tested, never stop trusting God."

"A lot of you might not be aware of the passing of my wife. It happened three years ago. She was diagnosed with cancer barely one year into our marriage. It was the most difficult thing I ever faced." He noticed he had everyone's attention. "I questioned God. I felt betrayed by His silence and I felt hurt that He wouldn't heal the love of my life. I focused more on the pain than on God. Didn't see the love He offered through loved ones. I was reminded of His sufficient grace but it was healing that I wanted. So that was why I left BYF. I couldn't keep standing here and preaching the goodness of God when I queried it."

Micah paused. Searching for words to express how he currently felt.

Tell them, Micah. Be open.

He took a deep breath and clasped his hands loosely. "Well, the last couple of months have been eye-opening for me. Through a devoted man of God, I realised God is good. Always. He has given me the healing from my pains. Yes, it's a process, but it's one I'm willing to go through. I have learnt to trust Him irrespective of what happens. It would be hard, because reality then trumps," he pointed at his head, "knowledge and you forget all else when tragedy occurs. But the lesson is to never lose sight of God. Even if you can't see Him or feel Him, know that He can see you and He's there for you."

Chapter Twenty

Maureen let the scripture take root in her head. Her heart. The Passion Translation giving new meaning to a truth she once knew. *But if we freely admit our sins when his light uncovers them, he will be faithful to forgive us every time. God is just to forgive us our sins because of Christ, and he will continue to cleanse us from all unrighteousness.*

Back from work and exhausted, she sat on her bed. A friend from church had messaged her; Pastor Micah was back. Maureen was happy at the news, but was too ashamed to face him. How could she tell him what happened after he advised her?

She only had herself to blame for her mistakes.

Taking off her sticky clothes, she opted for a shower. The last few days had been gruelling. The battles in her head leaving her weary. Somehow, she had forgotten that passage Leke had pointed her to. Forgotten or probably too guilty to apply it to herself. Prior to the incident, she had been the girl who went for evangelism, willingly volunteered for events in church and celebrated whatever change the Holy Spirit was willing to make.

Everything looked like she had only played it safe all the while, and when life's trouble came she had crumbled. Unable to stand firm to the enemies' wiles like the popular parable Jesus taught of the farmer whose seeds fell among the gravel and eventually withered and fell away because of a time of temptation.

Just like her.

She stepped out of the bathroom and wrapped her towel around her body.

What had Pastor Micah said the other time? That temptation was something all of them had to face.

You faced yours and failed, and you call yourself a Christian.

Maureen snapped her eyes shut as she sunk to her knees on the terrazzo floor of the bathroom.

Shut up! Go away! God will forgive me.

You don't even believe it. Why should God forgive someone like you? You think God loves you? You would just do it again and again and again and again.

No! I rebuke you in Jesus name.

She could almost feel the enemy laughing at her weak rebuff. Doubts filling her head.

God, how am I sure I won't fail You again?

The Scripture came to her again. Like God was telling her to come to Him first.

She felt the sting of tears in her eyes. "God, I'm sorry. Forgive me. I – I confess my sins of fornication, lying, self deceit. I ask for forgiveness and for you to wash away my sins. I receive Jesus again in my heart. Lord please accept me as your child. I'm sorry. So sorry."

In the strangest of ways, Maureen could almost feel arms around her. A peace overshadowing the guilt and condemnation that had eaten her up for weeks. She sobbed in reckless abandon.

God still loved her.

Surrender to Me. Stand up to the devil. Resist him. He would turn and run from you. I am with you.

The words, whispered against her heart, brought the greatest peace of all.

* * *

Call her, Micah.

"It's just for the church," Micah said, convincing himself that was the reason he thought of Zainab. Why she had been on his mind for a while. Her warm smile and easy going nature.

He tapped on the contacts icon and scrolled to her number. He could imagine Kiki giving him a cheeky smile. *We both know that's not true.*

"Hello."

Micah told himself to act cool. "Hi Zainab. How are you?"

"I'm fine. Micah?"

"I'm the man." *What?* He coughed. "Yes, I mean yes it's me, Micah." He was sure he sounded like a fool.

He could almost hear her grin. "Okay, the man Micah. What's up? How's Lagos welcoming you back?"

He leaned his back on the counter and scratched his head. "Really good. I've had power supply regularly for two days now."

She snorted. "The welcome back party will soon come to an end."

"*Haba*, don't pronounce that *na.*"

"I'm not trying to be negative *o*. That's just how things are and you don't need to be a prophet to know. How's your church? BYF right?"

Micah folded his arms. Glanced up at his wedding portrait of him and Kiki and felt a twinge of sadness. Suddenly, he grew serious. "BYF is fine. Could be better. Have to reach out to a lot of the youths who stopped attending while I was away. Trying to get my members back. I was wondering if you could come over to BYF to minister one of these days."

Zainab asked what day he had in mind. He could hear papers in the background. Micah mentioned a nearby date.

"Sorry, I'm ministering somewhere that day and also on the next two weekends. In between that, I have weddings to be at different places. Makeup for a trad and white on the same day and another for a pre-wedding shoot. I could choose the latter date but I don't want to come tired and straight from a makeup session. I don't know if you get what I mean?"

"I do. What of a Wednesday then? We meet for Bible Study." He thought about it again. "No, I think I would rather have you come on a Sunday instead of Saturday."

"Okay, let's settle for the third Saturday in October."

"Perfect."

"Great. I'm penning it down now."

Micah didn't want the conversation to be over yet. "How's your dad?"

"He's good. Don't you guys communicate? Since you're like best friends now."

Micah drew out a chair from the dining table. The legs scratching against the wooden floor. "Why do you say that?"

"Because he talks about you often. I guess he sees you as one of the sons he never had."

He smiled. "I seem to have a relationship with him I can't boast about with my dad."

"I understand a little. My step-father was also not very accommodating."

"Your dad said so."

He felt her hesitate then ask, "Is there anything you guys didn't talk about?"

Micah opened his mouth to respond then heard a male voice in the background addressing Zainab.

"I'm sorry I have to go. Nice chatting with you again. See you in October. You could do me a reminder and give me details of what you would like me to talk about."

"Would do. But I guess praying and saying what God wants is best."

She ended the call and Micah dropped his phone on the table as the power supply tripped off.

"Great. Just as she said"

* * *

"Sorry I'm late."

He took a seat just as she ended her call.

"Still having car troubles?"

He nodded. "Coming from the mechanic's. Car should be working well in a day or two."

"*Eh-ya*. Sorry."

"*Abeg*, it's one of those things."

Leke decided to tell Zainab about Maureen. Hoping for some clarification to his constant thoughts about her.

"What do you think it means?"

He sighed and looked Zainab in the eye. The one woman he had become comfortable with after Emem. The woman who had unknowingly taught him a lot about life and God in the short time they had come to really know one another. "I don't know. I feel that this is so weird, but I feel like maybe she's my wife."

"Why does it feel weird?"

"Because we are seeing each other and I'm suddenly having a strange feeling about another woman being my wife." She smiled. "Or am I the only one that finds this weird?"

"I find it more funny than weird."

He sat back and crossed his arms. "Why is that?"

"Well, because God has a sense of humour and I already kind of knew something like this was going to happen."

"Are you serious?"

"Yes."

He stared at the stainless steel bracelet on Zainab's wrist and then chuckled.

She took a sip of her orange juice with the help of a black flexible straw. "Tell me about her."

Leke placed his hands on the table. "This is so weird."

"Are you still on about that? I'm way past that."

"So when were you going to break the news to me?"

She shrugged and dropped her glass; rays from the sun resting on her arm. Her short sleeve blouse exposing a little of her tattoo. "I was waiting for the right time and praying you won't go off at me."

"I wouldn't do that."

"Just taking precautions. Now, tell me about her. What's her name?"

"Maureen."

"Nice." She linked her fingers and rested her jaw on it. Her bare lips spreading to a smile. Not the least bit angry. "Tell me more. How did you two meet? What does she do?"

Leke told her as much as he knew. "I think she's going through a tough time. I keep having the nudge to pray for her."

"Then don't stop. Settle the matter in the Spirit and it's all good."

* * *

Leke: *Hello. How are you today?*

Maureen: *Hi. I'm fine.*

You?

Strange. I was just about to send you a message.

Leke stretched his legs on the couch.

Leke: *Perfect timing then*

I'm good. What's up?

Maureen: *Good things. Very good things.*

I rededicated my life to Christ.

That Scripture was my undoing. Thank you.

Leke: *Thank God. I'm glad to hear that.*

Maureen: *It's like a heavy weight has been lifted off me.*

Thank you for heeding to God. I'm in no doubt now that God loves me and has probably forgiven me.

Leke: *He has. Psalm 107. As far as the east is from the west, so he removed our transgressions from us.*

Maureen: *True.*

Leke: *Can I call?*

Maureen: *KK*

"Hi. I thought calling would be better."

"It's cool."

"So, what happened? Do you want to talk about it? I know you don't know me and it would feel weird to divulge your personal life to a stranger, but if you would like to I'm willing to hear you. I won't judge you."

"It's okay. I don't want to assume you have bad intentions. Especially after how we met and all." She breathed heavily. Her voice shaky when she spoke, "I don't know how to say this. No one really knows. I had – I'm no longer a virgin."

Leke blinked hard. That hadn't crossed his mind, but thinking back at the dream he had, it seemed to make sense.

"My boyfriend and I. My fiancé now. It just happened. What I wanted to do was break up with him and I ended up sleeping with him. Very stupid of me."

"Hey, don't beat yourself up. Mistakes happen in life. You have to know that."

"Yeah, but I felt that couldn't happen to me. Me the good girl that always attends church. Loves God with her heart and would not want to disappoint Him. One open door comes and I fall."

Leke searched for the right words to say. "You are still precious to

God, Maureen. Very much so. You mentioned you wanted to break up with your boyfriend. Why? Why did you end up engaged?"

Is she pregnant?

"We don't share the same values. He's not a Christian. I've finally settled that truth with myself. At least he doesn't live and want to live like Christ. But he bears the Christian title. Why did I want to marry him? Since I already gave up the goods there was no point acting morally good and giving the excuse of him not being a Christian. Cos I had dropped the ball as well"

"Hmm. . ."

"I guess it sounds silly now that I think it over."

"Do you still love this guy?"

"I like him. But I think it would be wrong to marry him even though I've committed myself to this. We have had family Introductions. Wedding preparations are underway. I can't just announce that I want to call it off. My mother would insult me."

"I think the pain of insults is easier to recover from than marrying against God's will." He went on to tell her about Emem. How it had been a blessing in disguise he was unwilling to see at the time.

"What if he hates me?"

"Actually he would. I guess he should. When pleasing God, we would surely step on some toes of human beings. You are not of the world, only living in it and setting the right example for others." Leke was wondering where all these were coming from. Definitely Zainab had robbed off on him

"I'll pray about it. Thanks a lot. Sorry I used up your credit."

"I'm not sorry."

"Well, take care Leke."

"You too."

Chapter Twenty-One

He toyed with the idea of calling her. What if she had a boyfriend? What if she was engaged? And why was he thinking of calling her? It wasn't like he was interested in any relationship.

I'm also not asking for her hand in marriage.

Pastor Eghosa had told him Zainab was single, but what if that was in the past? Micah halted his line of thoughts and called her.

"The man Micah." She teased. "What's up?"

"Would you like to go out with me?"

She was quiet.

Micah drew his phone from his ear, checking to see if the network had disappeared or he had run out of airtime. "Are you there?"

"Did my father put you up to this?"

He frowned. "No. Why would you think that?"

"Nothing. I assumed wrong. Sorry. But did he?"

"No. Why would assume your dad would make me ask you out?"

"Well, according to him, I've been single for too long and since you guys have been spending so much time together I just thought he had somehow planted the idea in your head. ."

Micah couldn't help the laughter that erupted from him. "Seriously? Your dad isn't the domineering type."

"Okay. Now that you're done laughing at my expense, can you tell me why you want to go out with me? You hardly know me."

How could Micah explain he sensed a connection between them? That she was the first woman who had caught his attention since he lost his wife. Couldn't explain that he was attracted to her.

"I want to get to know you. I would like to if you permit it."

"Hmm, okay. Sure."

He pumped his fist in the air. "Cool. When is a good time for you?"

"This evening is fine."

"This evening it is."

There was nothing much to say after that and they ended the call. Micah suddenly noted the clamminess of his palm. He was nervous. He hadn't gone out with any other woman in the last eight years. What was he going to say? Where would he take her to? He didn't even have her address. He picked his phone and sent her a text, asking for her house address. Then he gazed up at his wedding photo in a large black frame, hanging high up on the wall, Kiki's smile wide and appealing as it had always been.

I told you you'll be fine, her eyes seemed to say.

"Yeah, you did." His heart feeling slightly heavy. "I still miss you, Kiki."

We'll see each other again. I love you.

Micah pressed his fingers to his lips and raised them up to Kiki's. "I love you, dear."

* * *

"I'm sorry. I can't get married to you, Detan."

This time she was wise enough to do it in her mother's house. She had prayed for three days, accompanied with fasting, and knew breaking it off with Detan was the best thing she could do for the both of them.

"You have started again with this nonsense talk." Then he gave a mischievous smile, "or are you trying to let what happened the day you came over to repeat itself? He winked at her. I'm more than willing."

The memory stung. "That will never happen again."

Detan dropped his car keys on a side stool and leaned forward. The smell of his cologne invading her personal space; causing her spine to tingle with the memory of how he had made her feel when their bodies touched.

"Please, stop the jokes. When you said you wanted us to talk, it sounded urgent. What is it you want to talk to me about? I'm supposed to be at the tailors' for measurements for my suit. Have you gotten in touch with the events planner? She said she tried reaching you but you haven't been answering her calls or replying her messages."

"I-" She started to say but he interrupted.

"Then I think the-"

"I don't want to get married to you," she said loudly. The fan rotating above their heads as the blade swooshed through the air and the television from her mother's bedroom a few feet away were the only sounds that followed her statement.

When he finally spoke, his jaw clenched, his tone was cold. "Where is this coming from? Our parents met. We set a date for the wedding, spent a lot of money already and now you are saying you *don't want to get married*?" He let out an expletive that raised the tiny hairs at the back of her neck.

She hugged herself. Hoping her next words won't further anger him. "I told you when I came over, the day we slept-"

"Sex! The day we had sex!"

Maureen could no longer hear the television. *What if her mother heard them? She was yet to break the news to her.* "Please lower your voice, Detan."

He cupped his chin, a hand on his thigh to support it. "Talk. I'm listening to you."

God, please help me. Give me the right words to say. Boldness cloaked her in that moment. She squared her shoulders. "I told you I wanted to end things because I don't believe you are a Christian. Even though you profess you are. Your actions speak against you and I can't be married to a man who can't lead me spiritually or wash me with the water of the Word of God. I apologise for not mentioning it sooner. I will pay back whatever it is you have contributed towards the wedding. It will take me awhile, but I would pay."

"You are calling things off because I'm not following you to church?"

"No, because you haven't given your life to Christ."

He eyed her. "Who told you I've not?"

"You don't need to tell me. Your actions say it all."

"Maureen, don't be stupid. You're a beautiful girl but if you keep behaving like this, you would end up an old hag. Stop throwing religion in people's faces ! Go to church, read your Bible, pray in the morning, fast," he counted the list off his fingers. "Very soon, you would be telling to me cleanse myself after sex. *Abeg*, leave all these things. I can take care of you financially, sexually, materially. Just shove the spiritual stuff aside."

As he spoke, she was finally able to let go of all the emotions she had towards him. Had she been so blindly in love not to notice he would never love her the way God wanted? She would have laughed at her silliness but thought better of it. The action would definitely be misconstrued.

"Stop staring at me like that."

She folded her hands in her lap. "How am I staring at you?"

He gave a bitter laugh. "We have done the introduction and we are getting married. That's final."

"You aren't my husband yet. You can't bully me into doing anything."

He stood and loomed over her. His fist clenched by his sides. His gaze threatening. "Don't let me do what we would both regret, Maureen."

She shrank back. Fear gripping her heart but trying hard to show a strong stance. "Detan, please sit down."

He bent low and she flinched when his hand caressed her bare neck. "Don't try me, Maureen. Don't test my patience."

"Or what would you do?"

Detan jerked back, surprise etching his features as he stood to his full height and stared at Maureen's mother. Maureen rubbed her neck. Her heart beating wildly against her chest.

Her mother walked into the room. "What do you want to do to my daughter?"

"Good afternoon, ma. How are you?"

"Afternoon. What were you doing a minute ago?"

"Nothing ma. Just a lovers' quarrel"

Her mother says something in their native language which Maureen recognises as an insult to Detan. "Lovers' quarrel? I don't believe you force someone to love you. So because my daughter has said she's not interested in marrying you, you want to kill her? Is this how you would treat her in marriage?" She hissed. "Lay one finger on her again and I will call the police! Now, get out of my house."

"Mummy, it's not like that."

Maureen stood and pulled the engagement ring from her finger and handed it to him. "I'm sorry, Detan. I really am."

He looked like he wanted to say something but one look at her mother's face and he snatched his keys from the stool and stormed out, leaving the ring in Maureen's hand.

Maureen took a deep breath and faced her mother. "Mummy."

"Sit down. Tell me what caused this drama. I was in the room watching TV and I heard your fiancé shout. What is going on?"

Tears gathered in her eyes as she juggled the ring with her fingers. "I called off the wedding because I couldn't go through with it. Detan is not who he claims to be."

"And you realized that two months to your wedding?"

Maureen nodded. "I knew before but, I told myself I would make it work. That I would pray for him and he would change."

Her mother exhaled heavily.

"I'm sorry I disgraced you."

"You didn't disgrace me. You have shown me all the years I invested in you was not a waste. You are a strong and capable woman. I wished you had called it off way before now, but then we all make mistakes. Whatever mistakes you have made, just know you have blood running through your veins because you're human," her mother said, reaching out to comfort her.

Maureen knelt before her and clung to her mother's embrace.

"It's okay, my darling."

After a few minutes Maureen drew back. "He didn't take his ring."

"Send it to him via courier. Good riddance to rubbish!"

"He's actually not a bad guy, mummy. We just don't agree on some things."

"Well, that's the end of that."

* * *

Zainab chose one of the clothes Adesewa picked out for her during their shopping spree. A black jumpsuit that accentuated what little curves Zainab had. She did her make-up and oiled her hair. This time, she had shaved the sides and left a lump of hair in the middle. She dumped her boyish bracelets and for once used a gold band. She took a picture and sent it to Adesewa.

Adesewa: *Totally on fleek! I'm proud of you. Have fun. *kisses* Gist me later. ;)*

The restaurant was one she had never been to. It gave them a view of the ocean. It was beautiful and had cool tunes playing in the background. Zainab kept telling herself to take it easy despite brimming with excitement.

"You look beautiful."

Goosebumps rose up her arms. "Thanks. You don't look so bad yourself."

He had on a black leather jacket over a white shirt and blue jeans. His head shiny from the lights hanging over them.

"Thank you. Are you ready to order?"

"I'm cool with whatever."

"Can I make a confession? I feel too nervous to eat."

She chuckled and nodded. "Same."

"Let me make you laugh some more. At home, I was worried about where to take you, what I would say and how to act. I was practically perspiring down my back."

She slapped a hand over her mouth and bowed her head in laughter.

"So yeah," he spread his arms, "have a good laugh at my expense."

She raised her head, tears in her eyes. "I guess we're even then."

"I guess so."

A waiter approached their table with menus and Micah ordered appetizers and drinks.

"So you're a make-up artist. How did you get into that?"

"I have a passion for making women feel beautiful irrespective of what's going on with them on the outside. I love the blend of colours and how happy a woman feels. But after giving my life to Christ, I realized it way more than that. Inner beauty is much more important."

"Nice. And you used to be a tomboy?"

"My dad told you?"

He nodded.

"Well, I'm still a tomboy. It's still in my blood. I'm at home with simple clothes and less exposure of my body. I'm just not into tight or fitted clothes. I know there are guys who appreciate women who dress a certain way and all, but I guess it's just who I am."

Somehow, Zainab felt the need to defend herself and justify the way she was. Knowing somehow Leke might not have accepted her that way. She had seen a picture of Maureen and seen how chic she looked.

On the other hand, Micah seemed unperturbed at her words.

"And there's nothing wrong with that. God made us to be united in Christ and become more like Him, not robots who act exactly the same with no unique personality. I would honestly like to know you better. All tomboy of you."

"So what's your history?" she asked. She called her dad to ask about him, but had failed to mention the date. Her father only told her he had lost his wife years ago and was going through a tough time. She wondered if he hadn't dated because he missed his late wife or there was some other reason.

"I'm a widower actually. Lost my wife to cancer three years ago, the hardest thing I had ever been through."

"Oh. I'm sorry."

"It's okay. I'm gradually learning to let go. It was hard for me to accept it at first. I blamed God, but God opened my eyes. He loves Kiki more than I could ever love her."

She rested her chin on her palm. "And this is your first date since your wife?"

"Yes."

"I'm guessing this must be hard for you. Starting over."

"Is it so obvious that I'm nervous?" She smiled. "What about you?" The waiter returned with Micah's order and the smell of freshly made finger foods tickled her tummy.

"I was in a relationship. Yeah, I guess I can call it one. We were trying to see how things would go. Waiting for go-ahead from God. But then it wasn't meant to be."

God, is this the better You have in store for me?

Things never discovered or heard of before, things beyond our

ability to imagine – these are the many things I have in store for you.

"So this is like a new beginning for you and I then."

"Yeah, I guess so."

Chapter Twenty-Two

"Just love up on God." Zainab raised her hands, her body swaying to the song in her heart. "Worship Him in the splendour of holiness. Glorify His holy name." She thought of the last couple of months and how faithful God had been to her. His love for her overwhelming. "Thank You, Jesus."

Zainab opened her eyes and gazed at the crowd of young men and women with hands raised and eyes closed. Some kneeling. Some laying on the floor. *God, please wash over these youths with Your blood and let Your word pierce to their marrows to bring an everlasting change.*

I will do that which I will do.

"Hi everyone. You can be seated. I appreciate Pastor Micah for inviting me here. It's a privilege to be here and be used by God to minister to you. I wasn't given a specific theme but to speak as directed by God, so I will talk about being used by God and being in step with the Holy Spirit."

She cleaned the sides of her mouth with a handkerchief and took a deep breath. "My life has been a spiral of ups and downs. I grew up in Abuja with my mother and step-father. I was into marijuana, fornication, lesbianism, a little of porn. My life was literally a hot mess until God took over." Zainab purposely stared at Micah to see his reaction but he sat there smiling at her. She felt her heart constrict. He wasn't showing disgust. Just comfortable with her sharing.

She shifted her gaze to another part of the audience. "I had a void in my life that I filled up with things that made no sense and didn't matter. I searched for my life's purpose in the created instead of going to the Creator. Three years ago, I encountered, not religion, but a relationship with Jesus. You see, God wants to use you. He wants to use each and every one of us, but we determine how much we can be used by our level of commitment and relationship with God. By our obedience to the Holy Spirit. In fact, our Christian life can never be as it should and can be without the Spirit of God. The Holy Spirit worked through the disciples in the book of Acts.

You say, that was way, way back. That doesn't happen with us now. And some of you are saying yeah, but God can't use me. I'm just ordinary. But I'm telling you that God *can* use you and *would* use you as long as you let Him. You can't surrender to God and be in control of your life. No. You have a new Captain and that's the Spirit of God. Especially now that you are a new creature and you have the Spirit of God bearing witness with your spirit. The Holy spirit leads, and not your flesh. Your head says it's impossible but your inner man is saying yes. And so, He says lay hands on that woman and you do. He says speak to the ears of that deaf man and you do! It gets to a point where you go about and pray for people to be recovered without waiting for God to tell you because you are working in line with God's will and you know his desires. In other words, you are already in tune with God."

Zainab cleared her throat. "You are selfless. You are not thinking of people's opinion about you sharing the Gospel or when you lay hands on the sick, whether they get healed or not. You are all about sinners going to hell and doing what you should. The Spirit is operating in you greatly and you can't help but let Him out."

She shared her encounter with the woman she had done make-up for and what happened. "I knew what God wanted me to do and went

236

ahead to tell her. I didn't care if she refused to pay or not give a referral. Her soul was important to God and therefore, it was important to me."

At the end, Zainab asked them to say a prayer, freeing themselves up to be led and used by God. Long after counselling a few people, Zainab waited for Micah in his car while he took care of a few things in church.

"Sorry, it took so long."

"It's fine. The life of a pastor is busy."

"Right. Your dad is a pastor."

She nodded.

"You want to get something to eat?"

"Actually, my friend asked if we would like to come for lunch at her place. She's a very good cook. You two would get along fine because you cook well."

He chuckled and started the engine. "Okay. Where is her place and how soon can we get there 'cause I'm starving?"

* * *

During the worship session, Maureen raised her hands in surrender and abandonment to God. God speaking over her, *Thou hast turned my mourning into dancing: thou hast put off my sackcloth, and girded me with gladness.*

God had brought her back to Him. Taken away the sorrow of her past mistakes and welcomed her into His loving arms in a dance!

She had spared a sideways glance at Leke as he listened intently on what the speaker was saying. Maureen had invited him to church that Sunday and was pleased when he confirmed his attendance. Surprised when he mentioned working together with the speaker, Zainab Baruwa-Phillips.

She leaned close to him as they made their way out of the church to the car park. "Thanks for coming."

He turned to look at her. "Me too." He winked and Maureen looked away shyly. Wondering, if perhaps, her meeting with Leke could possibly mean more than him helping her out of a difficult path in her life.

Detan wasn't on speaking terms with her and had asked her to pay back every contribution he had made towards their wedding. Tobi had called as well, asking if she could change her mind, odd, but Maureen also sensed a certain glee in her voice at breaking things off with Detan.

"Want to grab something to eat somewhere?"

"I'll like that."

Whatever the future held, Maureen would most definitely let God lead.

* * *

Adesewa gave Zainab thumbs up when they arrived. She had just finished talking with Micah and sharing recipes with him of her chicken sauce.

"Hopefully, it stays in the family and you aren't disappearing from my friend's life."

"Ade!"

Micah chuckled, his eyes finding Zainab's. "It's fine. I'm not going anywhere, except she kicks me away with one of her leather boots."

"You still have that?" Adesewa queried and Zainab groaned. The two men in the room laughed at them. It wasn't till past eight that Micah parked in front of her house.

"Thanks for a wonderful time," he said.

"Thanks for hanging around."

"I meant what I said to Ade, I'm not going anywhere."

"Despite my disgusting past?"

"Like you taught, it's not important to God, so why should it be important to me?"

He leaned close and kissed her softly on her cheek. "Good night."

She got out of the car and waved him off. Then when he was out of sight she screamed in delight, not caring if her neighbours thought her crazy.

* * *

Weeks later . . .

"Hey babes." Zainab said, her breath smelled of her chamomile green tea. They hugged and he took in her scent. A mix of lemon and nutmeg. She always seemed to mix her two bottles of perfume from time to time.

"You smell nice."

"Thank you." She walked into the kitchen. The counter top littered with brown boxes of various sizes. "Where do I start?"

He pointed at the cupboard. "Over there."

"I have never seen these many spices in my life!" she said when she opened his cupboard to reveal bottles of spice in different shapes and sizes.

Micah found that hard to believe. "Not even in the supermarket?"

She scoffed. "I boycott all those areas. Seriously, I doubt the local *bukka* deals spends time marinating her food with all this."

"Don't worry, I will show you their importance someday soon."

Belinda walked into the room with a black bag full of clothes. Her forehead glistening with sweat. "If I had known you were hiding these clothes I would have finished your life since. See the work you are making me do."

Micah went to stand by his elder sister and rubbed her shoulders. "I'm sorry."

239

"It's okay. At least I'm glad you are moving forward. I'm happy for you." Then she leaned in and whispered, "and I think she suits you as well." Gesturing to where Zainab stood as she placed the spices in a brown noodle box. Mouthing their names and shaking her head.

Micah smiled. "I think so too."

He recalled what God had told him after his dinner date with Zainab. He remember his dream the other day about the ruby and it all seemed to make sense now.

I make everything beautiful in my time. Like now. This is your ruby. . .

Micah took the picture frame of Kiki and gently placed it with the other pile of photographs. The moving van surely on their way and he wasn't done packing. He was no longer hearing Kiki telling him to dance with him. This time he was hearing a different voice with a different tune.

Dance with Me, Micah.

He smiled. Confident. Assured that God would never leave him nor forsake him.

Always Lord, always.

* * *

Micah roused from sleep, not knowing when he dozed off. The smell of Kiki's body wash from her night bath greeting him. He gazed at her. Taking in her short eyelashes and the serene look on her face. His heart picked up pace and he grabbed her hand, checking for a pulse.

"I'm still here," she whispered softly and Micah let out a sigh of relief all the while knowing the moment he dreaded was inevitable.

"You scared me."

She turned her eyes on him. A smile filling her face and lighting up her tired eyes. Her lips chapped. "I thought you don't scare easily."

240

"I told you I'm not like you who's afraid of every living insect on the planet."

She chuckled lightly. "There just seemed to be too many cockroaches back home. You know, I had never seen an albino cockroach before." She shuddered. "So disgusting."

Micah laughed.

She reached out and took his hand. Licked her lips. "Promise me something, Micah."

"Anything."

"Promise me you will move on. I'm not asking you to forget me; I'm just saying you shouldn't stop living your life. You have so much ahead of you."

"Kiki, please . . ."

"I have to say this. I know if I don't, you will keep sulking and being moody. Have kids and change their smelly diapers."

"You're getting delusional."

"No, I'm being realistic. If you don't do that, I'm going to tell God to increase your libido so you can't help but want to get married."

He covered his face, bewildered by her ability to still make him laugh at a time like this, "Oh my god."

"So you better do it."

"I'm not promising anything," he said, playing along with her. Not wanting to spend this moment in an argument.

"I love you, Micah."

"I love you too."

* * *

Tobi knew life differently now. Having tasted something new and fresh with Lola. It was as though she was living life anew. Last night, she spent more time with Lola after work. Talking and dreaming of a future together.

"You know we can do this. We can live the kind of life we want. No restrictions. I care about you a lot, Tobi. I'm in love with you."

Tobi blinked twice. "You know things can't work out here -"

"Then let's leave the country. Let's start our lives over. We can be where no one raises a brow at two women holding hands and kissing in public. We can even get married." Lola caressed her cheek Her touch sending sensations down Tobi's back.

"It sounds like a dream."

"It could be our reality. Think about it. We empty our accounts and move to America. We start afresh."

Tobi shook her head. "What if we don't get jobs on time? What if we are moving too fast? No, Lola let's take it easy and get to know each other better. If we leave, then there's no coming back. We would leave our families behind and our loved ones. Are you ready for that?"

"I am if you are. I told you I love you. I'm willing to go all the way for and with you." Lola dropped her hand and leaned back on her seat. "Aren't you willing to do the same?"

Tobi released a breath. "I am. I just don't want us to make drastic decisions."

Tobi licked her lips, stilling thoughts of their conversation for a moment. Trying to reason out the possibility. Leaving Shola would crush him. But yet, she would have her freedom. She would have Lola.

"We can't get God to accept our sinful ways and look for ways to justify it. The Bible is to help us correct our ways, not for us to find ways to make our sins acceptable to us and to him."

Tobi distanced Zainab's words from her mind and heart. Everyone was entitled to their own opinion. What if Zainab was the one who misread the Bible? What if God truly accepted Tobi for who she was? What if there was no harm in being a lesbian? What if people were just judgemental and prejudiced to the real truth of homosexuality?

Be not deceived: neither the sexually immoral, idolaters, adulterers nor homosexuals, will enter My Kingdom (1 Corinthians 6:9-10). I don't reject you, I reject what you do, beloved.

No, it's a lie. You love us. You would accept us just the way we are. Even pastors say so.

If you yield freely to My Spirit, you will abandon the desires of the flesh. For the flesh seeks to destroy you, but the Spirit gives life.

Why am I listening to you? You don't care about me. I don't believe in You. I'm not interested in someone who cares nothing about my happiness. Leave me alone!

"Did you just hiss?"

Tobi looked up to find Shola staring at her with a frown. She shrugged.

"What's on your mind?" Shola gave a wet kiss on her neck and settled beside her on the couch. "You have been seating here and staring at a blank TV screen for a while."

"Nothing much."

"You don't want to talk to me?" He took her hand in his and rubbed the back of her palm. "Come, to think of it, it's like you have been moody for the past few days. Have I offended you?"

"What makes you say that?"

"i don't know. You've been off these few days."

She rubbed her eyes. "I'm just tired."

"Physically or emotionally tired?"

"Emotionally."

He moved his fingers up her arm. "Need some help to ease the tension?"

"Gosh, Shola not everything is about sex!" Tobi got up and distanced herself from him.

"Okay? Are you on your period?"

She swallowed hard. "No."

"Then wh-"

"I want a divorce." She stared into his eyes and said it again. "I want a divorce, Shola."

Mouth opened, he only stared at her.

Author's Note

Hello, dear readers,

Pain. Things happen in life and we can't seem to understand at first why they did or see their purpose despite the Bible saying, 'All things work together for good to them that love God'. I empathized with Micah when he lost his wife and baby. I felt for him when he had to watch her die and the memories he made with her. The love they shared. Micah went through inner battles and struggles with his faith and almost went off track, if not for God ministering to him through Pastor Eghosa Phillips.

Dance With Me took a toll on me. I was practically heading to depression while writing the first ten chapters. I scaled through, and I could feel God speaking to me through the book and teaching me things. At the end of writing this book, I fell ill. I was in and out of the hospital for days. Took drips and injections. And I could feel God telling me to trust Him. I believe good would come out of all this.

The Spirit of God is wonderful! I remember screaming and telling my husband while writing this book that I want the gift of the Holy Spirit, specifically Word of Knowledge. I loved how Zainab went about the work of God so boldly and selflessly. We all need to learn to walk in the Spirit. To follow His leading whenever and wherever.

Zainab may just be a character, but her walk with God is one I want to emulate. I believe God is telling us something through this book.

The need to draw closer to His Spirit especially in this day and time when the world is getting darker and sin wants to rule. As children of light, we must shine the truth for others. To be used by God to do great exploits.

Homosexuality is fast becoming a norm in our world. Our children are growing up in a world approving same sex marriage. Laws are being amended to support this. I am not homophobic. It just saddens my heart to see people not understand who God is, His love, grace and desires. His love embraces us all but His grace enables us to say no to sin. Sin being a choice that doesn't make God happy. I pray our minds and hearts are opened to receive God's truth. Not what man declares as truth, but what the Spirit of God reveals as truth. Stay tuned for the sequel of *Dance With Me*.

Like Zainab, you may have a terrible past or worse, but know that God loves you and wants to use you. If you are willing, He is able.

Please share your moments from this book with me and others.

Till next time,

Tope Omotosho.

Facebook Tope Omotosho
Instagram @topeomotoshowrites
Email Topeomotoshowrites@gmail.com
Website www.lifegodandlove.com

Reader Study Guide

1. *Dance, with Me,* starts with the pain of Micah losing his wife. Have you ever experienced the pain of losing someone? What did it feel like? Like Micah, did you think God had betrayed you or let you down?

2. A good number of us have pasts. Do you feel bad about your past mistakes? Perhaps like Zainab you feel no man would be willing to accept you? What does 2 Corinthians 5:17 mean to you?

3. It's been said God doesn't disapprove of homosexuality. Is this true? Do you believe homosexuality is a sin? Do you believe the Scriptures Romans 1:26-28 and Leviticus 20:13?

4. Is God faithful even in times when we feel He isn't? Do you feel He is still there for you even in your darkest moments and deepest pains?

5. Like Zainab, do you yield to God? Ready to go where He says or do what He wants? How obedient are you to the plans God has for you?

6. Zainab felt bold to talk about God and share the Gospel in her line of work. Can you do same? Are you willing to speak up about Christ at your place of work when prompted?

7. Leke was disappointed when his relationship with Emem didn't

work out. How do we feel when we don't get the things we want? Or when we believe we have what we desire but God has other plans? Do you believe in Proverbs 3:5-6?

8. Do you yearn for a closer work with God? Do you have friends who push you to want more of God in your life? Just like Leke and Zainab?

9. Have you been tempted to walk away from God when you suffered a loss or great pain? Have you found your way back? How?

10. How often do you rely on God's Spirit to lead you in life? Are you willing to dance with God and let Him lead you?

Glossary

Haba - why?

Uni - University

Nutter - nuts

Sef - placed at the end of a statement or question when irritated

Abi - Right?

Britico - British citizen

Na you sabi - That's your problem

Ehn—ehn - so what?

Amala and Ewedu - Nigerian dish

O jare/ Jere - comply/ said at the end of sentences for emphasis

Ke - exclamation e.g pregnant ke

Jor - Please

Ehn-ehn - go on

Beta-soup - Better soup. tasty soup

Suya - Spicy skewered meat

Puff-puff - fried dough

Akara - Nigerian beans fritters

Ponmo - Cow skin

Na so I see am - That's how I saw it

Bukka - road side restaurant

Oya - get ready/move/action (depending on usage)

Ahn-ahn - an enquiry or an exclamation

Egusi - Nigerian dish

Aso-ebi - matching attires

Ofada-rice - Nigerian dish

Ankara - African fabric

Shebi - Right?

Oga - Master/boss/leader

Danfo - Yellow commercial buses

moi-moi - African dish

Dake enu re! - Shut up your mouth!

Gele - Head-tie

So gbo mi? - Are you listening to me?

M gbo Tobi? - Tobi, is that true?

Efo Elegusi - Nigerian dish

Pele - Sorry

Abeg - Please

Ehn? - What?

Eh-ya - What a pity

Also by Tope Omotosho

Other Titles by Author

With These Shoes: Now You Know Where It Pinches! (Coming soon)

Crumbled (Available in paperback and Amazon Kindle)

He Sees Me (non-fiction)

My Conversations with God

Separated

Ready To Say I Do (non-fiction)

I'll Keep Loving You

Once Upon a First Love

Always One More Time

With These Shoes . . . I Thee Wed (Book 1)

E-books Can be gotten on OKadabooks.com and Bambooks.io

Crumbled, Once Upon a First Love and I'll Keep Loving You are

Crumbled

Almost everything in Shola's life seems to be falling apart. With a rain of emotions breaking him, Shola faces the temptation of returning to his past life of women and alcohol, yet no matter how sweet it was, he must also remember it's a past that almost cost him his life. But will Tobi's long kept secret be the final blow that pushes him over?

Tobi is fed up with her marriage after hiding her true sexuality for years. She has only wanted one thing in life: freedom, and she's so close to getting it. The itch to leave her husband for a woman appeals to her day by day. One thing is clear, she must also deal with the consequences of her actions when everything comes crumbling.

This is one story of crumbling hearts, and a touch of hope.